Other Books by Mary Stolz

WHO WANTS MUSIC ON MONDAY?

Mary Stolz

WHO WANTS MUSIC ON MONDAY?

Harper & Row, Publishers
NEW YORK, EVANSTON, AND LONDON

This is for Emily and Reginald Barrett
and for
Elizabeth Alexandra,
Katherine Anne,
Janet Alice,
David Shield, and
Mary Alison Barrett

WHO WANTS MUSIC ON MONDAY?

Chapter One

They'd divided their room with string, even making a narrow hall so that Cassie, in getting to her side, wouldn't step in Lotta's side, which had the door. It required squeezing not to overstep, but Cassie always managed. After the strings were laid down, she never entered Lotta's territory without permission. Lotta, sloppy about rules as she was neat about possessions, frequently came into Cassie's without even asking.

Lotta was sitting on the floor now (on her own side of the room), wearing a flowery flannel robe. Barefoot, with bits of tissue between her toes, she was giving herself a pedicure. She didn't turn or speak as Cassie came in, bright-cheeked from the cold. That was part of their agreement. If they had actually had separate rooms, they wouldn't have called to each other through the walls, would they? Though Lotta sometimes forgot, Cassie rigidly observed the barrier of the strings, and she went to her closet without a word.

She got out of her gray-and-yellow plaid skirt and a yellow sweater so pastel it was almost white and looked at them glumly. It wasn't that they had not been perfectly good when handed down from Lotta to her. They had, as Lotta's things did, seemed almost fresher and smarter than on the day they were bought. Lotta did that to clothes. Mrs. Dunne said her elder daughter would undoubtedly be a designer one day, because clothes came alive for her. Cassie considered that silly, but looking at these, she decided that they certainly died when they got to her.

She yanked an old pair of olive-green toreador pants from the shelf, poked around on the floor until she unearthed a cherry-colored sweater that was getting too small. The only time she ever got anything with a decent color to it was on her birthday or at Christmas, and last Christmas she'd wanted new ice skates and a book on the compositions of Cézanne. It isn't that I regret my choice, she said to herself. It's just that I regret my clothes.

Aware that Lotta was not above cheating, that she'd look through the string whenever it suited her, Cassie took some care to hang the plaid skirt properly. It had been a favorite of Lotta's, and she still took an interest in its well-being.

Pushing a hand through her rumpled hair, cut short for convenience, Cassie sat at her desk and prepared to do homework. Their brother, Vincent, had made this desk for her and a dressing table for Lotta. Lotta had put a rose-and-white dotted-swiss skirt on her dressing table, and Cassie put nearly everything she owned on her desk. Pebbles, pencils, stacks of colored paper, a great assortment of magic markers, scissors, paste, books, clippings, paperweights, and a glass casserole with a baby turtle in it. On Lotta's dressing table were two pink jars and a silver comb.

"Oh, crumbs," Cassie muttered.

"You talking to me?" Lotta inquired, twisting around, nail polish brush poised in air. She was thinking that her toes looked like little rosy shells, but it was not the sort of thing a person said to Cassie, who didn't answer anyway or even look up from her book.

Homework, Lotta thought. Imagine. On Friday night. Lotta herself never looked at a book until Sunday afternoon, if then. But Cassie always slammed into her homework as if she actually liked it and spent the rest of the weekend outdoors, unless the weather was too foul even for her, which it almost couldn't be. Then, if she absolutely had to stay in, she put together those crazy portraits that no one could understand.

What a way to be, thought Lotta.

To be herself seemed even more wonderful when she considered Cassie. This completely truthful reaction made her feel guilty, and to compensate she decided to appeal to Cassie's taste. Cassie didn't have any, as far as Lotta was concerned, or if she did it was awful. Look at the colors she had on now. But being consulted always flattered people. Lotta got her new blouse out of the bottom drawer, gently took the tissue from it, and walked across the string.

"Do you like this?" she said. No answer. "Cassie, dear?"

11

Cassie looked up irritably. "What is it, Lotta?"

"I wanted to ask if you liked this blouse. It's my new one. I got it with the money from little Abby Keogh's birthday party."

Cassie scarcely glanced at the blouse. "Nope." She turned back to her notes.

"Why not?" Lotta said. Really, it was too annoying. You went out of your way to be pleasant, to pretend you were even the least bit interested in a person's opinion, and what did you get for thanks? Grunts, criticism. No, it was too much. "And just why don't you like it, please?"

"Too pale and powdery." Cassie looked at the blouse once more and then at her blond and fluffy sister. "It suits you, at that."

"I suppose you mean that to be an insult, doubtless?"

Cassie shrugged. "Not really. You are a pale and powdery type. You aren't getting any complaints, are you?"

"No, I certainly am not. For your information, I'm getting compliments by the galore." Lotta felt her temper slipping, snatched it back and smiled. She smoothed the folds of her blouse. It was the most delicate of lemon shades, with soft blue roses at wrists and collar. It was beautiful. With her light blue skirt and white cardigan she would look as fresh and fragrant as a—as a peony.

It sometimes occurred to Lotta that she could pay herself nicer compliments than any of the boys she knew were able to. J. H., for instance, when he saw her tonight, would purse his lips and say "Wow" or "Man" or, if he happened to be in a talkative mood, "Girl, that is really solid!"

12

Now quite out of countenance, Lotta scowled at her sister, who'd started the trouble.

"Can't you ever say anything nice about anything?"

"For goodness' sake!" Cassie burst out. "Did I ask you across the string? Then don't complain. You asked what I thought of the blouse, and I told you what I thought of it. Do you want me to lie?"

Lotta took a deep breath. "I just hate to think what your life is going to be like, Cass. Mother says you're the most tactless creature she's ever known."

Cassie bit her lip, picked up a pencil, and attempted to get back to work. "Suppose you let me worry about my life, Lotta, and you go back to your bubble bath."

Head high, Lotta stepped back across the string. Without having to look, she knew her sister's skinny form was slumped across the desk in that awkward position she always took to study in, leaning on one arm, hand clutching her mustard-colored hair, legs tangled around the chair legs. Poor Cass. What a mess she was. Skinny, sharp-featured, with that spiky hair, grubby fingers, never a trace of make-up. And those clothes! Horrible colors, and not even clean. What made up to Cassie for being Cassie? Not that she seemed to mind. She acted pretty sassy most of the time. But could she be, really, contented with herself? Looking like that? Having those peculiar interests and no friends to speak of and, really, no chance that a boy would ever adore her?

As she catalogued her sister's shortcomings and poor prospects Lotta became peaceful, even a little sad. Poor, poor Cass. Lotta looked at her own image in the mirror. There

13

she was, that familiar, adorable girl. There was her blondness, her—prettiness. There was no other word. Except beauty, of course. But Lotta felt that what she possessed at present was not beauty itself, but the promise of great beauty. This modesty so moved her that she felt even sorrier for Cassie, who showed no promise at all except in art, and if *that* was all a girl had to fall back on . . .

My goodness, Lotta thought, a little smile curving her lips. She'd forgotten Cassie. The smile was for herself, for her life, for the dazzling years that lay before Lotta Dunne, blond and sweet and modest, showing promise of great beauty.

She fluffed the two toy kittens J. H. had given her. One violet, one apricot. Their cute little faces with blue glass eyes looked at her until she could almost see affection in their gaze. J. H. had eyes practically the same color, the palest blue. And certainly he sometimes looked a little glassy when he stared at her.

"Lotta," he'd say. "Lotta, you're the *prettiest* girl." Sounding a little helpless about it, sort of angry in a way.

Lotta crossed her arms, laying a hand on each slender, rounded shoulder. Head lifted, hair falling back, she closed her eyes and smiled. "Lotta, you're the *prettiest* girl," echoed in her mind.

Cassie, happening to glance up and across the string at that moment, looked quickly away in embarrassment. Lotta was a female Narcissus; there was no other explanation for those trancelike states before the mirror. And she didn't even care if other people saw her carrying on like that. What must it be like to be so sure that you were beautiful, so sure that there was nothing else worth being?

Would I want to be that beautiful? Cassie asked herself seriously, and answered, No, I would not. Not if it meant almost no time left for anything else. She frequently asked herself this question. It was unavoidable if you were caged with a creature like Lotta a good part of your life. Usually she replied in the same fashion.

And yet—and yet—

Lotta went off to take her bubble bath, and all at once indifferent to rules and to strings, Cassie walked over and sat down at the brazenly dainty dressing table. There was no mirror in her own part of the room. She used the one in the bathroom, usually just to look at her teeth when she was through brushing them. Her hair she combed without looking. She'd never put on make-up in her life. Now she sat at the pink-and-white vanity table and addressed herself to the problem.

"Very well," she said aloud. "What have we here?"

If she saw that face in front of her for a moment—in a crowd, not knowing it—what would be her reaction? Would she, indeed, have a reaction? Yes, she suspected she would because the face was so like Vincent's, that dearest one of all. But leaving her brother out of it? She leaned forward, looked directly into the mirrored eyes. Grayish. Too close together. Provided with rather skimpy lashes, but nice arching brows. Teeth, good. Nose, satisfactory . . . haughty and well shaped. On Vincent it looked noble. What else? Hair like a mesquite bush, thin long neck, sloping shoulders.

Rather, she decided, like a Modigliani portrait—excellent in an art gallery but decidedly a drawback in high school. She did not need glasses. Her complexion was all right, so far, but there was plenty of time for it to cause her anguish, as Vincent's had and still did him. Her ears, she could confidently say, were good. Small and flat. How far could a person go on eyebrows, teeth, and ears? How far a person wanted to go, and in what direction, was more to the point. She at least was free to walk away from the mirror, which Lotta never was. Was that compensation for looking like herself and not like her sister?

She went back to her desk, pulled her trigonometry notebook toward her, and stared past it. Cassandra Dunne. Not so pretty. Well, not pretty at all. But a good mind. She was taking all advanced courses at school and would graduate at the age of fifteen, which some people—friends of the family and her own friend, Fritzy, for instance—thought was going to be simply disastrous. Cassie didn't think so. She had lots of interests. Books, music, art, languages. Oh, Cassandra Dunne should have a fine life, a fascinating life. It was all up to her. If she's smart, of course, she'll get away from that beautiful sister at the first opportunity—

She threw her notebook across the room. It hit the wall and fell to the floor, halfway across the string. Although she had no desire to move (it would have been good to sit staring with daft, blurry eyes at nothing), she had to get up and retrieve it before Lotta came back. It was peculiar how sometimes she could skate or walk or play hockey for hours without tiring, just getting lighter and freer, and at other times it

16

seemed too great an effort to close her fingers around something thin and weightless, like this notebook.

She straightened her shoulders, took a deep breath, narrowed her eyes as if at an adversary, and went to work. By the time Lotta returned from the bathroom, trailing scent and powder like a cosmetic counter, Cassie had finished the weekend math assignment.

Lotta padded over amiably on her shell-like toes, peered at the orderly array of figures, and said, "It's not to be believed how anybody can dote on arithmetic this way."

"It's not arithmetic, it's mathematics, and I don't dote on it, I'm just good at it." Not until the words were out did Cassie realize how they sounded, and she tightened her jaw in despair, trying to think of some way to soften the effect without seeming to apologize. Nothing occurred to her, and besides Lotta drifted away, back across the string, with sincere and obvious indifference.

I shouldn't let her get me wrought up this way, Cassie said to herself. I should be calm and unconcerned, the way she is. Still—it happened, and repeatedly. It was Lotta's talent for girlish stupidity that was maddening. She was a senior in high school and certainly knew the difference between mathematics and arithmetic. But this was the sort of ignorance she affected that seemed, beyond all bounds of credibility, to *charm* people. She pretended not to know how to add or subtract and would say to some limply admiring young man, "I just sort of go through life *hoping* people will give me the right change." Watching the young man's jaw drop with stunned delight at this statement which *had* to be either hypocrisy or imbecility, Cassie would be filled with outrage. For whom, or against whom, she was not sure. Each time it happened she promised herself never to react again.

"It's just," she'd said to Vincent when he'd been home last time, "that she sounds so fatuous. It's mortifying. And she turns those boys into cretins, right in front of our eyes."

"I imagine," Vince had answered with that ready laugh of his, "that even Circe couldn't have turned into swine men who weren't already well on their way to being pigs."

Lost in admiration of Vincent, in the delight of having him home, Cassie had forgotten Lotta for the time being. And now here she was caught in the same old snare.

"I will not, ever again, for *any* reason," she mumbled to herself, "let Lotta make me lose my temper. I shall be temperate, restrained, dignified, at all times."

"You say something, Cass?" Lotta asked. She was dressed now, and brushing her yellow hair till it sparked.

"I hope to tell you I said something," Cassie replied, but wouldn't explain.

At dinner Mrs. Dunne said that her sister, Muriel, was coming the next day for a week's stay. "She was so sorry not to be able to see us at Christmas or New Year's. I mean, that's what she said, but just between us I suspect she was doing something more exciting than visiting the family . . . not that there's anything wrong with that, an unmarried girl and all (Muriel Ferris, a divorcée of thirty, would always be a girl to her sister), but what I *mind* is—" She'd forgotten what she minded. "So if you girls will clean up Vincent's

18

room, change the linen if that wasn't done when he left, see that at least one drawer is empty, maybe two, if you can find some place to put his junk—I can't imagine what Vincent *wants* with all that stuff, like the stamps. He never even looks at them anymore, but when I suggested that he might give them to some needy child for Christmas, why he practically bit my head off. I don't understand people who aren't generous," she said, glancing at Cassie. "I just do not understand them and I never will."

"Mother," Lotta began, "I won't be able to—"

"It isn't lack of generosity," Cassie interrupted, "just because you don't want to give away something you've worked to put together."

"But he never *looks* at those stamps."

"He may, someday. He may want to go on with the collection or give it to his children. How do you know? Anyway, it's his. He made it and paid for most of it, and he ought to be able to decide what to do with it."

"He's just the way you are, about those pictures you do," Mrs. Dunne complained. "Secretive or something. Possessive. Which reminds me, Cassie—*don't* you think it's about time you gave one of those things to Muriel? You know how she wants one, and I just can't believe you can be such—such a little piggy," she said playfully. "What difference can it make to you if you give one or two away? You have thousands."

"Mother, that isn't the point."

"Well, I'm sure I don't know what the point is."

"No, I'm sure you don't," Cassie muttered.

It was a contest that had been going on for some time.

Aunt Muriel wanted one or more of Cassie's collage portraits to hang on her apartment wall in the city, and Cassie didn't want to give her one or more or any.

"I absolutely *covet* them, Cassie. You *can't* deny me," Aunt Muriel had said last time, with that pleading little who-could-resist-me smile that she'd handed on to Lotta like a family spoon.

But Cassie could resist and did. "Honestly, Aunt Muriel, they aren't good enough to hang on anybody's wall."

"Oh, but darling, they are. *I* think they are. I think they're simply utterly enchanting." She'd picked one up, held it at arm's length, and did seem delighted. "How can I find words to overcome that modesty of yours, Cassie? What do you want me to say?"

"But I'm not looking for reassurance," Cassie had explained. "I'm not even modest. It's fun doing the things and they mean a lot to me. But I'd—I simply couldn't bear to have them *hanging* some place." Why were people so dreadfully hard to convince? If I had any place in this house of my own, Cassie had thought irritably, then I could just do these silly, immature, entirely personal things by myself and put them away and not have to go through the horror of listening to Aunt Muriel try to guess which is a portrait of whom, try to inveigle one out of me for a conversation piece. I wouldn't have them *pry*ing this way.

Aunt Muriel had dropped one, selected another—which happened to be an impression of herself. Cassie had taken mauve paper, pasted on it a picture of a steamroller. In place of the driver she'd put a bunch of violets, and behind the steamroller she'd drawn some people who looked like plants, springing up alertly, though logically they should have been flattened for good. Aunt Muriel had studied this harmless steamroller driven by a fluttering bunch of violets and said, "Charming, absolutely charming. Cassie, if I guess who one of them is, will you sell it to me?"

"If you guess"—Cassie had sighed—"I'll give it to you."

Aunt Muriel had guessed wrong. Three times. Cassie, knowing that by her action she convicted herself of vanity and selfishness, bundled the portraits together and put them in her bottom drawer. "I'm sorry, Aunt Muriel."

"But may I commission one, then? Darling, do one of *me* and let me pay for it. It would be my pleasure."

Well, it certainly wouldn't be mine, Cassie thought. "Aunt Muriel, if I did one to order, don't you see, it wouldn't really be mine. Really be what I feel, I mean."

"My, you do take yourself seriously," Mrs. Ferris had said, but she smiled so affectionately that the bite left her words. "Well, if you won't, you won't. Perhaps one day you'll change your mind."

Later Mrs. Dunne had come to Cassie. "You're unbelievable," she said. "You really, truly are. I'm shocked beyond words. You must have a hundred of those things, and you won't give *one* to somebody who's been as generous to you as Muriel. When I think of the things she's given you girls over the years, and Vincent, too, and now the very first time she asks you for anything . . . How *can* you, Cassie?"

"Mother, you don't understand," Cassie had cried out.

"No. No, I most certainly do not. Selfishness is something

21

I never understand. Except that your aunt wants one very much, I don't understand anything about this. And I certainly don't understand *you*. You'd think she'd asked you for a— a finger or something."

They'd gotten nowhere that day. And we're going to get nowhere now, Cassie thought. But her mother was implacable. She was like an invading army. You subdued her at the drawbridge, and there she was at the top of the wall. She retreated, and before you could sigh with victory, she'd mount an assault from the rear.

"You could just give her *one*, couldn't you?" Mrs. Dunne was saying now. "One you aren't fond of, Cassie. It would please her so much and wouldn't deprive you of anything."

"Why should it be pleasing for me to give something I'm not fond of?"

"Muriel wouldn't know it," Mrs. Dunne said with surprise. "You surely wouldn't tell her."

"I'd know it."

"Oh, you are so—so stuck-up," Mrs. Dunne said in frustration.

"Mother," Lotta put in, "I've been trying to tell you that I just can't help with Vince's room."

"And why not, please?" Rebecca Dunne snapped.

"Don't you remember? Irene and I are doing a party for the Storch child tomorrow afternoon. I can't handle that and work around here, too. And I have homework besides," she added as an afterthought.

Cassie, already irked by her mother, found this intolerable. Homework! *Homework!* Lotta might have done her homework this afternoon, instead of all that grooming, mightn't she? "And a date tomorrow night, I suppose." The words were out before she could stop them, and sounded, naturally, spiteful and jealous.

Lotta twisted a yellow curl around her finger, desisted at a glance from her mother. "Well, sister dear—yes. Now that you bring it up, I have a date tomorrow night and a date tonight, too. Any objections from the peanut gallery?"

"You're darn right I have objections," Cassie shouted, just as her mother said, "Do you feel you're being entirely reasonable, Lotta?"

"Being entirely reasonable isn't precisely my *aim* in life," said Lotta. "But I'm happy to listen. Where am I being unreasonable? I work hard at these birthday parties, darn hard—"

"We know that, dear," said Mrs. Dunne. "And we're proud of you." She glanced at Cassie, quickly looked away. "But the fact remains that if you fill up your life with— with outside things, that leaves Cassie and me to do all the work at home."

The real fact, Cassie thought, is that Mother loves having a pretty, popular daughter who's in partnership with Irene Stevens, subdeb of this city, running birthday parties for the children of mothers who can't cope with parties themselves. The fact is Mother's proud of Lotta for being blond and adorable and so sought-after that she can't find time for the homefolks even when she's home. Well, in a way it was understandable. Lotta, who took after Aunt Muriel, was, except for her, the only ornament the family could boast. Vincent

23

wasn't a good-looking boy. He had a high-hearted way about him that seemed to Cassie to make him handsomer than merely elegant features could have. But not *worldly* handsome. Mrs. Dunne's looks were serviceable and neat, but she was no television mother, slender-waisted and difficult to distinguish from her own daughters. Mr. Dunne was a chunky man whose face might have been anybody's. Cassie had never even attempted to do a portrait of him. Probably it was not to be wondered at that having hatched a swan, Mrs. Dunne tended to crow over it.

I wonder, Cassie said to herself, whoever made up that bit To understand all is to forgive all. I understand—I guess I do—what it is that has cast me in the role of Cinderella Dunne. I don't feel in the least forgiving.

"It does seem to me," Mrs. Dunne was saying to Lotta, "that you might at least share some of your profits with Cassie. After all, she is left with most of the chores."

Betrayed from this quarter, Lotta reluctantly offered to ante up some cash in return for ducking her household responsibilities.

"Let's see," she said, and frowned, the pink tip of her tongue showing. "We charge five dollars plus expenses for a party. That leaves about two dollars and fifty cents each for Irene and me—"

"What do you mean, *about?*" Cassie inquired. "It comes to precisely two-fifty apiece, unless you're paying social security."

"I can see no other future for you except to be a bookkeeper," Lotta said coldly.

24

"Let's get back to your proposition."

For a moment Cassie had intended to reject any offer from Lotta as smacking of charity. But Lotta's tone, and the briefest reflection, served to change her mind. It could scarcely be called charity, since tonight she'd be doing the dishes and tomorrow getting Vincent's room ready for Aunt Muriel. It was simple justice, and she wondered why she hadn't thought of it before. Not that she had even thought of it tonight. She gave her mother a grateful glance and turned attentively to Lotta.

Lotta wriggled. "I'll give you fifty cents. That only leaves me—"

"Ha! Ha-ha!"

"Oh, Cass. You sound so silly."

"See if this does—I'll split with you. Fifty-fifty. Take it or leave it."

"Mother!" Lotta cried. "That's not fair. She isn't being fair at all."

"Suit yourself," Cassie said. "Only I serve notice, as of now, that I'm resigning my position as Cinderella Dunne. So I'll do *half* the dishes tonight and *half* of Vincent's room tomorrow and—"

"You see what you get, Mother, for interfering?" Lotta said, her face pink and glowing. "You see? Everything was going along fine—"

"I was being exploited; that's what you mean by fine, I suppose?" Cassie said. She was losing interest in the conversation and the financial gain, but it wouldn't do to let Lotta know.

"Now, wait a minute, wait a minute," Mrs. Dunne said, flipping her hands in front of her as if trying to put out a fire. As, Cassie thought, she probably feels she is. "Just a minute. Let me think. I do think it's disgraceful the way you two go on at each other. I'm sure I never *heard* of sisters behaving to each other in this fashion. My sister and I never had words. Never. We were always seeking little ways of pleasing and helping each other. We were so close that people used to remark on it."

Cassie carefully kept from looking at Lotta, who, she knew, would also be trying to suppress a smile. Aunt Muriel and Mother had not one thing in common other than their parents, and there was no question of their ever having been close sisters. For one thing, the age difference separated them. And then there followed all the other even more important differences, in looks, in outlook, in values, in everything. But Mrs. Dunne was going on, at some length, to tell her daughters about a beautiful sisterly relationship that may never have existed in fact but did, apparently, exist in at least this sister's mind.

Covertly Cassie eyed her own sister and wished, as she had wished before, that Vincent had got some of those looks. She remembered a scene, during Christmas vacation, when she had wished it almost—no, quite—in the form of a curse on Lotta.

Vincent had come downstairs, wearing his new sports jacket—a handsome dark green blazer—and a bright bow tie. He'd powdered his face in some way, and it looked much better than usual. And he was in one of his marvelous gay moods.

"You look like the King of the Cats," Cassie had told him proudly.

"Not, perhaps, the effect I'd intended. But 'twill serve, 'twill do." He'd smiled and brushed away a speck from the jacket.

The phone rang, and Vincent picked it up. His face brightened even more.

"Betsy!" he said. "What's the matter, can't you wait? I was just about to—" Like a flame snuffed out, a curtain falling, the end of everything descending, joy and beauty left his face. He became a short, sallow boy with a blemished face badly covered. His eyes behind his glasses blinked rapidly.

"Well, of course I understand," he said in a moment. "Sure, sure . . . naturally if your mother's sick, you— Yup, I know. When? Oh, I'll be back at Intersession, probably. Sure, sure . . . I'll call you. I tell you, I do understand." He swallowed hard, smiled vaguely at the receiver. "Yeah, sure thing. Well, I hope she feels better soon . . . Well, your mother, of course—"

It was a conversation that seemed to Cassie to go on all night, but was over pretty soon. Lotta, coming downstairs, asked, "Is that for me, Vince?" just as he hung up. "Oh, yours?" she said. "Say, Vince, I was wondering if maybe on your way to pick up Betsy you could—"

Can't she see? Cassie had wondered. What does she *see* when she looks out of her adorable blue eyes? Look at Vincent's *face*, she wanted to scream at Lotta. And then she wished something that she knew in her heart was wicked, that Vincent himself would have been appalled at. She stared at Lotta on the staircase and wished her ugly—

27

I want—she'd crooned inwardly, as if she had demonic powers—I want you to be pasty and plain and bespectacled and skinny and *hurt*, so that Vincent can be beautiful and happy.

"For heaven's sake," Lotta had said, looking herself over. "What's wrong? Did I forget my lipstick or something?"

Vincent gave a funny little snort. "That's the amazing thing about girls," he said. "No matter what happens, they take it personally."

"Well, *I* don't," Lotta said indignantly. At that Vince really laughed. Lotta, missing the point, flounced past them to the living room. But Cassie stared at the floor with bitter eyes.

"Now, now, Cass," Vincent said. "One of life's minor tragedies. Not even a major minor tragedy, if you follow me."

"I hate that girl," Cassie said slowly. It made her shiver a little, to use the word "hate" and to think that possibly she meant it. Children used it easily. They hated oatmeal, geography, dentists, and even, sometimes, their parents. But they didn't mean it. They didn't know what it meant. To say you hated someone, knowing what was meant by hate, and to say it of your—

"Betsy?" said Vincent.

"Yes," said Cassie, letting out a quick short breath, like someone reprieved at the brink of a disastrous admission. "Betsy."

Vincent shrugged. "You don't hate her, Cass. And she gave me a nice round reasonable excuse. I always accept excuses. Saves time and face and heartache and all that."

One thing was certain. Any heartache Vincent suffered he

would handle without help from others. Without, in any case, help from his family. "Oh, the cares of the world rest lightly on Vinnie," Mrs. Dunne was apt to say, and Cassie couldn't remember when she had seen him anything but lighthearted, jaunty. Was he different with his friends? Did he show them any true sorrow, any pain, any fear? She wanted to say, Trust me, Vincent. But you didn't *say* things like that to people.

"Cassie, are you listening to one word I'm saying?"

Cassie started, looked at her mother apologetically, and said, "No. Sorry, Mom. I wasn't."

Lotta's lips curved down wryly. Even caught off guard, even dreaming, Lotta was never to be surprised into unseemly truths.

Mrs. Dunne clicked her tongue, looking displeased. "Then possibly you'll design to listen now?"

"You mean deign, I think."

"Cassie, don't be impertinent. I guess I know what I mean."

"But—" Cassie glanced at Lotta, who had the appearance of a cat amused by the blundering of a dog. "Okay, I'll design to listen."

"You think you know so much more than other people, don't you?"

"No, Mother. Honestly. That's something I *don't* think. What were you saying? Before, I mean."

"I was trying to work out some reasonable solution to this problem."

What problem? Cassie wondered for a second. Oh, yes. The division of labor and cash.

"—and trying to make you see that while I wish to be fair to both of you—" Mrs. Dunne stopped, almost as if expecting a denial of this from Cassie. Getting none, she continued. "If you stop to remember, Cassie, that Lotta is older than you and—"

"But—"

"Please. Let me finish. Lotta is older. So she began helping at an earlier age than you did. With the housework, I mean. So if you are going to make—bookkeeping—of this matter, why then Lotta's ahead, as far as housework is concerned."

"Your logic isn't very sound, Mother, because there's every indication that I'll catch up with Lotta, and surpass her, if it comes to that. What happens then? Do I get retroactive justice?"

"I am not finished, Cassie. Besides having started to help before you did (she'd apparently decided to ignore the future), Lotta *needs* more things than you do, being older and"—she stumbled slightly—"and more in need of things, because of having dates and all—"

"Forget it," Cassie interrupted. "I don't want anything from Lotta. Not money or fair play or anything."

"Oh, you aren't fair," Lotta breathed. "That's the way you always do. You start things and then walk off leaving everybody with tag ends they don't know what to do with."

"Make a corsage of them," Cassie suggested, getting up to clear the table. "You can wear it on your date tonight. Should be quite a fun thing."

"Oooh—" Lotta shook her head. Her blond hair swung

softly. "I wouldn't be you, Cass, for anything in the world."

"And here all along I've thought you were just waiting for the day when we could change places."

"Oh, honestly!" Mrs. Dunne said, covering her eyes with her hands. "I simply cannot stand this. I have a good mind to—"

"To write to your father," said both girls together.

"That's nice. Laugh at me. Make fun of your mother."

"Mother, dear," Lotta said persuasively, "we're not laughing at you." She was always willing to make an attempt to soothe wounded feelings. Cassie, who, if she felt in the right, was never able even to try, couldn't decide if Lotta was a dissembler or a saint. "I mean," Lotta was going on to their mother, "it's one thing to tell Daddy the children are misbehaving when they're still children. But I, for one, am not a child."

"I, for another," said Cassie. "I'm not one, too."

"You're both impossible," said Mrs. Dunne. "Sometimes I wish I'd never had any—" She wouldn't finish the sentence, and they all knew she didn't mean it anyway. As I, Cassie assured herself, still burdened with a sense of guilt about the wish she had wished Lotta on the stairs that night in December, didn't really mean a malediction. I want Vince to be happy, to have everything in life that he wants and deserves, but not at Lotta's expense.

Cassie did the dishes, and as an extra heaping of coals of fire on her own head, washed the kitchen floor. She was just finishing when Lotta, looking a snow maiden in her pale, cool colors, stopped at the door to say good-bye.

31

"Oh, for Pete's sake, Cass," she protested. "Are you doing that just to make me feel bad?"

Exasperated at having her motives misread (not entirely sure they had been misread), Cassie shoved the mop in the pail of soapy water and only missed splashing her sister's finery.

Lotta jumped back in the hall. "Cassie," she said furiously, "what's the matter with you? You act as if the devil had gotten into you."

"Well, if he ever does," Cassie said, "I want to tell you that you will be the first to know."

Chapter Two

When Lotta had gone, with J. H. jangling behind her like, Cassie thought, a skeleton *invited* to the feast, Cassie wandered into the living room where her mother was at the desk writing out checks. Mrs. Dunne wore the apprehensive look she always brought to this task and seemed glad to be interrupted.

"For the life of me," Cassie said, slumping into a chair and throwing one leg over the arm, "I cannot fathom what Lotta sees in that character. He has no more individuality than a fence picket."

Mrs. Dunne frowned. "He comes of a fine family."

"Oh, Mother. You sound like such a snob when you say things like that."

"I hope it isn't snobbish to want your daughter to see nice people."

"J. H. isn't nice because his father made some money in the real estate business. Of course," Cassie added in an attempt to be impartial, "he isn't not nice because of it either. The fact is, he's not actually nice or not nice. In short, he is a cipher."

"Well," said Mrs. Dunne, unexpectedly sardonic, "at least he's a cipher who behaves himself and drives carefully. At this stage in Lotta's life I don't much care about anything else. Cassie, must you sprawl that way? I really don't think girls should be allowed to wear pants. It encourages them to be unladylike."

Cassie put her feet primly together, then slumped until she almost balanced on her neck. A silence fell in the room, and they could hear the winter wind outside. *A wind with a wolf's head howled about my door,* thought Cassie, staring at a night-blackened window, which mirrored back a picture of her mother, a lamp, a corner of the fireplace.

"I could make us a fire," she said, not moving.

"Cassie, dear—I'm going out. That is, unless you'd mind just awfully. Mrs. Fitzsimmons and I thought we'd go to that lecture at the school tonight. Would you like to come along? It's R. G. Dawson, that explorer who spent all that time at the North Pole."

"Greenland," Cassie corrected. "I heard him at Assembly. Very inspiring."

"I suppose you're being sarcastic."

"Why should you suppose that? All I said was, he's inspiring."

"You sounded as if you were laughing."

"I can't help how I sound," Cassie muttered. A voice in her mind, probably Vincent's, said, You most certainly can. Cassie straightened in the chair, looked at her mother, and smiled. "No, really. You'll like it. He has movies of seals."

Mrs. Dunne, still slightly miffed, consulted her watch. "Why don't you ask Fritzy over?" Cassie moved impatiently, and her mother said, "I'm only trying to help, you know."

"Yes, I know, Mother. But I don't need any help."

There was another long silence. Cassie wondered whether to ask about her father's letter. There'd been one in the mail that morning, but as her mother hadn't said anything about it, maybe it was one of those downhearted notes he wrote so frequently. If it was, Cassie didn't want to see it.

Mr. Dunne was a salesman. Cassie imagined he wasn't a very good one, because the subdivision in which they lived wasn't especially good. All right, of course. It was a place she meant to get away from, the sort of place she would never live in once she did get away, but aside from not having a room of her own, she found it acceptable for the time being. Vincent's room was empty most of the time, now that he was in college, but of course no one thought of the room as possibly being available to one of the girls. Vince came home on vacations. Sometime he might bring a friend. He hadn't yet, but Cassie was always hoping he would. Anyway, lots of his things were there, and the room was his. Cassie accepted the justice of that. If he didn't have a room at home, maybe he wouldn't feel welcome, maybe he wouldn't come back at all. Besides, sometimes they used it for company. It was Aunt Muriel's room when she visited.

35

Her father was away almost as much as Vince, on the road.

"How sad it must be," a neighbor had said a few years ago, "to have your daddy away on your birthday."

"Oh, I don't mind," Cassie had replied brightly, partly because it was true, partly because she hadn't wanted to spoil the party her mother had made for her. Instead, Mrs. Dunne had spoiled it with the look she gave Cassie at that "I don't mind."

"But, Mommy," Cassie had protested, appalled at her mother's expression, "I only—"

"That'll be quite enough," her mother had said, sounding sad and angry at once. "Go back to your guests."

But Cassie had run upstairs to cry, and Vince (he'd been sixteen? seventeen?) had come into the bedroom—stringless then—and sat beside her, patting her shoulder.

"Poor kid," he said gruffly.

Sniffling, pushing her face into the pillow, but warmly, beautifully comforted at his presence, his concern, Cassie sobbed, "I just was—was trying—to be—"

"A good sport," Vince said confidently. "Mother didn't understand, Cass. I'll explain to her."

Cassie had rolled to her back, screwing up her face in an effort to get things straight. "Well, that," she said slowly. "But, besides—"

A smile he tried to control twitched at Vincent's lips. "Cassie, my nice and thorny little sister, must you be absolutely letter-perfect honest about everything in life?"

Cassie looked at him in bewilderment. "I should try to be, shouldn't I? Shouldn't everybody try to be honest? Do you want me to lie?"

Vincent shook his head and got up. "Boy, have you got a long way to go," he said. He wouldn't explain what he meant. He just told her to wash her face and get along back to the party, that he'd smooth things over with Mother. He didn't say how, and Cassie didn't ask.

Well, if she hadn't known what he meant then, she pretty well knew now. For all the good knowing did her. Maybe being born tactless and truthful was like being born left-handed. The condition could be altered, but only at the cost of a violent wrench to your whole being.

Looking now at her mother's round, sad face, feeling somehow responsible for the sadness—Lotta never seemed to cause that wan expression to appear—Cassie said cheerfully, "You got a letter from Dad today, didn't you? I thought I saw one in the box this morning."

"Yes."

"Well, what did he say?"

"The usual."

"But what?" Cassie tried to use Lotta's coaxing tone but suspected she only sounded sharp. Really, if there was any relationship more difficult than a family one, she couldn't think—

"He wants to know how we all are. He says he misses us, and he's lonely. Your father has a lonely life, you know. Traveling the way he does, hardly ever with his family, spending his evenings in strange towns—"

"Well, Mother . . . they can hardly be strange anymore. He's had the same territory for twelve years."

"Pick, pick, pick," said Mrs. Dunne, getting to her feet. "Cassie, that's all you ever do."

"But I was trying to—to comfort you," Cassie said indignantly.

"By saying that your father never gets a better territory? That's your idea of comfort?"

"Mother, I had *no* such thing in mind. That's your own— dissatisfaction speaking. All I meant—said—was that the towns couldn't be strange to him anymore bec—"

"Cassie, I just can't listen to you anymore. Honestly, sometimes I wonder why people ever have children." With a little half-sob Mrs. Dunne went into the hall for her coat.

Cassie looked after her, feeling grim. What Mother wouldn't say with Lotta around, she'd sometimes get out when just Cassie was. Even if she didn't mean it—and come to that, who could say if such a statement couldn't be made and meant by any parent once in a while—but even if she did not entirely mean it, she allowed herself to say it out loud. Vincent held that lots of people permitted themselves to say, in grief or anger, unforgivable things, and then when they'd thought it all over, asked to be forgiven.

"And what do you do when that happens to you?" Cassie had demanded.

"Forgive them. You can't hold people accountable for every word and action. There's nothing to do but forgive them."

Is he right? Cassie had wondered. Can he possibly be right? Weren't people accountable for what they did and said? Could even Vincent go through life forgiving everything . . . careless cruelties, indifference, injustice? But when she asked him, Vincent shrugged.

"I can't use up my time resenting it all," he'd pointed out. "There'd never be a spare hour for anything else—like dreaming or making a living or playing tennis. Besides, Cass, do you mean to say that you're trying to go through life expecting it to be *fair?*"

In the face of all opposing evidence Cassie was trying to do just that.

"Cassie," said her mother, coming back into the room, pulling on her thick driving gloves, "I'm sorry I said that. People have children because they want them, and I wouldn't not have you for anything in the world. It's just that . . . oh, you *are* an exasperating girl sometimes."

"I know, Mother." She did know. She must be, because she was constantly exasperating people.

"Well, off I go. Have a nice evening, dear. Maybe there'll be something good on television. Lock up after me."

"Sure. Have fun."

When her mother had gone, Cassie locked the front door and the back. Then she took some ginger ale and a bag of potato chips and went upstairs, observing, even in Lotta's absence, the demarcation of the strings.

Lotta's side of the room glowed softly. (She used a pink bulb in her bed-table lamp.) The bed was turned down trimly. The two fur kittens waited on the pillow. Lotta did things with cozy grace. She'd make an admirable wife one day if she married the right kind of man. J. H., with some age and polish on him, would do.

"What sort of man will *you* marry, Cass?" Lotta had asked one day. Recognizing this as a polite preliminary to a discussion of Lotta's own future husband (Lotta probably saw her sister unwed to the end of her life), Cassie had said, "Any good-humored man with a reasonable income."

Lotta, who had never read Jane Austen, wrinkled her nose. "How dull. Well . . . not for me. I," she said forthrightly, "am going to marry somebody rich."

"Why?"

"Oh, Cass—what a stick you are. Well, so I can have beautiful things. So I'll never have to do dishes or cooking. So I can have the linen changed every day and not have to do it myself. So I don't have to do my own hair—"

"What are you going to do instead of all these things you aren't going to do?" Cassie had asked curiously. Actually she could see Lotta in another subdivision. A very expensive and probably exclusive one. Lotta was a country club, resort area, exclusive neighborhood type.

Lotta had looked momentarily nonplussed and then had said with a smile, "Be happy, darling. That's what."

"Oh. Well, that's a good ambition."

Lotta sometimes turned down Cassie's bed, too. But usually—as now—it was so cluttered with books and clothes and art materials that even Cassie experienced brief dismay at the sight of it. I could straighten it up, she said to herself. I could get to work and neaten up my whole side of the room. That'd surprise her, all right. The thought dispersed even as it formed, and she settled in her armchair with the potato chips and ginger ale.

The wind prowled in the darkness outside. She could hear nearby branches creaking in the cold. There was almost no traffic. Cassie crunched and swallowed and thought about forgiveness.

Perhaps the quality of mercy flowed like a tide through Vincent, and perhaps—just possibly—it was mercy plus something else. She wouldn't call it cowardice. But maybe the quality Vincent called forgiveness was an admixture of forbearance and propitiation. It was easier to be lenient than to protest. But it seemed to Cassie that you had only to look at a newspaper, at the faces around you, at a history book, to see that things were done, and done all the time, that just were not forgivable. From the Roman carnivals of blood through the slave trade and Dachau, down to plain little acts of simple human meanness.

Her own mother was not a wicked woman, but she did wicked things that she considered only her normal right to do. She opened people's mail. "And why not?" she'd said in surprise to Cassie one day, holding a letter from some boy to Lotta. "It's to my own daughter. Why shouldn't I read it?"

"Because it isn't yours," Cassie had said shakily.

"Don't take that tone with me, dear. The fact is, the letter isn't yours either."

"I wouldn't dream of reading it, for that reason. Mother, don't you see it's wrong to—to invade people's privacy?"

"If Lotta is getting letters that I would blush to read, perhaps it's a good thing I do open them. Not that she is," Mrs. Dunne had said, sounding a bit confused and very annoyed. "Girls your age should not have secrets from their mothers."

"Everybody has secrets from everybody!" Cassie had shouted. Shouting was a mistake with her mother, because it gave her a chance to cry and so win the argument by default. Having started, however, Cassie was unable to stop. "Our minds aren't in the back of windows!" she yelled. "Or our feelings either, and we're entitled to some decent—" She tried to think of another word for privacy, and into the hesitation flowed her mother's tears. Cassie always retreated before them.

Her mother opened mail and looked in people's bureaus and asked personal questions. Nothing she did was malicious or intended to be unkind. Her questions were not unanswerable, but having to answer them was sometimes almost unbearable. And it all seemed to Cassie a small form of a tremendous wrong. People did not respect one another. That was why the world was in the mess it was in. That was why there were wars and racism and family fights. Vincent often accused her of oversimplifying in order to prove she had an answer. But this was not oversimplification. This was hard, plain logic. If you respected another person, you would never try to deprive him of his dignity, his possessions, his rights, his beliefs, his life. And if everybody just realized that—who would steal or go to war or murder or say to a man of another color, Don't study or breathe or live near me?

"Maybe," said Cassie, not quite aloud, "a little oversimplification is just what the world stands in need of."

The telephone rang, and she had to go downstairs to answer it. Some boy for Lotta. Cassie explained that her sister was out, did not say with whom, promised to leave a note, and hung up. Lotta, who appeared to be going steady with J. H., certainly kept her hand in. Well, that seemed sensible. If you were terrified of hunger, you made sure of extra provisions. Since about the age of twelve Lotta had been unable to face the briefest period of being boyless, dateless. She seemed to find the measure of herself in a datebook and would have reacted with cold astonishment to the knowledge that her quite unsought-after sister frequently found her pitiful.

Back upstairs, Cassie remembered that with Aunt Muriel coming tomorrow, she'd better shove a few things out of sight right now. There on her desk was the portrait she'd done of Lotta a few days before. It had a *roi soleil* sunburst at the top, some yellow ducklings churning drowzily in the center of the page, a daisy with petals falling in a he-loves-me-he-loves-me-not effect, and down at the very bottom a mole, blindfolded. The blindfold was shocking pink and tied in an enormous bow under the creature's ear.

Cassie studied this work thoughtfully, then stowed it with some others in the bottom drawer of her bureau. She pulled out, in order to make room, some old copies of *National Geographic*. Sitting on the floor, she leafed through these, concentrating in particular on some photographs of lovely thin-legged animals from the Andes. Their mild eyes looked out of the pages directly, it seemed, into her eyes. They looked very innocent, and Cassie thought, as she had thought before, how many of these guiltless lives would go if—*when,* according to Vincent—mankind blew his planet part. "Man could never just destroy himself," Vincent said. "When we go, we're going to take the whole works with us . . . make no mistake about that."

Cassie pulled a drawing pad toward her, picked up a piece of charcoal, and drew three goats coming down a mountain path. They had long beards streaming behind them like skaters' scarves and very long, very thin legs. She never could draw in proportion, and retained a childlike tendency to caricature, to symbolize. She was not self-critical about her drawing or about her portrait collages. She did them because they were fun, because in some way they ordered things for her, and then she put them away and did more. Well, it was one area of privacy no one could violate. Who, for instance, would ever conceive that anyone could conceive of Lotta as a mole?

She had to answer the telephone once again. Someone for her mother. Then she took a shower, washed her hair, and dumped all the stuff off her bed to the floor. She decided to let the turtle have his freedom for a while. As always, when first set down on the vast expanse of the floor, he withdrew in total horror. Nothing showed outside his decorated shell except the tiny spot of a black nose and the minute claws at the end of his webbed feet. He carried a symbol on his back, a heart enclosing the initials J. H. and L., and had been a Christmas present to Lotta, who loathed him on sight. They hadn't known how to get rid of him, so Cassie had put him in a glass casserole and undertaken his care until spring, when she intended to release him in the pond over at the nature preserve. She hoped he'd grow old and strong and that one day the pointless painted heart would wear away.

Tentatively at first, then with increasing confidence, the turtle set off for a walk, lifting the webbed feet carefully, the tiny loop-shaped head turning from side to side. Chin in hands, Cassie watched his promenade.

Lotta was having a marvelous time at the party. She'd met a boy from a prep school who had already asked her to write, and who, though politely attentive in the early part of the evening to his own date, had been making it steadily clearer to everyone whose date he preferred. J. H. was wearing a look of strained indifference that foretold one of those nice little quarrels on the way home that would end in coziness and one of his marvelous long kisses.

Lotta really did just love J. H., captain of the basketball team, handsome in that divine craggy way of certain movie stars, and lavish with his spending money. It wasn't that she couldn't have loved a poor boy (she had, in fact), but it certainly was handier not to. When she and Ray had been in love, for instance, they'd been lucky to get to a drive-in movie once every couple of weeks. And he'd had to work every weekend, so that she practically never saw him anyway—as she'd explained to him on that last, perfectly frightful date. No, J. H., for now, was ideal, and she wouldn't have risked him even for a prep-school boy, except that he wasn't in the least being risked. He was growing by the minute a surer thing.

Lotta sighed a little and smiled at the boy beside her with such an air of shining pleasure that he suddenly, huskily, and to his own great surprise, said, "Look, will you come up to school in June for the Senior Prom? *Please.*"

"Well, for heaven's sake," she said, and laughed. "How can

you say a thing like that? You only met me two minutes ago."

"I feel as if I'd known you all my life," he whispered.

People actually *say* that? Lotta thought. I must remember to tell Cassie. She looked at the boy's own date, playing the piano at the far end of the room and not looking playful or pleased.

Following her glance, the boy shrugged and said, "Just a date. We aren't a thing, you know."

"How would I know? I don't know anything about you."

"But I want you to. Please, will you come in June?"

"I couldn't say, just like that, Bud."

"Brad."

"Oh, of course. Brad. I'd have to ask my mother, and—and anyway, how do you know you won't change your mind? If you're this impulsive, you'll have time to ask a dozen girls before June."

He groaned and set himself discreetly (not wanting to get that big center too annoyed) about the task of convincing her that this was Kismet. Lotta listened enchanted. All this was to her the salt, the savor, the breath of life.

Lotta's favorite indoor, outdoor, all-weather sport was boys. She lived exclusively for the existence and attention of males, those she knew, would one day know, even those she'd never know. The entire masculine world was not too great for the compass of Lotta's admiration. For them she dreamed and dressed herself and spent those mirror hours practicing slow smiles and a mysterious limpid gaze that reduced her (so far regrettably small) cast of masculine characters to helpless

46

stammers. Who knew what lay ahead? Who could tell what raptures, what victories, what splendors were in her future?

J. H. complained that she practically never looked at him. He said that when they were together her eyes were like moths fluttering around, looking for something else to eat up. A silly way to put it, but sort of cute. And oh, he was right, he was right. Other boys had complained of the same thing, and some had even left her, in a rage. But they weren't going to change her. One day someone would change her but not J. H. and not anyone she'd met so far, including this puppy type at her side. She smiled into his eager eyes.

Brad from prep school was stunned at his own success. He'd never known a girl so attentive to his conversation. Everything about her asked him to say more. "And so what we did," he continued, moving closer, forgetting J. H., "what we did was, we got a bowling ball and rolled it down the stairs right toward the hall-master's door. Oh, man, was he bugged!" Looking at her, he experienced a faint misgiving. "Are you sure you want to hear this?"

"Oh, yes," Lotta murmured dreamily. "Do go on."

He went on at length, ending with another, more pressing invitation to the Senior Prom. "Honestly," he said earnestly, "I can't remember when I've had such a great conversation. It's been a real ball. I honestly do feel like I'd known you forever, and that's a fact."

Lotta looked at him affectionately. For over an hour he'd talked. He'd told her wild tales intended to make prep school synonymous with reform school. He'd told her where he'd been born, what his hobbies were, what he thought about when he thought. He'd told her so much that she really did feel she knew him. He'd never asked a single question. He was adorable.

And on the way home she and J. H. quarreled splendidly. The sort of quarrel that ended with J. H. desperately apologizing for the way she'd hurt his feelings. To Lotta's way of thinking this was the only proper outcome to a male-female argument, and as she allowed him to kiss away a small, touching tear, she smiled in the familiar darkness of his car.

Chapter Three

"I don't understand her," Mrs. Dunne said to her sister, Muriel. "I try, but it's no use."

The two women looked at Cassie going off down the road, ice skates over her shoulder, walking in that light, half-running way she had when leaving home.

Muriel Ferris, who had no children of her own and did not try to understand other people's, sipped her tea and said, "Odd how she doesn't mind the cold." She shivered at the thought of the hours ahead of Cassie, tearing around on some frozen pond with the wind biting her face, numbing her fingers.

"You're a big help," Mrs. Dunne said, with a short laugh to show she didn't actually want help.

"Sorry," Muriel said, and then, "Why don't you stop trying to understand her? I think the different generations should settle for just getting along, if they can manage that. It's naïve to expect understanding too. I seem to recall that Mama was always complaining that she didn't understand us, and we weren't especially different or complicated. We were just our age, and it wasn't hers. Probably Cassie doesn't understand you either."

"She doesn't try."

"You can't know that."

"Anybody who was trying to understand other people wouldn't talk and act the way Cassie does. So indifferent to people's *feelings*. Look at what she said about your hair. I didn't notice you enjoying that."

"Oh, well." Muriel held out her cup for more tea. She forgot, between visits, how much Rebecca talked about her children. "I'm sorry I got upset about such a trivial matter."

And she was sorry. Cassie had taken her by surprise. One got out of the habit of expecting candor, especially unflattering candor. All Cassie had, in fact, done was notice that her aunt's hair-do was different, which was more than anyone else had noticed.

"I liked your hair better the way it was," Cassie had said, tipping her head a bit, the better to criticize.

Muriel had said nothing for a second. Then, seeing Rebecca's outraged expression, and to forestall an outburst, she'd asked quickly, "Why not, Cassie? I spent a lot of money to have it styled."

"But it *isn't* your style," Cassie persisted. "Bangs don't become you. Your forehead is too low."

50

"Cassie!"

"Well, but Mother . . . that's not an insult. A low forehead has nothing to do with intelligence. That's just an old wives' tale. Besides, Aunt Muriel welcomes honest criticism. She's said so, lots of times."

"Not when I haven't asked for it, dearie," Muriel said, half piqued and half amused.

"Apologize to your aunt, this second," Mrs. Dunne instructed her daughter.

"Oh, Becky, for heaven's sake," Muriel said. "Can't we stop this? Anyway, the child's right. I *am* always saying I welcome honest criticism. Can't think *why* I say it, as obviously I do not. And I had the faintest tremor of doubt myself when Maurice had finished me this time, only I didn't want to hurt his feelings."

"Too bad other people aren't so thoughtful," Mrs. Dunne said, attempting to impale her daughter with a glance.

Cassie refused to be pinned. "Sorry, Aunt Muriel," she said, picking up her ice skates. "I only mean that you used to look lovely with your hair swept back, and this way—"

"Cassie!"

"All right, Mother, all right. I said I was sorry." She flipped a hand at them and was gone.

Now Muriel put her empty cup on the tray and thought that for a girl who was plain as a poker, Cassie had remarkable assurance. How she had come by that assurance was equally remarkable, since she got little assistance in that line from her family. Becky and Roger loved her, of course, but could never in this world have been subtle enough to give a

51

homely girl the humor and persuasion of a good-looking one. And having Lotta around all the time would be taxing. There must be something in Cassie herself . . . a throwback to a strong-minded woman in their family's past. An abolitionist, a suffragette had handed down her spirit to this tough little descendant.

Becky was still looking harassed. To divert her, Muriel said, "Where's Lotta?" One could always catch Rebecca with that bait.

"She'll be along in a few minutes. She and her friend Irene Stevens are running a birthday party this afternoon for the Storch child." Becky's irrepressible pride in Lotta glowed in every syllable. "They've started a business."

"So enterprising," Muriel murmured. "Does she make a lot of money?" She never knew what to say about Lotta and as a consequence fell into banalities. To her, Lotta was a far less interesting girl than Cassie. No doubt one day Lotta would be a beauty. And unlike Cassie, she was good-tempered and accommodating. Sweet as a teacake and just about as heady.

"Oh, no. They really charge very little," Mrs. Dunne said. "And now that Cassie's decided to demand a share—" She broke off with an expression of self-reproach. "What's valuable for Lotta," she continued, "is the association with someone like Irene. She meets all sort of fine people. I mean, living here in Forest Acres, everybody is the same as everybody else, you know. Same incomes, same . . . attitudes, you know." She frowned a little, wondering if Muriel would see that she was not being undemocratic but simply analytical. "I am not complaining, mind. It's just how things are."

"People who live in subdivisions shouldn't expect variety."

"Muriel, I will thank you not to sneer."

"Dear, I'm not sneering. Tell me about these birthday parties," she wheedled.

Briefly it seemed Rebecca would prefer to sulk. Then she relaxed and even smiled. "Well, Lotta and Irene were sitting around one day last summer, wondering how to make some money. I mean, Irene comes from one of our better families, you know, but she's not spoiled moneywise. She baby-sits and all, just like the other girls."

Very leveling, Muriel Ferris muttered, but to herself. Useless to protest Becky's snobberies. She couldn't help them. In some peculiar way there was an innocence about them. She simply was impressed by what she called "our better families."

"And they were saying how boys can wash cars or windows or work in garages or supermarkets, you know—" Mrs. Dunne went on while Muriel stifled a yawn and stared out the window. "So they were saying how there must be something girls could do besides baby-sitting, which gets *some* boring." She stopped, looking pleased with herself for the bit of slang. "And then Irene said, well, she plays the piano and Lotta plays the flute, so why didn't they give concerts, and Vincent—he was here then—said nobody with ears over ten years of age would listen to them, or I guess he said nobody over ten years of age with ears. So then they had the whole idea. I mean, they'd play for people *under* ten. It all began in such a simple way."

Mrs. Ferris yawned openly this time and wished she hadn't agreed to stay a week. The ties of blood when examined closely so often proved to be knots. She never remembered that when absence blurred the picture. "Becky," she began, "is Cassie still doing those collage portraits? I was hoping—"

"Here's Lotta now," said Mrs. Dunne. "Darling, do come in and say hello to your Aunt Muriel. Bring Irene with you."

Irene, Muriel decided, was a diminished Lotta. Not quite so blond, not quite so pretty, just not quite so. But young and fetching. These are the girls, she thought, who sail lightly along the surface of their youth, never suspecting the existence of undercurrents, riptides, rapids. The cheer leaders, the prom and hop belles, the flirts, who look forward to the next date, the next dress, anticipate college as a more glamorous extension of high school and marriage as a state of being adored by a perfect man.

I should know, she thought, having been just such a girl myself.

"I understand you've become entrepreneurs," she said. The two girls looked blank. "You've gone into business for yourselves." Schools were not what they used to be. Or was it the students who weren't what they'd been? Should "entrepreneur" be a word beyond the grasp of people this age?

"Oh, yes," Lotta said, plumping down on a sofa and patting the place beside her. "You sit, too, Irene," she directed with a queenly air. "We have a marvy setup," she went on to her aunt. "Mother's been telling you about it?"

"All things considered, I think you're very brave in your choice of endeavor. The thought of children's birthday parties is too appalling."

"We figured lots of mothers feel that way too. That's how

54

the whole idea came about, really. You know, if you're *giving* the party for your very own Johnny, it *is* apt to become cream of frenzy. Is Johnny *really* having a good time, or is he having *too* good a time, and *is* he behaving like a perfect little gentleman . . . so many questions and all that ice cream and shrieking besides. Mothers simply go under. Now, Rene and I can be detached, you know, since none of the little frights belong to us. And children do tend to behave better with strangers than with the family."

"A condition not limited, after all, to children," Muriel said.

"Heck, no," said Lotta cheerfully.

"She doesn't," Mrs. Dunne pointed out, "really mean to call the children frights. Do you, dear?" she asked, frowning at Lotta.

"Some of them aren't," Lotta admitted, ignoring the frown. She was reliably good-natured and never took offense at what an adult did or said. Muriel suspected that this was the result of an indifference to them so total that reaction was out of the question. Cassie appeared to take everyone, of any age, as an individual to whom a response of some kind was inescapable. But to Lotta, Muriel thought, that whole authoritarian world of people no longer young, really young, was a horde of shadows, indistinguishable one from another, without significance. In the company of her elders she had a lamblike mildness that seemed affectionate but was probably in fact a state of trance that occupied her until she could escape.

I, thought Muriel Ferris once again, should know. Then,

55

feeling that more reaction on her part was called for, she said, "How do you make your contacts, girls?"

"They run an ad in the local paper once a week," Mrs. Dunne explained. She was rosy-cheeked with gratification. "Let's see, now . . . there's one around here someplace. Yes, here we are—" She read aloud: " 'Two girls will conduct children's birthday parties. Reasonable, experienced, Call—' " She broke off. "We use our telephone number, because Irene's father isn't away most of the time the way Roger is. Men tend to be awfully grouchy about anybody's phone calls but their own, I find." She put the paper down, patting it with satisfaction.

"How many tots can you handle?" Muriel asked listlessly. If she hadn't known Cassie would stay far too long, she'd have asked to go along to the ice-skating pond. Maybe she'd still bundle up and walk over. The walk alone would be enough on a day like this, and by then perhaps Cassie would be ready to start back. It was either that or retire to her room (Vincent's room) and read or take a nap. But Becky became injured if one closed a door against her during the day, so probably the walk— She turned her attention back to Lotta, who was explaining that it depended on the assortment, how many they took.

"Assortment?" said Muriel, wondering if she'd lost the thread.

"She means," said Irene, "that we'll take up to twenty-four of boys and girls together. But more than twelve of just boys . . . wow!"

"Boys just stand still and everything starts coming unglued," said Lotta. "So far we haven't had a real disaster, and boys are pretty good at getting out of scrapes, but still—"

"You could always apply for a gun permit," Muriel suggested. The girls laughed and Becky said, "*Really*, Muriel."

"The point is," Lotta said, "that boys are good at getting out of scrapes that girls wouldn't get into in the first place." She looked at her watch. "We better get the stuff and be ready for when J. H. gets here, Rene." She went to the closet under the hall stairway and came back with a shopping bag and her flute. "Now, let's see. . . . The favors, the place cards, the itty-bitty presents, the balloons . . . where are the balloons?"

"I have them," Irene said, indicating the shopping bag she'd brought with her. It was from Jensen's, very handsome and unused-looking. Mrs. Dunne looked from it to Lotta's brown paper bag that had carried home a large assortment of groceries. A shadow skimmed her eyes.

"Dear," she said to Lotta. "I'm sure we must have a bag from one of the better stores that you could use."

Muriel Ferris's mouth dropped, and even Lotta seemed surprised. "What's wrong with this one?" she asked.

"Well . . . Irene's bag is so pretty and . . . and chic-looking."

"For heaven's sake, Mother. How crazy can you get?"

"I only said—"

"Well, don't."

Mrs. Dunne bit her lip, averting her head at the unexpected brusqueness of Lotta's voice. I imagine, Muriel thought, with a rush of helpless pity for her sister, that this

57

often happens to Becky. Her children get impatient at her silliness, make no attempt to hide their impatience, and she learns nothing to help her against the next rebuff. Poor Becky.

Irene was delicately investigating her chic shopping bag, muttering an inventory. "Scratch pads for the word game, little colored balls, snappers. . . . Well, I guess we're in order. What's keeping J. H., do you suppose?"

"He'll be along," Lotta said tranquilly, and as she spoke a cowlike moan sounded outside. Muriel Ferris started nervously.

"Bye, Mom," Lotta said, taking a moment to lean over and kiss her mother's cheek lightly. "Bye, Aunt Muriel."

"Don't boys ever ring doorbells anymore?" Muriel said as the girls disappeared.

"Only at Halloween," Becky said, getting up to clear the tea things. "Young people are much more casual today than we used to be."

"Casual's a word for it, I suppose," said Muriel, not much liking the way Becky had put her thought.

Mrs. Dunne, with some conscious satisfaction, went on to make matters worse. "Muriel, don't be so picky. You sound like your own maiden aunt."

Cassie hurried along, the skates that she'd hung around her neck bumping on her thin chest. She wore a red-and-green striped stocking cap pulled down over her ears and forehead, the not immaculate cherry-colored sweater under an old yellow corduroy jacket, and purple stretch pants. In a little while her blood began to race and a peculiar tangy warmth seemed to come from the cold itself, making her step lighter, as it always did. She walked everywhere she could, all year round. Even to and from school, nearly two miles from home. If you could stand the first couple of blocks, when all you wanted to do was turn back and dive into one of those warm, smelly, noisy buses, this other feeling seemed then to take and rush you along till you felt as if you skimmed the ground. Even when, as today, the sun seemed to go out all of a sudden and a wind that hadn't been there a moment ago now made you gasp for breath, even then the feeling of being light and brilliant kept you skimming along.

She wished she hadn't said anything about Aunt Muriel's hair. "If you can't say something nice, say nothing." That was Mother's advice. It seemed to Cassie, who liked variety, most monotonous and, strictly speaking, dishonest advice. If you said only the good things and suppressed the critical or disapproving, restraining all disagreement while you waited for something you could acclaim to turn up, why then you were dealing in half-truths most of the time.

Of course people went around saying things they didn't mean, or not saying things they did mean, all the time. They didn't call it dishonesty. They called it tact. Once in a while Cassie tried to get a grip on tact, but it slid from her grasp with the ease of an eel. Tactful people—even Vincent— seemed to her as agile, as elusive, as slippery as eels. How friendly, for instance, her mother would sound telling a woman she didn't admire that she wouldn't be able to attend the canasta party after all.

"It isn't that I don't *want* to, goodness knows, Mrs. James, but you know . . . my church work, the children, the difficulty of running a household when your husband is on the road so much— I know you'll understand—"

She'd go on, sounding so real, and Cassie would listen, telling herself that Vincent was right, that this was what people had to do, or else they'd arouse hard feelings and hurt feelings and all sorts of feelings better left unaroused. But only the night after she'd begged off with Mrs. James, Mother had told Mrs. Fitzsimmons, whom she did admire, that she'd just love to join the bridge group. "Oh, of course I'm not too busy. I mean, I'm busy, of course, but a person has to make time for pleasure, too, don't you think? No, my work on the church bazaar finished up last week and I'm free as air." And Mother frequently remarked (not to her children) that she'd become so accustomed to having Roger on the road that the real trouble came only when he was home. "He seems to get the children's backs up the moment he steps in the door, poor Roger. And, of course, with just the two girls at home, it's easier to keep house. Not that Cassie is neat, but she isn't a *boy*."

Lotta, breaking one date in order to keep a better one that had come along—a really sinful thing to do—never sounded sweeter or sorrier or more sincere than in the moment of sinning. "Ray, darling," she'd coo, "truly, when I said yes for Saturday, I but utterly for*got* that this aunt of mine was coming for the weekend. I mean, I practically never see her, and she wouldn't understand at all if I just left as soon as she got here. I mean, I can't hurt her *feelings*, can I? Yours? Oh, but Ray, I expect *you* to under*stand*." As if Lotta or Aunt

60

Muriel would for a second expect either to alter her plans for the other. Ray would understand, or claim to, and Lotta would go out on Saturday evening with J. H., who'd take her dancing or someplace to hear jazz. Places she'd never run into Ray, because he couldn't afford them.

Not, Cassie said to herself, arriving at the deeply frozen pond, not that I hold any brief for Ray, a two-hundred-pound blob of blood and sinew with a warm wind where his brain should be. And not that J. H. is any better or worse, just twenty pounds lighter and a good deal richer. What I hold a brief for, she explained to herself as she laced her skates and put her shoes on a large flat rock among a lot of other shoes, what I *do* value is honesty.

She pulled her mittens back on and struck out across the reaches of ice. For a moment, before the skimming and the soaring and a sense of speed close to flying overtook her, she thought about these matters still and frowned. A young man who had liked the look of the back of her—the slender tension of her body as she sped forward, the shabby brightness of her dress—dashed to overtake her and look back. At the sight of her sharp-featured face with its furrows of discontent, he fell behind in disappointment. With her cap pulled down that way and the lines in her forehead she looked to him sort of like a monkey.

Cassie, not observing him, his interest, or his loss of it, leaned into the wind and went on with her thoughts. Her father, for instance. How was a person to take him? Jolly as anything when company was around, turning immediately gloomy when it left. How could you believe anything when the man who put his arm around you and said to his boss, "You remember our baby, Cassie, don't you, Mr. Gunner?" gave you such a look of impatience when the boss had gone? "At least you could have *acted* pleased to see him," he'd said last time this had happened.

"But you weren't pleased to see him yourself," Cassie had protested. "I heard you telling Mom that the old bore infringes on your time as if he had you indentured."

"Cassie," Mr. Dunne had said slowly, "do you have to practice being this disagreeable, or does it come to you without effort?"

Cassie, like her mother, preferred life when Mr. Dunne was on the road. She had learned to keep this to herself, which was, perhaps, a step in the direction of tact. She certainly hoped so.

The sun was out again, glinting and refracting on the smooth surface of the pond. The cold air seemed almost to spark and was pungent with the odor of pines that grew close to the shoreline. All the brightly dressed skaters whirling and dashing, skimming and stumbling, looked to Cassie's eye like a Flemish painting or a Grandma Moses. Very gay and detailed, full of a wonderful winter brightness, biting and flashy. It suited her splendidly to be lost in the picture, to speak to no one, not even to notice if she knew anyone. It was good to be for a while among people who had no reason to talk to her.

About an hour later the same young man, skating past her, was once again caught by the air of flying freedom in the slight figure. Once again he looked back and this time wondered for a moment if it could be the same girl, though he knew it had to be from her clothes. The crazy green-and-red cap was still jammed down so that no one could tell the shade of her hair, and it still gave her somehow the look of a monkey. He wondered now that he had found it unattractive. Maybe she looked more like a fox. Anyway, like some little animal, wild and unselfconscious, the funny clothes a natural covering and the expression one of—joy? Not that so much as belonging. Like any creature in its proper element. She was a marvelous skater, and he would have liked to meet her. He even turned and started back with this in mind, but she was away and gone without even seeing him.

J. H., operating on a high level of romantic concentration, was low on other things, such as manners. He would (he thought) have submitted to the bastinado for Lotta but not to the torture of courtesy. Pulling up to the curb in front of her house, he leaned on his horn without troubling even to reach across the seat and open the door. Opening doors for them! It gave him a laugh. Helpless females, huh? Lotta, for all her kittenlike appearance, was strong as an ox, and J. H. felt he'd be the guy to know, having been wrestled to a standstill by her many a night in this very car. If he hadn't known he was really crazy about her, there were times when he'd almost have said he couldn't stand her. Her or any of the rest of those pretty, spoiled-rotten types who took and took from a guy and thought nothing was due in return but sweet smiles and an occasional kiss that promised plenty and delivered nothing.

Drumming his fingers on the steering wheel as he waited, J. H. failed to interpret his rising resentment. He attributed this sour feeling to the fact that Lotta and her sidekick failed to shoot out the second he arrived.

"Who do you think I am?" he demanded when Lotta and Irene, loaded with shopping bags and other junk for the birthday party finally made the scene. "Father Time?"

"Sweetie-pie," said Lotta, opening the back door and stowing away their gear, "I think you're Mr. America, with a distinct dash of Prince Charming mixed in."

J. H. rarely looked for sarcasm and didn't now. As they settled in beside him, however, Irene definitely sniffed. He leaned around Lotta and glared at her. "You mind your manners, or you'll find yourself running behind the car."

Irene pursed her lips at him invitingly. "J. H.," she said softly, "how can you talk to me that way? I've been but just longing to see you."

All the girls had these low, sort of breathless voices these days. Half the time you could hardly hear them. Feeling badgered but unable, as usual, to formulate the reason why, far less to counterattack, J. H. gave his attention to the one thing he was sure of here—his car. As they drove along, the girls chattering like squirrels (*Female* squirrels, J. H. said to himself irritably—male squirrels probably just went quietly about their business.), he listened to the lovely familiar hum of the engine, every inch of which he knew by heart. If only a girl could be like an automobile. If only you could tend them and take them apart and put them back together again and *know* them the way you did an engine and a chassis that were your own. . . .

64

He smiled a little at his own fancy. Lotta, alert to his slightest expression, his least alteration of mood, knowing him, in fact, as well as he knew his car, put her hand on his and squeezed it. "See?" she said softly. "You aren't really mad. And besides, we practically knocked down Mother and Aunt Muriel in our race for the door, didn't we, Rene?"

"Absolutely," said Irene. "I doubt if they've picked themselves up yet."

"Well, it felt like ages," he grumbled. But she was right. He wasn't mad anymore. A man who could stay mad at Lotta would be—not a man, he concluded with masterful simplicity.

"Lamb, that's because you were missing me," Lotta explained, snuggling slightly. "I've missed you too."

Irene lifted her eyes but said nothing.

Boy, said J. H. to himself, starting to get angry all over again. Boy, the stuff she thinks she can get away with! Like that crud from prep school last night. Swarming over him like a bee and then buzzing back to me as if nothing had happened. The evening had, in fact, ended with *him* apologizing to *her*, though how she'd maneuvered him into that was more than he could tell.

"J. H.," she went on, "do me a great big favor, will you?"

"What sort of favor?" he growled.

"But I want you to promise *before* I ask. Come on, now, sweetie. You know you can't resist me."

Oh, *man*, said J. H. in a silent shout. How do you like that? Sometimes he wondered if it wouldn't be better just not to bother about Lotta, or any girl, ever. He had a swell car and had had more rebounds this season than any other guy on

65

the team. In practice today he'd made nine out of ten foul shots, three out of three lay-ups, and one half-court shot that no one else even would have tried. Why wasn't that enough?

He slid his glance down to Lotta's blond and fragrant head, so close to his shoulder, and sighed a little. "Okay," he said. "What do I have to promise?"

"Oh, you *are* wonderful, J. H.," Lotta said, sounding sincere. This time she was, but the sound was always the same. "It's an awfully little thing, really. You're coming back for us at five?"

"Natch. I said I would, didn't I?"

"Well, *would* you mind not blowing your horn? I mean, would you come up to the door and ring the bell?"

"Why?" J. H. demanded irritably. "Why should I make like a gentleman here if I don't—" He broke off at Irene's giggle. "No, I won't go up to the door and ring the bell, and that's that."

"But, J. H. You promised."

"Come off it. You be on that stoop at five, see? Or I'll blast the birthday party into orbit."

Lotta exhaled a long soft breath. She shrugged. "I'm sorry, J. H. We'll find someone else to drive us home."

"What do you mean, you'll find someone else?"

"Seems clear enough to me, doesn't it to you, Rene? Now look, J. H. Irene and I are running a business, and the impression we make counts. If people think we run around with a lot of mannerless boors, why we won't get the sort of—of trade we're looking for," she said firmly.

"Well, I'll be a—" J. H. was almost speechless with anger. Get someone else, would she? Mannerless bore, was he? "Listen, if I'm good enough for you at home, then I'm good enough for you here. If you're so slam-bang anxious to make a good impression, why don't you try making one on your own mother? Why don't you ask me to ring *your* doorbell?"

"For one thing, you'd have to be ringing it practically every night. Here you only have to make the effort once. Anyway, it's too late for you to act like a gentleman around my mother. She'd probably get suspicious the minute you started. She'd think we had something to hide."

"If you don't have the twistiest mind of all time," J. H. said, honestly indignant.

"Do you realize," Lotta said, abruptly changing tactics, "that if Irene and I can make a go of this, J. H., I may even be able to help send myself to college? I mean," her wistful voice went on, "you and Rene, you'll just go—"

"If anyone will take me," said Irene. "With my grades I'll be lucky to make a charm school."

"You'll go to some nice finishing school," Lotta said. "And J. H.—why even if his parents didn't have the money, he could go practically anywhere on an athletic scholarship, at practically any sport." J. H. ran a hand over his smooth crew cut. "So, you see," she said to him, "you have two ways to go, and Rene'll get in somewhere. But *I* won't. My grades aren't super, and my family doesn't have any money—"

Every time she said this, and she said it fairly often, J. H. melted like a snowman in a spring thaw. He found it so touching, so naïve, so . . . so darned sweet. True, of course, but how many girls would admit it the way Lotta did? Never ashamed, never trying to put on a show. Nice as pie to that cuckoo sister of hers, who wasn't always so darned nice back. Come to that, Lotta never complained, never said anything mean about anybody, and that was a fact. And here was the poor kid, trying to make a little money so she could go to college. He didn't like to point out that she'd started sort of late.

By golly, J. H. said to himself, if I had my own money, I'd send her myself. Since I don't, the least I can do is ring a doorbell when she asks me. In fact, he said to himself critically, from now on I'm going to ring the blasted doorbell no matter where she is. So there.

In this mood of high purpose, he circled the Storch driveway, instructed the girls to stay where they were, dashed around the car to open the door and assist them out.

"My goodness, J. H.," said Irene. "You do overreact to stimulus, don't you?"

But Lotta gave him her hand and a glimpse of her lovely knees as she slid across the seat and out. "Thank you, love," she whispered, lifting her eyes to look directly in his. "Thank you, J. H."

Feeling, in a way, knighted, J. H. grabbed her shopping bag and accompanied her to the door. Oh, Lotta knew how to behave toward a man, all right. She could enrage a person almost past endurance but then make you feel splendid, special. He was crazy about her, and as he drove away he felt his love like something constricting his breath. He wanted to yell or leap in the air or run the fastest mile on record. His feeling for Lotta often gave him this sensation of wild physical exuberance, and today he went to the gym and played handball for an hour. Only then could he relax a little, only then did that feeling of a hoop around his chest lessen its grip.

"I don't suppose you'd give me the recipe?" Irene asked as they sorted party favors and began to inflate the balloons.

"Recipe?"

"For turning a big strong man into a taffy pull?"

Lotta smiled and lifted her softly darkened brows. "I'm not sure it's translatable. Anyway, you know perfectly well that what works with J. H. won't work with someone else. I guess it's a matter of mood more than anything else."

"With a dash of hypocrisy, to taste."

Lotta shrugged. "People who try to get along in this world without a dash of hypocrisy—to taste, as you say—end up like—"

She stopped. Even with Irene, to whom she would tell most things, she retained her determination never to sound critical. She tried not even to *be* critical. It was a role she'd begun to act so long ago that by now it was almost not acting. She would never put into words for anyone what she felt about her family.

But she was never, either, going to get like them. And especially not like Vincent and Cassie, who constituted one of the major disappointments of her life. She would have adored an attractive, dashing older brother, a pretty and popular young sister. But Vince and Cassie—in her most secret mind she knew that not only was she not proud of them, she didn't even properly love them. A conformist like

69

Lotta realized that she should love her family in spite of everything even if she couldn't love them because of anything. Only she didn't. She was pleasant to her father when he was home, forgot him when he wasn't. She got along nicely with her mother, who thought they had a beautiful relationship, and where was the harm in that? But her brother and sister—those two had let her down. Their plain, serious faces offended her when she contrasted them with the brother and sister she might have had. Their bluntness was embarrassing. Vincent, she supposed, she could have forgiven bluntness and plainness if he hadn't been her relative. She might simply have enjoyed his good spirits and sense of humor. After all, some of the nicest boys she knew weren't madly good-looking or frivolous. But to have to introduce to people as her *brother* a person so insignificant, so blotchy—

Look at Irene's older brother. The one at college. Tall, handsome, with a teasing fondness for his little sister and his little sister's friends. There was a brother to be proud of. He didn't, in truth, seem to have as nice a disposition as Vincent, but he showed up so well. She was ashamed to be ashamed of her brother, and that made her resent him even more. It was an awful circle of ill feeling they had caught her up in, those two. Even if they didn't know it. And Cassie was worse. Cassie didn't even *try*. That hair, those tacky clothes, that air of slovenly superiority. With some effort Cassie could perhaps achieve a sort of gaminlike distinction, but she missed it all along the line and didn't even seem to *care*. Sometimes it almost seemed that she deliberately made herself as unattractive as possible, just to be annoying.

Well, certainly none of this was the kind of thing she'd confide in Irene or anyone else. You couldn't help the sort of family you were born into, but you could help the way you behaved until you got away from it. Long ago Lotta had opted for an attitude of sweetness, gentleness, with a little conscious courage showing at the edges. It was a subtle role and she carried it off well, she felt. If the dash of hypocrisy was something rather more than a dash, even her best friends weren't going to find out.

"My goodness," Mrs. Dunne was saying to her sister, having followed her up to Vincent's room, "my goodness, it does seem pleasant having you here. What are you doing, reading?"

Muriel looked up from her book. "Yes. It's—"

"Don't let me interrupt you," Becky said, smoothing the bedspread, where the imprint of her sister's traveling case remained, and emptying the ashtray. "I believe in letting people have their privacy."

"Becky, I only used that ashtray once. Are you going to empty it after each cigarette?"

"Oh, it's no trouble."

"No, but—"

"Don't you think Lotta's looking beautiful? Honestly, I sometimes wonder how in the world a daughter of Roger and me could be so beautiful, you know? Are you perfectly comfortable here? I'm sorry you have to share a bathroom with the rest of us. I realize you aren't used to—shall we say, roughing it?"

"For goodness' sake, Becky. What a silly thing to say."

"So I'm silly, am I?" Mrs. Dunne laughed lightly. "Well, maybe I am, and maybe I'm not. But anyway, I'm happy, and that's something, isn't it?"

"I should think it was everything," Muriel replied, putting her book aside.

"Oh, don't stop because of me," Becky said. "I was going anyway. I only came to see if everything was all right, and if the girls had cleared Vince's room properly. I meant to get up here this morning, but what with one thing and another —you know how it is—I never had a chance. And anyway, you'd think by now Cassie could clean up a room without being checked up on, wouldn't you?"

"I thought you said the *girls* had done it?"

"Oh, well, that was how it . . . You see, it all became a terrible rumpus, even *asking* them."

"I'm sorry if I—"

"You just be glad you don't have children, Muriel. You just be glad. I said to them that you were coming and would they get the room ready. If we had a guest room, of course, none of this would happen, but we don't and we all have to make the best of it, including you, of course. I know in your own apartment you're used to the best of everything—"

"I don't know what gives you that idea."

"But here we make do with what we have, and we're cheerful about it. At least we're cheerful all except Cassie, but she's a natural complainer."

"I don't think—"

"You should have heard her when she realized that she'd

have to do the room alone because Lotta was doing the birthday party for the Storch child. . . . My, I wonder how it's going. Not that there's anything to worry about; those two girls do a job that— I think I'll try to get Lotta some sort of smart bag to carry her things in, for the parties, I mean. Something personalized."

"What did Cassie say about having to do the room?"

"Oh, I don't really remember. She demanded a share of Lotta's birthday party money. As a matter of fact, I was the one who suggested it, but I didn't think— I suppose it's fair, in a way, since Lotta does get out of a lot of the housework because of her birthdays. But what does Cassie *want* with money? She doesn't care about clothes or anything."

"Maybe paints and—"

"If you ask me, and even if it isn't nice to say, sometimes I think she's just jealous of Lotta. And I suppose you can't blame the poor child. I mean, she's my own daughter and I love her dearly, but a sister like Lotta *could* be a handicap to a certain type of person. Of course if Cassie would study her sister and learn from her, maybe even imitate her a little bit, then she wouldn't have to be so jealous. But everybody has to be what they have to be, wouldn't you say?"

"Yes."

"If Roger could only get a raise, I can't tell you the difference it would make to us. I mean, the girls could have separate rooms, for one thing."

"Why doesn't one of them take this room?"

"We considered it, don't think we didn't. But after all, it is Vincent's, and we do want him to feel free to come home.

73

And Cass keeps hoping he'll bring friends. And there's company. There's you. We can't just put people up in the living room, can we? No, the girls will have to just try to get along together until Lotta goes away to college. *If* she goes, of course. Where the money's to come from I can't say, and it isn't as if Lotta was one of these bookworms and could get a scholarship or anything. Well . . . did you find your towels and everything? Do you think you'll want an extra blanket?"

"I'm not sure, but—"

"Well, if you do, all you have to do is ask, you know that of course." Mrs. Dunne, who'd been standing all this time, sat on the edge of Vincent's bed (Muriel was using the other one) and said, "Tell me, have you seen much of that friend of yours—what was her name? The one that got the job in Paris? My, what a wonderful life she must lead, running around the world that way. I don't suppose Roger and I will ever see Paris, or anyway not till we're too old to care, I tell him. Actually, I don't think Roger would care if he *never* saw Paris. Vincent said when a man spends so much of his time in romantic Detroit—that's where the home office is— why should he want to see Paris? Of course that's just Vinnie's way of talking. He thinks he's quite funny. Sometimes he is, too. What was it he said last time he was home—oh, it was a scream—now, what was it? Give me a minute, and I'm sure to remember, because I do remember we all practically died laughing—"

A week, Muriel Ferris was saying to herself. I must have been out of my mind.

Chapter Four

In the second semester of his second year at college Vincent Dunne had only fitful, insubstantial ideas of what it was he wished to do or to be, of what he wanted from life, except to be happy—a sensible, reasonable desire, condoned even by Samuel Johnson, no casual condoner.

Vincent was not especially happy at present but felt this was the result of certain physical defects he was still hopeful of outgrowing. He was young enough yet, a doctor had told him, to have a sudden spurt of growth, and it was a known fact that bad complexions were a burden of adolescence, a period he would shortly have done with. He did not expect suddenly to become handsome, but good looks were not of the first importance in a man. Six—even four—more inches and an end to acne. That was the extent of his physical wishes. Hardly hubris, he'd tell himself, looking in the mirror as he shaved. Nothing to bring the wrath of the gods down upon his head.

As to where he was going, what he was preparing himself for . . . He would end up somewhere, doing something, because everybody did. Questioned by his distressed mother, his vexed and choleric father, he'd indicate a leaning toward the sciences. So far as the college was concerned, he was a zoology major. But he suspected that what he meant by a leaning toward science was a disinclination for arts. He loved to read. He liked to listen to music, to go to an occasional picture gallery and look at nonobjective pictures, which suited his sense of quandary. That was all. A composition for his English course was agony to him, a letter next to impossible. He played no instrument, had no desire to express himself in oils, and though once he'd briefly considered architecture as a career, that had been the result of reading a book about Frank Lloyd Wright. There was a man who'd had an interesting life.

"Architecture, is it?" his father had bellowed. "You couldn't pick a riskier profession, could you?"

"Nothing risky about it," Vincent had replied. "I'd be sure to starve."

"I suppose that's your idea of humor?" Mr. Dunne had demanded.

"Well, just for a moment there . . . but no. Now that you put the issue so forcibly, no, I don't really think it's humor."

"Vincent, when are you going to settle down and take some of your obligations and responsibilities seriously?"

"Glad you brought that up, sir. Actually, I was thinking of sometime in April. Around the fifteenth. If we don't have rain, of course."

He couldn't help it. There was something about his father, that gloomy, disgruntled, reactionary man, that brought out the picador in Vincent. With everyone else he was prepared to be gentle, to think the best, to make concessions in order to avoid dispute, in order to nurture any fruits of friendship or accord.

But there was something about his father—

"*If* my recollection serves," Mr. Dunne had gone on that day, "you have now been a geneticist, an oil engineer, a metallurgist, a doctor, a psychologist, and a trial lawyer. All pretty high-sounding, all right. But what I want to know is, what are you going to *be* when you get your nose out of the air? And when's that going to be? Do you think you have the rest of time to decide in? Or maybe you think I'm going to stand you to a graduate school? Seems to me you fellows go to school longer and longer, and if you ask me, it's just to put off getting out and actually making your way. A bunch of ostriches calling yourselves scholars. You make me laugh."

There was enough truth in that to make Vincent uncomfortable. Graduate school seemed to be becoming not the exception but the rule, and though he dared not mention it around home, Vince was pretty sure he'd have a go at one himself if he could figure out which one and if he could earn the money. That last he could probably do. Lab jobs, tutoring, summer work. He already, with his scholarship, earned part of his way just working summers. If he dug in and made a real go of zoo, some foundation or industry might even pick him up and see him through another two or four years of research. Dr. Vincent Dunne, the eminent zoologist. Or even Dr. Dunne, a zoologist. Was that what he wanted?

He thought that when the penultimate moment arrived, leaving only the ultimate in which to decide, he would choose according to what book he'd most recently lost himself in. Or, by some grace of fortune, found himself in. It would depend on whether he'd been reading Fabre or C. P. Snow, Aldous or Julian Huxley, Freud or Clarence Darrow. What seemed to him the most peculiar part of all this was that while he was interested in the outcome, he had great difficulty forcing himself to feel involved. The college years, which he loved even if they were not bringing him great emotional happiness (he supposed he meant by that that he didn't have a girl), would pass. With luck he'd get a few more (to stave off, as his father rightly guessed, the moment when his head had to come out of the warm collegiate sand for good). And then he'd take his place in the world, as other people did, because that was all there was to do. There was no way to explain to his parents that just how he took it did not seem important to him. Vincent Dunne, the architect, or Vincent Dunne, an architect. Vincent Dunne, Supreme Court judge, or Vincent Dunne, a lawyer. Did it really matter?

With *the* nuclear physicists and *the* heads of government guiding the times, would his future even be there when he reached for it? Was this world long for this world? A good question, and no answer at the back of the book. Yet the people he admired were not those who lay down and moaned,

What's the use, we're done for. Nor were they those strange types who seemed exhilarated and freed of responsibility by the threat of destruction so great that nothing they did or left undone could matter. Vincent admired people who were concerned and curious about the world, who behaved as if mankind would endure and might even become better.

But he could not imagine explaining to his parents that it seemed less important to him what he did than what he was. Putting aside his scholarship and his summer jobs, they were making sacrifices to send him to college and were justified in expecting him to find it all of the keenest importance.

"If you don't care what you do, then be a garage mechanic, be a truck driver." He could hear his father saying it, and had to grant that by parental lights it was a fair ultimatum. Only he didn't want to be a garage mechanic or a truck driver. He wanted to go to college and someday be a scientist of some sort.

Once, in an unaccustomed attempt to smooth his father's almost permanently ruffled feathers, he had said, "Well, what do you suggest, Dad?"

"You know damn well what I suggest. Be a salesman. Sell anything . . . it doesn't matter what. Just sell something. Soap, ideas, machinery, politicians . . . *sell* them. If you're a salesman on your toes, you can go anywhere, be anything. President of some big company, easily. It's the salesmen who get ahead in our society, and don't kid yourself otherwise. All these scientists—they'd drop to the bottom like lead weights with their know-how and their jargon if it wasn't for the salesmen putting them and their ideas across."

"To whom?"

"To everybody. To the government, to the people, to foreign powers. The top dog today is the businessman. The salesman, in other words."

"But I don't think I'd be a salesman on my toes. I think I'd be a salesman on my flat feet," Vincent had said thoughtfully.

A look of deep and painful disappointment possessed his father's face, and in a moment he'd nodded, like someone who's been momentarily caught up in a vision and then crudely dumped back to reality. Vincent felt sorry for him, this not very successful salesman idealizing his unidealistic profession.

"I'm sorry, Dad," he'd said. "But you know yourself it takes a certain kind of man—a man like yourself—to be a good salesman."

Mr. Dunne had looked pleased. He agreed that not everyone could do it, and for a while there'd been peace between father and son, like the peace between nations—wary, distrustful, but desperately hoping for accord.

"Ho, Vincent! Wherefore sits thou in the gathering gloom? Hast the electric power been cut off?" That was the voice of David Gates in the hallway.

Vince reached over and turned on a lamp as his two roommates came in.

"I was seeing through a glass darkly," he told them.

"Is that Shakespeare or the Bible?" asked Enoch Burke-Runciman. "I never can pin these overquoted quotations on their proper pages."

80

"I think it's the Bible," said David. "But I wouldn't make book on it. Good Book, that is. That's a pun," he added.

"And very funny too," said Vincent. "You raise my spirits immeasurably with your wit and wisecracks."

"Anytime, cousin. Anytime."

Vincent looked at these two good friends and thought how strange it was to realize that there had been a time when he hadn't known them. Enoch had been growing up in England, David in South Carolina, himself here in the northeast. Vincent had had friends before but not like these. Not people whose minds he knew, who knew his. Among ourselves, he thought, we don't even employ the harmless social lies and masks with which people make their images more presentable to the world. And to themselves.

Enoch, who around the college tended to live up to his hyphen, admitted to Vincent and David that it had neither history nor validity. "My father just stuck it in there to doll things up. Like so many other things about us, it's sheer pretension." Vincent carried off, with what success he did not know, but with unvarying determination, the role of misogynist. To these two he could say almost easily, "What girl would be bothered with me?" and allow them to know, if he never said, how much he wished a girl would. And David, the light-stepping, high-hearted man-about-campus, here in this room could be morose and dispirited without apology. In the security of this friendship Vincent was sometimes tempted to think it enough.

What he wanted—who did not?—was to be loved. If his mother had heard him say this, she'd have burst into tears.

His sister Cass, who doted on him, would have been deeply, deeply hurt. But he didn't mean, sometimes felt he didn't even want, love from his family. That kind of love had too many strings attached. He wanted to be passionately loved and accepted, altogether, with all that was wrong with him, for himself, by a girl. Failing that, he wanted to believe that one day he would know this kind of love with a woman.

He didn't believe it. Not for a minute.

But David and Enoch had shown him that there was much even in a life that lacked passion. David had a girl who loved him and several who would have been glad to apply. Enoch had had a succession of trueloves. Nevertheless their relationship with him was important. It was real and tough and honest, and they made him feel that though a man might not be born to inspire great love, given will, intelligence, and unshakable friends, he could aspire to anything else.

How much could a person ask from life?

Enoch, lying back on his bed, arms under his head, yawned and said, "It's snowing, chaps. Let's go out and build a fortress. Let's pelt with snowballs the girls as they go past."

"I have to study for this zoo prelim," Vincent said.

"Oh, tut. You can pass it with your head tied behind you."

"Maybe if I tie yours behind me too. That just might do it."

"Excess baggage, that's all I'd prove to be. How about you, Dave? Isn't anyone for snowballs?"

David looked out the window, looked at his desk. "I don't know. I get this feeling every once in a while that I'm undermotivated scholastically. I especially get it after my father has called to tell me I am."

Enoch, with an index finger, drew a bead on his lamp. "You know something? I was asking myself the other day if I know any oldest son, or only son, or almost any son, in any culture, in any country, who gets along with his father. And do you know the conclusion I came to?"

"Yes," said David and Vincent together.

"No, but don't you find it a fascinating facet of our times?" asked Enoch, sitting up to signalize the beginning of a discussion. "Why should this be? *Why* can't we get along with our fathers? Poor devils, they work hard enough for us, most of them, and try to take all this pride in us. My father, when I'm home, always throws his arm over my shoulder and says to people, 'This is my son Enoch, my oldest boy.' You know, *le roi* presenting the dauphin. Picks me to pieces all the rest of the time."

"I'll tell you what I think it is," said Vincent. "I think that by nature men our age ought to be entirely free of their fathers. In the old days when a boy arrived at maturity, he either killed his father with an ax or got driven off by him. Simple as that. Now it's a lot more complicated."

"By complicated," said David, "you mean we depend on them financially."

Enoch winced. "You put it crudely, Dave. But have gone to the heart of the matter, as usual."

And, as usual, David had. Vincent himself worked summers to contribute to his education. But Enoch didn't help a farthing's worth with his, and he was not an inexpensive type. The best clothes, the finest sports equipment, the choicest dates for Enoch. He seemed to take it all as his due, and maybe both he and his father felt that it was. On the other hand maybe old Mr. Burke-Runciman got resentful sometimes, maybe he felt he was being taken. And David was being put through by the combined efforts of his father and mother, who had both worked every giant step of their way through college and for some reason didn't want Dave to work even a baby step. He wasn't always so thankful as he let them think he was and didn't do so well in his studies as they had.

"You know," David said now, "I think it's our Puritan heritage in this country."

"What is?" said Vincent.

"My grades."

"You're putting a lot of responsibility on the Puritans, aren't you?"

"No, but the way I see it, in this country if a man isn't working himself to death, his conscience troubles him. And if his conscience troubles him, he attempts to escape. Like, you know how some guys sleep."

There were several men in the fraternity who slept like hibernating bears. They slept through breakfast, through classes, through life, it seemed to Vincent. Fairly often they slept themselves right out of college.

"Now other—escape artists, shall we say?—they play. That's me. And the more time I waste playing, the guiltier I feel, so the more I have to play to forget it. It must be something like being a drunk."

"Girls and greasepaint, kisses and kleig lights," Enoch said dreamily. "What *better* escape hatch?"

"It's the times," David went on reflectively. "How many

fellows do you know who are doing a decent, *honest* job of school? Or know what they want to do when they get out? Face it—most of us are going to school without any flaming love of knowledge. We're here to keep from getting out there and actually doing something."

"If you feel that way," Enoch said, "why don't you get out and start doing?"

"My friend, I am merely making a diagnosis. I don't intend to take the cure—not until they shove it down my throat. But it's the times, I say. The times are out of joint."

"They've always been out of joint," said Vincent, picking up his zoology text.

"Ah, but not fractured the way they are now," said David. "You'll admit that. Whether you say it or think it or just have an itch in the old subconscious, you can't get away from the feeling that you could work like a beaver building for your future and get there to find there wasn't any after all. Wouldn't even a beaver's energies get sapped if he thought the river would turn to sand or fire just as he shoved the last stick in place?"

"I don't know," Vincent said reflectively, the book still closed on his lap. "I think if you're a beaver you keep building the dam, and if you're a man you keep building your life. What else can you or I or a beaver do? Sit on our backsides and wait for the bomb to hit?"

"Here they are, folks!" chanted Enoch. "Step right up and listen to the Doom Sayers . . . brought to you at *gah-rate* expense and by special arrangement with the Eumenides! Step lively, step lively . . . all predictions guaranteed dire—"

85

"And another thing," David said to Vincent, both of them ignoring Enoch, "another thing—I'm not sure I even know what college is for anymore. A corridor to graduate school? Doing what? Wasting more time? A plain B.A. doesn't give you much more of a leg up—and don't ask me a leg up where because I don't know—than a high-school diploma. And if it's just a question of money, why not be a plumber or an electrician? Twenty-five hours a week and a pay scale like a Brink's robbery. Half the time I think we're going to college to work our way up to the lower-income groups."

"Will you say that over again in different words, Professor?" said Enoch. "Your meaning got away from me."

"*If,*" said David, "I *were* a professor, I'd be making less than a plumber. Clear now?"

"Unhappily, yes."

"And you're the guy," Vincent said to David, "who said last week that you love college because where else would it be perfectly right and acceptable to read Plato in the morning?"

David shrugged. "I believe that. I'm being honest. You want me to be consistent too?"

Vincent laughed and opened his book, removing himself from the conversation that continued to ripple back and forth between Enoch and David.

Boy, he thought, would my father have a sardonic old laugh over this. David saying practically word for word what *he's* always preaching at me. From Dave, of course, it was easy to take—both the roughness and the truth. Clearly Dave didn't intend to do a thing about it and neither did Enoch or Vincent himself. But there was something bracing about saying once in a while, among friends, that you were wasting a good deal of time. At home you had to put such a fancy face on it all. Especially since your father, narrow-minded and maddening though he was in many ways, still was neither a fool nor fooled. It occurred to Vincent that his father, in plain fact, was being pretty patient. But the thought was a glancing one.

"Enoch Burke Runciman?" his father had said, eyebrows surging together, mouth turning down in distaste. "What kind of a name is that?"

"It has a hyphen in it," Vincent had said. "I imagine you left that out."

"Hyphen, is it?" Mr. Dunne's face had flushed with annoyance but whether at Vincent, Enoch, or the hyphen would have been hard to say. "I asked you what kind of a name it is. Where does he come from?"

"England. Or, at least now the whole family lives in the United States. They come from Manchester, England. But they like it here in this country."

"Jolly, ruddy good of them," said Mr. Dunne heavily. His own Irish ancestry was not far back and generally he found it a matter of indifference, but now and then something within him stirred at the sound of the word *England*, and he reacted in a way that even he didn't understand. "Why can't you have a plain American for a roommate? Aren't Americans good enough for you?"

"Oh, sure," Vincent replied in a bright and reassuring voice. "My other roomie, Dave Gates, is American as all get-out. More American than we are, probably, if you count how far back families have been around this country. He's my good friend from South Carolina, and his family goes back practically to the Revolution." Vincent had hesitated, eyed his father, and been unable to resist. "He's a Negro."

"He's a *what?*" Mr. Dunne had bellowed, half rising in his chair. "What do you think you're—what are you talking about?"

"Well, about my roommates, weren't we? About how Enoch has a hyphen and David is—"

"And this is why I'm sending you to college, is it? So you can fall in with foreigners and colored? That's it, eh, Vincent?" His already flushed skin darkening, Mr. Dunne had leaned forward in an attitude of menace.

"I'd say it was one of the reasons," Vincent replied, thinking how like a turkey his father looked when enraged. "One of them, certainly."

When he and his parent got into one of these scenes, Vincent often experienced a quite horrible conviction that he was not only capable of cruelty but capable of liking it. He *enjoyed* baiting his father into a rage while he himself remained apparently calm and unperturbed. He imagined from what psychology he'd studied that he was *not* calm and unperturbed. He felt that probably something pretty corrosive went on inside him during these times and that one day he'd pay for it, in ulcers, high blood pressure, or something more drastic, like madness. Yet still the ugly mounting pleasure came as he watched his father's flushed face and shaking hands betray his helpless rage.

"And just suppose, you bloody upstart," Mr. Dunne had

88

said that day, "just suppose I say to you right now, you *choose* between going on with school and getting rid of your— your—"

"Shut up," Vincent snapped. "I'll suppose *that*," he'd added icily, "and I'll suppose what you were going to add, and the answer is, I'll go anyway."

"On what? The skin of your teeth? Elbow grease? A spot of honest labor? Hah! You'd be out in a month, trying to put yourself through. The first hardship you encountered, you'd be wiring home. 'Have encountered hardship, send money.' Put yourself through, indeed—"

"Maybe. I'd give it a go, just the same. And I'm rooming with Dave and Enoch no matter what you say, *see?*"

Mrs. Dunne, who had come into the room halfway through the argument, but with long experience had been able to pick up most of the matter, had sat down quietly and started to cry. It was her way of arbitrating, and it worked. Vincent had muttered some sort of apology to his father and skulked away, and after that there was no talk of cutting off support and no talk, either, of school since then. His father behaved, when they met, as if Vincent were someone of whose background and occupation he was uncertain, to which he was indifferent. He did not, anymore, even inquire about Vincent's grades.

The situation made Vincent uneasy, even sad. Samuel Butler had said that it isn't all that easy to hate your father. And Butler had certainly tried. Vincent, who hadn't tried to hate his father, and didn't, had at least assumed that he was secure in his contempt. But his father's silence and the continued arrival of the monthly checks shook that. In his darkest and most introspective moments Vincent wondered if perhaps the contempt wasn't flowing from the other side. He'd take the check from the envelope, hold it as if weighing its worth, and think, I ought to send this back. But he never did. He was a good worker and did quite well in his studies. Not so well as he could, and possibly should, have. Still, a good student. Nevertheless he was lazy and he knew it. His father knew it too. He supposed that if the threat had been carried through, pride would have obliged him to refuse further assistance and try to put himself through the rest of college somehow. Apparently that was as far as his pride went, and it wasn't a pretty thing to recognize.

He pushed the matter from his mind now—he was good at that—and concentrated on the zoology book. It was his best and favorite subject. The study of animalcules beneath a microscope's eye was better even than books. There you both lost and found yourself. For the time you fixed your sight and your intelligence upon this living (perhaps in the case of amoebae, never-dying) universe, you were part of history, not just the human animal's, but time's. *As it was in the beginning,* you could say to yourself, watching the beautiful green volvox execute with discipline and grace its billions-of-years-old revolution. Who, trying to sense the incalculable ages anteceding this revolving volvox, this undulant dividing paramecium, this indestructible amoeba, could feel that he himself, an observer grown and gone in a breath, was of consequence? With his eye to the microscope Vincent Dunne was nothing, his problems and confusions nothing. And he was part of everything, was close to the essential marvel, was absorbed and lost in the mystery, was found, a particular and individual member of it. But what happened to him, this for the moment sentient witness, was no more important than what happened to that whole world in a drop of water that you blotted from the slide when the class period was over. It was difficult to think that your career or even your complexion mattered after an hour or two in the lab.

The trouble was, of course, that from the universe of a droplet your vision presently narrowed down to the world, where you found, once again, yourself, that signal, significant, absorbing, and important being about whom everything was of consequence and who was probably immortal.

"Hey, Vince! You gone deaf or something? You *can't* be that industrious."

"Huh?" Vincent started, dropped his book, realized that without realizing it he'd heard David and Enoch inviting him to do something. "I didn't hear."

"We said," Enoch repeated patiently, "that we'd like the pleasure of your company over at the workshop this aft."

Enoch and David were devoted members of the drama group and workshop and were indefatigable in their attempts to snare Vincent.

"Come on," David said. "We're having tryouts for a Shakespeare Medley evening. *I'm* going to try out." Generally David was scene shifter, lighting manager, carpenter, director, but rarely actor. "It doesn't make sense," he added ruefully. "They want a colored guy to play colored roles, period. In short, Othello. I want to be Iago. You be Othello, Vince. How about it?"

"Me?" Vincent laughed, the thought of his own appearance

as an actor being so laughable. "I couldn't play Desdemona's hanky."

"Old buddy, if you could," said Enoch, "you'd be better than Garrick himself. You coming?"

Vincent shook his head.

"Give it a try, will you, Vince?" said David. "The world of greasepaint and footlights and all the great words. There's nothing like it."

"Stow it, both of you. I don't have to go out of my way to make a fool of myself. I'm built to be an actor like I'm built to play tackle for the Texas Oilers."

"That's *no* sequitur," said David. "An actor is an illusionist, not a muscle man. A good actor can make himself any size. By God, he can make himself any color too. A good actor could play Romeo if he was four feet tall and spotted like a leopard." He stood up. "Vincent, my boy, I offer you a challenge. Come over there with us, right now, and audition for something."

"Like, for instance, Peaseblossom?" Vincent said sourly.

"Rage is permissible, peevishness is not," said Enoch in a lofty voice.

"Okay, okay. What role would you two suggest I have at?"

"It doesn't matter," David said absently. He lifted his eyes in a reflective manner. "You know . . . I could read Oberon. I mean, who's to say what color Oberon is?"

"I thought we were talking about me," Vincent said.

"We were talking about the philosophy of acting."

"Oh."

"However," David went on, "I will talk about you. Glad

92

to. The trouble with you, Vince, is you think the world was made for tall guys and beautiful women. Well, it wasn't. And it wasn't made for white men either. It's for all of us. You, me, Enoch, Miss America, and the animal kingdom—right down to those green volvoxes you dote on. And the world's gotta make room for us all, see?"

"Some people don't look at it that way."

"They will. If there's time."

"Anyway," said Vincent, putting the zoology book aside, "the volvox has made his adjustment and kept his balance better than we're ever likely to do."

"But at what a cost," said David. "There he is, down there under your microscope, going about his dance just the way he did billions of years ago, and he doesn't even know he's doing it. I want to know what I'm doing. I want to know every single minute that I'm *alive*."

Vincent studied his friend's dark and radiant face. Eyes gleaming below half-closed lids, head lifted with a look of pulsing zest, David was the picture of a man dared, and glad to be.

"Okay," said Vincent. "To the workshop!"

The three of them went out and walked across the campus, lighted to a cold glow by the falling sun.

❦❦❦

Chapter Five

After the Storch child's birthday party business picked up in a manner that Irene found alarming and Lotta exhilarating. For the first time since she'd been—what?—ten or eleven, probably, Lotta found herself thinking about something besides boys, a development so unexpected that Lotta herself didn't actually notice until Cassie said one day, "You know, I wouldn't be surprised if you had the makings of an executive in you, Lotta."

"Oh?" said Lotta, pleased. "Why do you say that?"

"The way you've gone feet-first into this party enterprise. The fact is, I thought you'd last out one or two childish gatherings and then remember something important you had to do in the next county."

"So nice of you to have faith in me."

"But you're a real organizer," Cassie went on admiringly. "And I'll say this: I think you're brave as a momma bear. The sight of that many children determined to have fun would paralyze me, and having to pro*vide* the fun! I just do not see how you do it."

Lotta, who found the conversation most congenial, smiled and attempted to explain. "It's funny, Cass, but when I see all those kiddies there, expecting so much of—well, of the day, I guess, more than of me—why I just, without even *plan*ning, you know, suddenly realize what it is they need to have the fun."

"Dear, you plan most carefully. Even your reluctant hench-man there, Irene, plans. I've heard her contribute an idea at *least* once."

"Don't be so hard on Irene. She's not used to work."

And you are? Cassie said to herself, always aware of Lotta's extraordinary agility in evading the major share of house-work. And there really wasn't much a person could do about it either, without making herself sound a constant whiner. Lotta did about a tenth of what she ought to do and got away with it all the time. Mostly, of course, because of this showy career she'd embarked on. Still, at the moment Cassie was not feeling resentful, and she liked this unusual accord with her sister. It was won at the cost of flattery, but if the flattery was sincere—as in this case it was—why scorn the accord?

"I guess I know what you mean about realizing what it is they want," she said. "All the planning in the world doesn't replace the sixth sense. I notice that in drawing, sometimes. I sit in front of a drawing pad with no idea of—"

"Children are more important," Lotta said, meaning no offense, certainly not intending to be rude. Good manners were of major importance to Lotta, but she still thought they were something to be practiced outside the family. "Do you really think I'm a good organizer, Cass?" Visions of herself in an executive position—something to do with fashion— formed gracefully in her mind. She could see herself standing at a white, freeform desk, wearing a sable turban, talking into one of those sexy phones you saw in the movies. She had taken off her earring, and it dangled lightly in her left hand as she gave crisp, inspired directions to her subordinate. To Lotta nothing seemed more dashing and professional than to wear a hat in the office and take off your earring to answer the telephone. In fact, the whole picture was so stylish, so dazzling, that she caught her breath. "You really do, Cassie?" she insisted.

"For heaven's sake, Lotta. Do you want me to sign something? I said yes, I really do."

She hadn't really wanted to talk about her own interests— it always annoyed her when she fell into the error of doing so with Lotta—but on the other hand, Lotta never made the flimsiest effort even to pretend concern about another human being. How *did* she manage those parties so skillfully? Cassie thought it must have less to do with affection for children than for a certain image of herself that Lotta could, for the present, only work out in this fashion. And Lotta did have astonishing funds of energy when her self-interest was involved. She'd make a go of those birthday parties, partly to earn money, but mostly because she refused to fail once she'd started something.

"Yes," Cassie said. "I really truly do. I predict you will be an arbiter of fashion." She could imagine few drearier predictions, but Lotta simply sparkled and said, "But how *marvy*."

Cassie's unreliable temper snapped. "Is it within the realm of possibility that you find an alternative adjective for marvy?"

Lotta, never so quick to alter moods as her sister, was still feeling friendly. "What in the world do you mean, Cass?"

"I mean that nobody has to be limited to basic slang all her life. I'll lend you my thesaurus, and you can study it between flirtations, if there ever is a between."

"What a nasty little girl you are," Lotta said calmly. "Jealous, too, I imagine."

"Jealous? Of you?" Cassie gave a shrill hoot.

"I shouldn't be surprised. If you ask *me*," Lotta said, sounding, if anything, sweeter than she had when they'd been talking contentedly and without dissension, "If you ask me, Cassie, jealousy is one of your main difficulties. *One* of them, mind. Why else, for instance, do you go around dressed like something that fell off the hanger in a rummage sale? You're afraid of competition, that's why."

"What have you been reading? Freud in the classic comic strips?"

"I don't have to read to recognize envy," Lotta said and walked away, leaving Cassie bested and angrily aware of it. But why it always came to this when she and Lotta were together, she could not understand. She would swear that Lotta tried, as hard as she did herself, to avoid this kind of meanness. Neither of them liked the feeling that followed on such scenes. Lotta didn't want life to be ugly, Cassie didn't want it to be overemotional, yet they contrived, repeatedly, to see that it was both.

And I'm worse than she is, Cassie thought now. At least it must be so, because Lotta did not have such interchanges with anybody else, and Cassie seemed to have them with everyone but Vincent.

Maybe it's all my fault, Cassie thought, desperately trying to unravel the cause of this effect. What had she done? Tried for a second to mention something that interested her when they were supposed to be talking about Lotta. Asked Lotta to stop using that idiotic word. *Marvy.* It was doing Lotta a favor, really, to suggest that she jettison *that* from her vocabulary. She'd sound silly, wouldn't she, even to silly people like Irene and J. H.?

"Well, it's the last time I try to do you a favor!" she yelled after her sister, who'd gone downstairs.

"I hope I can rely on that, because it'd be simply marvy if you stuck to it."

"My goodness," said Mrs. Dunne, coming in the kitchen door from the garage. "Are you two at it again? What's the matter with everyone in this house? Lotta, as long as you're here, help me get the groceries in, will you, dear?"

"But Mother—I was just going to practice my flute. I'm rehearsing a new piece for the birthday party at the Wildings. It's absolutely essential that I practice. It's a fifteenth-century folk tune that—"

"Well, all right. Cassie," Mrs. Dunne said as her second daughter came down the stairs, "will you—"

"Sorry, I was just going to practice standing on my head. I'm working on a twelfth-century position which may be absolutely essential at some point in my career."

"She's so *funny*, isn't she, Mother?" said Lotta. "Maybe she could get a job as a lady comedian, and all the rest of us could live off her. No, I'll get the groceries, Mother. You go in and put your feet up."

"Thank you, darling," Mrs. Dunne said gratefully. "I am a little tired. Perhaps I'll just go in the living room and sit for a bit." She walked past Cassie with a shake of her head.

Cassie followed. "Carrying up a couple of bags of groceries doesn't constitute slave labor, you know."

"Oh, Cass. Please. Do let me just close my eyes and relax for a second. It's been a difficult morning."

"But, *Mother* . . . she's always putting me in this position where I look as if *I'm* the one who's lazy and gets out of all the work. For those two bags of groceries I'll probably have to do the dishes for a week to make you think we're even." Aware of how she sounded, aware that she worsened her position by the second, Cassie was unable to stop. "Don't you see how she does this, Mother? I'll bet it's been six months since she carried so much as a gingersnap up from the car, but what are you going to remember? I ask you, when you think about people carrying groceries up from the garage, who are you going to think carries—"

"*Cassie!* Go away. I simply cannot tolerate this nagging."

"Well, there's lots I can't tolerate, too, let me tell you."

"You don't have to tell me. I hear about it all the time."

"That's not fair, and that's not true! I only—"

"Lotta thinks of other people once in a while, that's all I'm trying to say."

"And I don't?" Cassie shouted, outraged.

"Oh, Cassie," Mrs. Dunne said hopelessly. "I really do not know what you think about. I really, truly, have no idea."

"Cassie," Lotta said, coming to the door, "why don't you let poor Mother alone for a second? She's tired. Mother, all the groceries are up now."

"Thank you, dear. That was very thoughtful of you."

"It wasn't thoughtful," Cassie said. "You asked her to do it."

At that her mother and sister bent on her looks of such cold patience that she stamped from the room. She went into the kitchen, and just as she'd expected, Lotta had carried up two bags of provisions, dumped them on the table, and considered herself discharged of household onus. And now what? If the stuff were just left there, all the frozen things would thaw, the milk would get warm, the—she poked in a bag—the juice from the meat would run out of its insufficient wrappings and make the rolls soggy. And who was to take care of it? If she went in now and pointed out a few facts to them, they'd say she was whining. If she left the whole mess here, somebody would be sure to say that since Lotta had carried the things up, surely Cassie could have—

"Oh, for the love of mud," she grumbled, and sighed, and began to put the groceries away. What difference did it make? What she did, whether Lotta did as much, what anybody thought of her, or even if things were fair? What possible difference could it make in her life if Lotta was limited to one adjective—marvy—and one interest—herself? With boys running a close second. What did it matter if once in a while her mother made too clear a preference she couldn't help?

It makes none at all, said Cassie to herself. Mother prefers Lotta to Vincent and me, she always has, she probably doesn't know it and couldn't do anything about it if she did. Dad and Mother both. They wouldn't admit it, but they're ashamed of Vince and me because we've failed to be beautiful reflections of them. I don't see what they could expect, being no beauties themselves, but I guess parents aren't strong on logic that way. Parents want brilliant, beautiful, popular children to be proud of, and whether they're brilliant, beautiful, or popular themselves apparently doesn't seem relevant. So here are Mother and Dad, who got that stunner, Lotta, by mistake, or by grace of Aunt Muriel, and instead of being grateful for one swan, they go into a flap over having to admit two ugly ducklings.

Well, I don't care, she said again. I'd rather be together with Vincent in everything than paired with Lotta in anything.

She would not allow herself to think that Vincent might not feel the same. Or that Vincent, indeed, lumped her with the rest of the family and was gradually extending his indifference to them all. It was only natural that a boy should get —get other interests when he went to college. She and Vincent were close, and had always been, and always would be. It wasn't something she made up to lull herself. It was a fact.

There was a sudden blare of an automobile horn outside.

101

For a second Cassie thought that J. H. had arrived and then remembered that he had taken to coming up the walk and ringing the doorbell for reasons that even Mrs. Dunne's indulgence of him couldn't relate to manners. ("I mean," she'd said to Cassie one evening, "why would he develop manners all of a sudden?" "Search me," Cassie had replied. "I can't even think where he'd have heard of them. That crowd he runs around with has about as much use for manners as a pig would have for a knife and fork.")

So it wasn't J. H., unless he'd reverted. Cassie wondered briefly if Lotta had added another beau to her string, then lost interest. There was still a good part of the afternoon left, and her homework was done. She could, if she hurried, have time to walk over to the nature preserve. The ice was off the pond now, but the ducks and geese who lived there even when it was frozen would be eagerly looking for handouts, and some deer who roamed a large enclosure would come to the fence for carrots, letting her stroke their long noses. There were a couple of peacocks, too. A glorious—and vainglorious —male and a rather edgy, apologetic female. Well, that's what—

"Hey! Everybody! Everybody come and *see* what I got!"

Irene, in an abnormally elevated state, burst into the house. "Lotta! Mrs. Dunne! Come on, come on, come and see! You too, Cassie," she said, as Cassie came curiously to the kitchen door. "Oh, I'm so excited I could but *die*—"

"What can it be?" said Mrs. Dunne, but Lotta, biting her lip, said, "I bet it's a car, isn't it?"

"Oh, and *what* a car, my pet. Just you come and see what a car it is."

102

"You mean you've been given a car of your own?" Mrs. Dunne asked, unable not to sound astonished. Generally she liked to behave as if nothing the Stevenses, or people like them, did could surprise or awe her. If Irene let drop the information that her parents were in London, Mrs. Dunne would nod and go on with what she'd been saying as if such a trip were of no more significance than a run into New York City for the afternoon. But she was totally unprepared for this car and openly gaped at Irene.

"Of my very, very own, madam. Of course, I can't drive it at *night* yet. But we'll make *quite* a splash in the daytime." Irene could scarcely contain her joy.

Thinking *splash* a peculiarly unfortunate choice of words, Cassie studied the girl's animated face. She'd often wondered what it would take to raise Irene's blood pressure or bring color to that magnolia skin. An autombile of one's very own, eh? That was what it took. Or looked at more broadly, a great big acquisition of one's own. Something nobody had? Or, anyway, that Lotta didn't have. I wonder, Cassie thought, if Lotta knows how jealous Irene is of her? Perhaps she's right about me. Perhaps in some obscure part of my being I am envious of her. If I am, it isn't causing me much pain. I have a feeling Irene's jealousy is with her night and day.

They went out to view the car, but Cassie scarcely looked at it. She was watching her sister. There was an expression on that customarily smooth and smiling face that made Cassie turn her head, like a cat estimating a strange sight. Not, she decided, so much an expression that was there as one that was missing. Confidence? Complacency? In a quite disarming sense, Lotta's usual look of self-satisfaction was rather nice, Cassie decided, now that it wasn't there. After all, Lotta didn't have many of the things she wanted—the things that money could buy. Yet she went about with that look of sunny well-being. Perhaps because she had things that money couldn't buy? Beauty, vivacity, adulation. The poise that came of having these qualities. Irene's father's money had never endowed her with anything but an imitation of high spirits. Trite, and true.

But at the moment, Lotta was definitely caught with her vivacity down. Cassie, who had no feeling at all about cars, tried to translate the emotion for herself. Suppose Fritzy had burst in just now, saying she'd been given an original Picasso cartoon? A most unlikely supposition, but suppose it anyway. Now, Cassie asked herself, how would I feel? Envious? That didn't start to describe what she'd feel. Heartbroken and out-raged would be closer. I would know that I, not Fritzy, was the one who deserved, who could appreciate, could really know and find meaning in, an original Picasso cartoon. That's how I'd feel.

She studied the automobile and then, with sad regard, her sister's face. Lotta was making a valiant effort. There were white lines along her jaw, and her eyes were far too brilliant, but she was trying.

"Rene! It's but absolutely *marvy!*" She shot a glance at Cassie, looked away. "It's divine, darling. *Simply* heavenly."

Mrs. Dunne was too absorbed in complete stupefaction to notice Lotta's tone of voice, and Irene was devouring her automobile—a red sports car—with eyes that had nothing to spare for the expression on her friend's face. But Cassie, watching, thought how her sister was saying to herself, It isn't fair, it is not *fair*. I would look gorgeous in that car, dashing around town, a scarf flying behind me, offering rides to friends, dazzling corner policemen. . . . *It should have been mine!* As I, Cassie thought, would have been saying of the Picasso, *It should have been mine!*

Poor Lotta, she thought sadly, and said, "I don't understand the hysterics, Irene. It's just a car, isn't it?"

Irene's eyes widened briefly before she exchanged with Lotta a look that clearly said, She's even more of an idiot than we took her for.

"You see, Cassie is above such things," Lotta explained to her friend. "She thinks you and I are subnormal in most of our tastes. Automobiles, slang, clothes . . . you name it, and Cassie's above it," she said icily, turning her back on her sister. "It's a dream, Rene. But a perfect dream. An utterly, utterly marvy little auto. Let's go for a ride, all right?"

Her voice and expression were close to normal again. If she couldn't have it, she could ride in it. The car wasn't hers, but Irene, for all intents and purposes, was. In no time Lotta would find that just as good, if not better. She'd look gorgeous riding around town in this red racing car, the object of all eyes, free to look around while her friend, her best, dearest, closest friend did the driving.

The two girls jumped in the car and drove off without saying good-bye. Cassie and Mrs. Dunne, left standing on the sidewalk, stared at each other.

"I suppose you were trying to help," Mrs. Dunne said at last. Cassie nodded dumbly. "It was sweet of you, dear. It's just that you're so—so tactless."

"Yes, I know."

"Fancy. Just *fancy* those people giving a seventeen-year-old girl a car of her own."

"An airplane wouldn't surprise me. I bet her family goes crazy at Christmas. What can you give someone who had her own television set at the age of four?"

"Sometimes I wonder," Mrs. Dunne said hesitantly, "if it's good for Lotta to associate with people who have—all these things that she can't have."

"Too late to wonder that, Ma. Anyway, Lotta will get them, never fear. She'll have everything Irene has, and more."

Mrs. Dunne took this for reassurance and brightened. But Cassie went into the kitchen for bread and carrots feeling oddly depressed.

The nature preserve had a little woods surrounding it. Not a wild one. From the deepest part of it you could still hear the far sound of traffic on the streets. Still, a woods. It had a brisk stream flowing through it that fed into the pond. Now, in late March, the narrow brook slid darkly here and there under brittle, thin ice formations, springing free again, curving like glass over rocks, running in bubbled cascades under and across fallen branches. Cassie leaned on a small stone bridge and watched the waters slide away beneath her. Somewhere a cardinal was singing. The cardinal was a winter bird, and there was not the faintest haze of buds on the bony trees. Yet you would not need a calendar to tell you this was the end of winter.

She walked on, past an old fieldstone mansion that had been the manor house of this estate. The whole thing had

106

been left by some rich old man to the city as a refuge for animals and people. Cassie looked at the turreted, gabled, many-elled house with its imitation stained-glass windows and its observatory and thought what a nice old man he must have been, in spite of his taste. The house was a museum now, housing a touching, second-rate collection of fossils, rocks, and stuffed birds. Vincent and Cassie had often speculated on what it must have been like actually living in the place. They'd concluded that from the beginning it had been intended for a museum. No matter that two or three generations of a family had lived there—it was a structure that inevitably had to become a school for boys or a museum.

Shaking his head over it, Vincent had said once, "It's the ugliest structure I've ever seen."

"When that house was built," Cassie told him, "people had different standards of elegance."

"Anyway, they had good standards of privacy. I suppose you could disappear in there for days before anyone ran you down."

"I wouldn't know about privacy. That was before my time too."

She turned now and walked down the path toward the pond. The deep ice was gone from the center, which now was covered with the thinnest shell of gray-white. Toward the shore it still was strong enough to hold the wildfowl up, and they rested on it comfortably, stretching their wings, their legs, their necks. They quacked and honked and waddled about like any aimless congregation, bird or human. In the center of the pond, breaking the fragile ice covering as

107

they swam, two swans went side by side in a slow, circuitous ballet. They ignored the geese and the ducks. They kept themselves to themselves. Do they *know* they're beautiful? Cassie wondered. The peacock always seemed to know. Were all living beautiful creatures conscious of being different, apart?

That was the sort of thing she had once discussed with Vincent, but it had been a long time now since they'd walked here. Even when he was home, Vincent never seemed to have leisure anymore for walks, for the ducks or the deer. For, Cassie thought, me. Well, that was to be expected. A person goes off to a new world and makes new friends and encounters new horizons, and all that. So naturally he doesn't have time for walks. Or his old friends—even if the friend was a sister—or even to write letters, she thought, slipping into bitterness without the least intention of doing so. You would think *anybody* could write a letter, in spite of his new horizons, wouldn't you?

Dotted among the trees and shrubbery, in a painstakingly casual fashion, were statues of gods and goddesses. Cassie paused to look at one, smiling in spite of her lonely mood. Yes, they'd had different ideas of elegance then, all right. This stone Demeter with her modest stone draperies, her uplifted, nearly noseless face, stone grapes spilling down her skirt, was reminiscent somehow of those very early movies you saw late at night on television. More American flapper than Greek deity, there she stood in the rain, the snow, the sun, and the night, growing more worn and preposterous with every season. But no doubt the generous old gentleman had

108

found her and her fellow immortals scattered in groves here and there throughout his property most classical and uplifting. Cassie walked around Demeter, wishing she'd brought a drawing pad. She never took one out in public when there was any chance of an audience, but today the woods, the park, the pond, all seemed quite deserted.

Even as she thought this a young man—a boy—strolled out of the manor house museum, hands in his pockets, and ambled toward the pond. He scuffed his feet and stared at the ground as he walked, then sat on a rock and stared at the swans. Cassie sighed, as people do who've thought they had a piece of the world for a moment unchallenged and then encounter interlopers. It occurred to her that to him she'd be an interloper too, and for a moment she considered leaving without feeding the ducks.

It was too late. A large white drake came toddling toward her, head stretched forward, beak opening and closing in an anxious, almost inaudible quack.

"Me, me, me," Cassie said to him softly. "Feed me, feed me, I'm starving!"

"Well, I am," the duck seemed to say, coming up to nibble fervently at her boots. Cassie opened the bag of crumbs and held some in the palm of her hand. The duck gobbled, gnawed about frenziedly when he found no more, then lifted his head and fixed Cassie with a glance so full of supplication and entreaty and confidence that Cassie laughed out loud. The boy on the rock, aware of her presence for the first time, turned.

He looked at the girl, at the white petitioner shuffling

around her, and smiled. "No end to their appetites, is there?"

"Not to my knowledge," Cassie agreed. "I think everybody in town feeds them and still they are not full."

"You know, there are people in this town who don't even know this place is here?"

Cassie knew. "I was just talking. Here, want to feed them?" She offered crumbs. By now there was a regiment of ducks and geese encircling them, all in a state of the highest perturbation. Only the swans remained aloof.

"Do you suppose they feel too refined for beggary?" Cassie said.

"Well," said the young man, "if your reflection gave you that"—he indicated the swan couple—"would you want to associate yourself with this?" And he looked down, rather tenderly, at a gray gander with wattles so goiterous as to make him not merely homely but grotesque.

"I certainly would," Cassie said sharply.

He smiled. "I only had reference to the bird kingdom."

"Snobbery's snobbery in any kingdom."

"Do you always make a point of your principles, even with strangers?" he asked curiously.

"I'm afraid so," Cassie said, sighing. "I don't precisely mean to; it's just how things work out."

"I think that's great," he said. "I envy you."

Cassie found no answer to that. She looked about and spied the peacock. Along the stone wall that extended from the bridge he came dragging his tail in a ponderous, bobbing fashion. The peahen, at once pursuer and servitor, followed closely.

110

"You'd think the least she could do is carry it for him," said the boy.

"His train?" said Cassie. "He'd probably consider it presumptuous of her to try."

"Have you ever seen him spread it?"

"Oh, yes," said Cassie. "That's when you forgive him for everything. That's when you know what beauty is all about."

In the spring, in the mating season, this now sullen-seeming, slow-stepping dandy would lift that great train, fan it to its fullest, and dance for his mate. Cassie had seen him once, on a windy day, when the glossy arc of his many-eyed iridescent tail had swayed forward across his body till it covered his imperious small head and then backward in a languid sweep as he revolved and stamped his feet. Backward and forward in a great hypnotic flourish had gone the tremendous fan of his tail while Cassie and peahen watched transfixed.

When they'd scattered the last of the crumbs, Cassie said, "I have some carrots for the deer."

He fell in beside her as they left the protesting congregation of ducks and geese. The daring drake followed for a while, insisting that there must be more, and then grumpily returned to the pond.

The young buck, when he saw them, paced gently down the hillside to the high wire fence, thrusting his black and gleaming nose through the meshes. He seemed to come for company as well as carrots, to enjoy their fingers stroking his nose, his large velvety ears.

"I cannot understand," said Cassie, looking into the smoky purple eyes, putting a fingertip on one slender, branching

111

antler, "how people can shoot them." She had said this to Vincent repeatedly. He always answered, "They don't look at them; that's why they can shoot."

This boy shook his head and said, "I think there's something basic for some men—and women, too—in killing. It must revive them somehow."

"Like vampires?"

"I suppose, in a way."

"I saw a little red fox here one day. He ran across the bridge and down that ravine there. He was so small and charming. And seeing him running free that way—I loved it. Do you know what Oscar Wilde called fox hunting? *'The pursuit of the inedible by the unspeakable.'* I don't even like to kill an insect. It makes me sort of freakish, I guess. At least my sister thinks so. But still—it's how I feel."

"What about eating?" he inquired. "Don't you eat meat?" She shook her head. "You *do* have the strength of your convictions. No fish either?"

Cassie shrugged. "I'm inconsistent, I know. I eat fish and chicken and eggs. But meat—no. I've given up trying to explain, because I can't. It's just how I feel," she repeated.

"I can understand," he said thoughtfully. "I don't agree, except about hunting. But I can see what you mean."

"That's more than most people can," she said pleasantly. "What are you doing here today? I mean, mostly the place is unfrequented in weather like this." She was beginning to be conscious of the cold and of the long walk home.

"I was just driving around and found it, so I came in. To think," he said deliberately.

112

"About what?" said Cassie. It was not a question she would ordinarily have put to a stranger. It was almost as if he'd prompted her, but she didn't mind and was rather curious to hear his answer.

"I'm trying to decide what to do with my life."

"What are you doing with it now?"

"Nothing. I went to college for a few weeks last fall. I couldn't stand all those college kids, so I quit and haven't done anything since."

"Are you rich?"

"Far from it. I'm sponging off my parents."

"Doesn't that trouble you?"

"I don't know. It's one of the things I'm trying to decide."

"I see," said Cassie, trying to sound noncommittal. She offered the buck her last carrot, and they watched in silence while he ate it.

"Have you been in that house?" the boy asked then. "The museum?"

"Lots of times. It's sort of touching, isn't it? All those dusty rocks and fossils and those tatty birds and squirrels posed in lifelike positions. Do you live in town?"

He nodded. "I've seen you before, you know."

"Oh? Where?"

"At the pond, one day in the winter. You're a very good skater."

Cassie never knew how to respond to a compliment, except to ignore it. She said now, "I didn't see you."

"No."

The buck gave a little spring, leaving the ground with all

four feet, and bounded away, snowy tail high.

"Well," Cassie said, sighing unconsciously. "I guess I'll start home."

"Let me give you a lift."

"No, thank you."

"But—"

"No, really. But thanks." She waved and walked away, not looking back.

"Lotta," she said that evening, when she and her sister were in bed, "tell me the truth; do you think I'm a freak?"

"Freak?" Lotta said uneasily. She never liked being asked to tell the truth.

"Yes. Do you think I'm—you know—odd, contrary? *Freak-ish?*"

"Well, my goodness," Lotta said. "How should I know? You have some funny ideas. Like not eating meat. Or not liking automobiles."

Or boys to drive me home in them? Cassie wondered. Was it odd of her to have enjoyed that encounter yet feel no need to prolong it?

"I didn't say I didn't like automobiles. I don't like or dislike things like that. A car is just something to get somewhere in, and I can't see what difference it makes what the thing looks like if it gets you there."

"Well, that's odd of you," Lotta said with certainty. "Oh, honestly, Cass, *can* you look at that dreamy bus of Rene's without dying of envy?"

"Yes."

"We drove *all* over town. Everybody was looking at us."

114

"That must have been fun. Good night, Lotta."

"Night, Cass."

Mrs. Dunne, on her way to bed, saw the light go out as she reached the girls' room. She wanted to walk right past but stopped, a bitter little frown creasing her forehead. If they couldn't bother saying good night to her, why should she trouble to say it to them? Oh, I don't understand them, she said to herself. Not Cassie or Vincent or even Lotta. Perhaps Lotta, who pretended better than the other two, was the hardest to know. She seemed so friendly, so thoughtful, so actually loving—and yet there was always this other feeling about her. At this hour, when the two of them had gone upstairs early and then not even taken time to call down a good night, Mrs. Dunne could admit to herself what in the daytime, in Lotta's presence, she couldn't believe at all, and that was that Lotta didn't care about anyone but herself and her friends.

"They only think of themselves," she had said to Muriel, lunching in town with her last week. "Just themselves."

"Who?"

"Oh—" She wasn't going to name Lotta. It was only a feeling, and she didn't always have it; but put it into words and who knew how real it might become? Some things you didn't *say*. "Oh, no one in particular. Young people. Vincent—we hardly ever hear from him anymore. Cassie, in a way. I tell them that the way to be happy is to think of others—"

"You tell them that?" Muriel had said with amusement.

"Muriel—you are *so* condescending. Do you really know so much more than anybody else?"

"Not at all," Muriel had said, sounding piqued. "But I should have thought that wasn't the sort of thing that got told to people. It's like telling someone with a disease that the way to be cured is not to be sick. Besides, at their age they should be thinking almost exclusively about themselves. Otherwise how do they find out who they are, what they want, or even what they can give?"

"I can't recall that you and I were so self-centered, so indifferent to Mama and Papa when we were girls."

"Now, Becky. We were quite as bad. Quite."

"I say no."

"Well, you're stubborn, and you're wrong, and you have a poor memory. Think what you want."

"Thank *you*," Rebecca had said stiffly, and Muriel laughed.

Now, hesitating in the hallway, Mrs. Dunne recalled that laugh with annoyance. Who was Muriel to lecture and laugh at her? She had no children of her own, apparently never knew or felt that she'd missed life's greatest blessing, so how could she understand anything of what a mother felt? The truth is, Mrs. Dunne said in her mind to her absent sister, the truth of the matter is that you lead a life yourself that is almost entirely selfish, with your stylish job and your apartment and your little dinners for friends. It was Mrs. Dunne's conviction, never borne out by Muriel's behavior, that the life of a single woman (and what else is a divorcée?) is sterile, without meaning or purpose. Sure that children were life's dearest treasure, Rebecca Dunne could never be shaken in her belief that Muriel was simply putting up a brave front.

Well, then, if you did have these treasures, these children, why should you deny yourself the pleasure of saying good night to them, even if they'd failed to say it to you?

I won't rebuke them, she said to herself. I'll just open the door and call in a friendly *Sweet dreams*. Feeling humorous and wise, above petty hurt feelings, she flung the door open and said, "Good night there, careless ones. Don't think I didn't notice that you sneaked off without so much as a *Pleasant dreams, Mommy. . . .*"

Lotta flipped over in bed and said nothing. Cassie grunted and said, "Sorry."

"Sorry what?" Mrs. Dunne said gaily. "Heavens, you don't think I mind, do you? I'd be a pretty peculiar mother, wouldn't I, if I didn't understand that young people have other things on their minds besides parents. I was saying to Muriel only the other day that this is the age when young people *must* think of themselves. Otherwise, how do they get to know who they are, and what they want. . . . Muriel seems to feel that people your age think of nothing but themsel—"

"Mother," Lotta said, yawning loudly in the dark, "all we're thinking of right now is sleep, okay?"

"Well, excuse *me*." The gaiety drained abruptly from Mrs. Dunne's tone. "Excuse me, *please*. Next time I'll know better than to try to say good night to my own daughters."

"Next time you might try knocking," Cassie muttered.

"What was that, Cassie?"

"Nothing, Mother. Good night."

"Good night, girls."

Still she lingered. The light from the hallway fell into the room and she could see the two beds, the string on the floor,

117

the two humped figures under the bedclothes. Lotta had pulled a pillow over her head and Cassie was leaning on one elbow, staring toward the door.

"Sweet dreams, children."

"Sure thing," Cassie said. "Same to you."

After she closed the door, Rebecca Dunne stood for a moment to discern if they said anything about her. She realized it was a foolhardy thing to do, that she might hear something perfectly awful said that they wouldn't mean, or not entirely, but which would nonetheless wound her terribly. It had happened before.

Tonight there was no sound. Apparently they really had been sleepy. That was why they'd sounded a bit short-tempered. It had nothing to do with her personally.

She prepared for bed slowly, wishing Roger were here. Roger was a disappointed man with a frequently gloomy outlook, but he was someone her age, someone who knew and cared for her, who occasionally sent her a glance of shared understanding when the children were even more baffling than usual.

She tried now to think of the years when she and Roger had been young and in love. It should be a talisman, such a memory, against the present. But though she knew they had been very much in love, nothing but her mind could recall that time. It was like remembering a movie that had moved you once to tears, as long ago A Farewell to Arms had moved her. You could tell yourself that you'd been greatly touched, and believe it, but no emotion remained. Nothing remained but cold and colorless facts. Once you had wept at a movie with Gary Cooper in it, once you had been in love with Roger. The movie had long since been blurred by successive ones, and love had been replaced by— She didn't know what had replaced love. Just life, probably. Just marketing, and worrying, and getting up and going to bed, and wondering why the children didn't bother to say good night.

"Oh, dear," she said aloud. A few easy tears slid down her cheeks. She wiped them away, took two aspirins, and got into bed, where she read for a while before going to sleep a novel about an English family. It was all love and joy and witty conversation. The mother, especially, was delightful, an easygoing, charming woman, constantly getting into scrapes that her doting husband and her grown and devoted children laughingly rescued her from.

Suddenly impatient, Mrs. Dunne slammed the book shut, turned out her light, and lay down tensely determined to sleep.

Chapter Six

The telephone rang and Cassie picked it up. "Here," she said to Lotta. "For you. J. H."

"Oh, dear. Tell him I'm not in."

"You tell him you're not in." Cassie thrust the phone at her sister and walked away.

Lotta scowled at the retreating back, put the receiver to her ear, and smiled. "Is this my J. H.? How nice of you to call."

"What do you mean, nice?" J. H. said testily. "I phone you every day, don't I?"

"Yes, you do, and it's always *lovely* to hear from you."

"Lotta, will you come off it? You talk like I was some guy called you on his way through town every coupla years."

"You're imagining things, lambie-pie."

"Am I imagining that I don't see you very much lately?"

"Well, you must be. It seems to me we see a terrible lot of each other."

Cassie, in the next room, shook her head. She herself on the average of once a day made some completely tactless comment and had not yet found a way to guard herself against this, as she never recognized a blunder until she'd made it. But Lotta—Lotta was almost never unintentionally rude and was not being so now. She knew just what she was about, saying that to J. H.

Well, thought Cassie, there's one thing to be said for being too plain to attract that kind of attention. You don't have to hurt people when you're tired of it or when your interest has been caught elsewhere. She got up and went into the kitchen so as not to hear anymore.

J. H., after a moment of shock, said, "Lotta, are you trying some fancy way to tell me to shove?"

"J. H., please. Don't talk like that. You know it is *not* so. You're just saying it to hurt me." Lotta's voice dropped shakily.

"Hurt *you?*" J. H. bellowed. "What do you think you're doing to me?"

"J. H., I wouldn't hurt you for anything in the world. Not for anything. And it makes me . . . miserable, just miserable, when you talk this way. You take all the fun and the b-beauty out of our friendship—"

"*Friend*ship, she calls it," said J. H. But he sounded less sure of himself. "Friendship. Is that what this has all been about with you and me?"

121

"After all, lambie, I *am* on the phone. And my little sister is right in the next room, and—oh, J. H., I just don't know what to say. You make me so unhappy I could cry." She sniffled delicately.

"Ah, Lotta," he said. "Don't cry. Please. I'm sorry. I take it all back." There was a pause, during which he tried to figure what it was he was taking back, but another sniffle from Lotta urged him into speech. "No, but honestly. If I've said or done anything—"

"But you haven't," she said unsteadily. "You're my wonderful J. H., and you haven't done *any*thing. I'm the one. I'm terrible and unreliable, and I don't know why you bother with me at all. Any girl in the school would just die to have you . . . care for her. Maybe you should just forget about me—"

"Lotta, will you stop talking that way?" he said desperately. "I love you. Do you hear? Don't ever talk about other girls to me."

"All right, J. H.," she said submissively. "It's just that I know what a bother I am to you—"

"Anybody who didn't think you were worth a bit of bother can go kiss a pig," he assured her in a fervent voice.

Lotta smiled. Even in extremis, J. H. couldn't put any grace or charm into his arguments. There was something sort of endearing about it in a way. He had so many nice qualities, and it was just too bad he didn't have more.

"Well, then, darling," she said, "everything's fine, isn't it. Tell me that you're happy."

"I'm happy," he said glumly.

"There, now. I knew you would be. Was there something

special"—she looked at her watch—"some special reason why you called?"

"So I have to have a special reason now?" he shouted.

"J. H.! You aren't going to start again, are you? Just when we had everything so cozy and—and sweet?"

He sighed. "No. I'm sorry. And what I called about— you're doing that bash at the Donaldsons' tomorrow, right? I'll pick you up. You and your shadow," he added.

"Now, please. You know I don't let people talk about my friends that way. Irene is my—"

"Your shadow, dammit. Excuse me. I didn't mean to swear."

"Well, I should think *not*."

"I said excuse me, didn't I? I haven't said anything else, come to think of it, this whole blasted phone call."

"That's hardly my fault," Lotta said coldly.

"Lotta, will you tell me what time I should be there?" He couldn't stop shouting.

"J. H., let me tell you this. You have no right to call me up and swear and yell at me this way—"

"I'm sorry, I'm sorry, I'm SORRY! There. Will that do?"

"I haven't the faintest idea what you mean. And I'm too tired of being yelled at to continue this. And you needn't bother to pick me up. *Or* my shadow, as you so kindly put it. We'll use Irene's car." She hung up on the start of yet another apology.

"Really," she said, wandering into the kitchen. "Honestly."

Cassie, scrubbing potatoes, didn't reply. Not that would keep Lotta from launching out on some justification

123

vital to her self-interest. Or her self-portrait, Cassie thought. She has to keep that picture in the right light at all times, for all people, herself primarily.

She wondered, all at once, what it was going to be like for Lotta, getting older and finally old. Even Aunt Muriel, who was only thirty, had begun to act nervous and defensive. Her eyes, when they rested on Lotta or Irene, were measuring eyes, even if she didn't know it yet, and she had a way of holding her head at an upward tilt, though there were only the faintest lines in her throat. Beautiful women in books, and no doubt in life, had a precarious time of it as they aged if they didn't have some insurance—like an interest in art or bird-watching or other people. It seemed to Cassie that they were in a way like medieval queens. Never sure if they'd wake in the morning to the adulation due a reigning monarch or the scorn accorded a deposed one.

It would break Lotta up, thought Cassie, if she knew that I worry sometimes about how she's going to face the problems of age. She's too young and gorgeous to think that that could ever relate to her. She'd say, as she's said before, that I was just jealous. And who knows, she might be right. It's a wise person who can sort out his own emotions and say, This is precisely what I mean and how I feel, *not* that. I wouldn't want to be Lotta, even to be that pretty. But I might want—well, do want—to be myself with my interests, and pretty too. Since that is clearly not to be, maybe I *am* jealous and just calling it concern.

She picked up a potato and began to peel it. Mrs. Roosevelt hadn't been an attractive girl. Everyone had told her how un-

124

attractive she was, which anyway hadn't happened to Cassie. The people in her family were horribly practiced in never mentioning her looks. But Mrs. Roosevelt had grown up to marry a handsome, intelligent, interesting, and great man. And she had become the greatest woman in the world, one that even her enemies loved, or anyway admired—

"Cassie!"

"Hmm? Oh, yes, Lotta? What is it?" she said dreamily.

"Look what you're doing. You've peeled that potato down to your thumb."

Cassie looked. "So I have. Thanks for saving the thumb. I was thinking about Mrs. Roosevelt."

"Why, for goodness' sake?"

"She's a nice person to think about. She was very wonderful, and she had a marvelously interesting life."

"What's that have to do with you?"

"I am a part of all that I have met."

"But you never met Mrs. Roosevelt."

"You didn't have to walk down a receiving line and shake hands with her in order to know her. You just had to look at her picture or hear something she said or read what she wrote."

"Oh, well." Lotta moved about restlessly. "You know, J. H. is getting to be too much, just too much."

"Is he? Why don't you set the table? You can talk at the same time."

When there were just the three of them, they ate their meals in the breakfast nook in the kitchen. The dining room was used only for company or when their father was home (which came to much the same thing). They did not even eat so well as they did when others were there. I think basically women don't have any real self-respect, Cassie said to herself. Self-regard and self-consciousness and self-delusion and no doubt lots of self-deception. But no self-respecting man would put up with the meals Lotta and Mother and I get by with. And even three of them together were *nicer* about it than any one of them would be alone. Whenever Cassie was left by herself to eat, she managed with a sandwich and an apple or a candy bar. She was pretty sure her mother and sister would do the same. Or any woman alone.

"I wonder what Aunt Muriel eats when she isn't having people in or going out to 'dine,' as she puts it."

"You know, I just don't understand you. What do you mean, what does she eat? And what's wrong with saying 'dine'? I'm dining out. What's the matter with that?"

Cassie shrugged. "Sounds arch."

"It doesn't to me."

"Okay. Well, what do you eat when you dine alone?"

Lotta considered. "I don't know. A sandwich, I guess."

"As I thought. What were you saying about J. H.?"

"I can't remember."

Cassie went back to peeling potatoes.

"He's just so . . . so all around me, you know?" Lotta said.

"I thought you liked it."

"I did. For a while. But you know, Cass—" She broke off.

"Do I know what?" Cassie encouraged.

"Well, it sounds awfully unmodest—"

"Immodest."

"Cassie, I am *not* going to talk to you anymore." Lotta threw down a fork and started out of the kitchen.

"Hey, come back!" Cassie shouted. "I'm sorry. Honestly. That was rude of me."

"It certainly was."

"Well, I'm sorry," Cassie repeated. "I can't help it. I hear something like that and the correction sort of slips out before I can stop it. Very wrong of me, I know," she said contritely.

Lotta slowly picked up the silver again and began to arrange it. She was pouting and out of countenance, but Cassie waited in silence, and presently Lotta said, "I was only saying that if it wouldn't sound too un—I mean *im*modest—the fact is that I get bored being adored."

"Coming from you it doesn't sound immodest. Just a necessary statement of fact."

Lotta looked mollified. "It's just that he's so steady, so reliable, so always *there*. I mean, there's no excitement in knowing J. H. anymore. I really do try to force myself to care about him the way I used to. I sit down and make a point of remembering how I used to be so mad about him, and how unattainable he seemed, and how thrilling it was when he first noticed me, and then when he actually fell in love with me. I mean, J. H. was one of the *great* conquests of my life, but I just can't recapture the old feeling anymore. There's no challenge left. It's really making me sad," she said plaintively. "I liked loving J. H., and now he's gone and ruined it all."

"Thoughtless of him."

"I should know better than to try to confide in you. You always have some sarcastic answer."

"Not always. I'm sort of sorry for J. H."

"So am I sorry for him. But you can't force yourself to love somebody, can you?"

"I shouldn't think so. Why don't you just tell him right out? Seems to me that would be kinder all around."

Lotta frowned. "Look, Cassie—I hope you aren't getting any ideas of telling him yourself."

"Why should I?"

"I don't know *why* you do most of the things you do, but I'm making it clear that when J. H. is told anything, *if* he's told anything, I will do the telling. None of your slips of the tongue, please."

Cassie had no answer for that. She said instead, "You aren't seeing J. H. tonight?"

Lotta shook her head. "I'm going to stay home with you and Mother. I'm going to wash my hair and do my nails and write letters. Really, I'm quite looking forward to a little peace and quiet for a change. I haven't answered about the last six of Brad's letters."

Cassie, who knew Bradley R. J. Kingston only as a boyish scrawl on incredibly frequent envelopes, said nothing. They worked for a few minutes in silence and then heard the sound of the front door opening, closing, and a step in the hall. Cassie had time to think, Mother's home early, before a male voice called out, "Is anybody home around here?"

The two girls exchanged glances of surprise and dismay.

"It's Dad," Cassie said unnecessarily. She went to the hall, followed by Lotta. "Hello, Daddy."

"Well, well, here are both my charming daughters," Mr.

128

Dunne said in a hearty tone. He always acted jolly on arrival. "Glad to see me?"

"Of course we are," said Lotta. "We didn't expect you until next week."

"Bit of a surprise, eh? Well, it's a surprise for me too. And a pretty nice one too. Your mother here?"

"It's Saturday," Cassie said.

"Oh . . . ah, of course. The bridge game, the *ine*vitable Saturday ladies' bridge game. I can just see them all at Gabriel's last trump bidding no-trump." He laughed and the girls joined in. "That's pretty good," he said, looking at them with happy satisfaction. "Have to remember it for your mother. Well, well. How've you been? Stricken any good boys lately, Lotta?" He laughed again, picked up his suitcase and sample case, and walked with a heavy, downright tread up the stairs.

"Oh, golly," Lotta said. "Good-bye, peace and quiet. I think I'll give J. H. a ring and tell him he can come around for me after all."

"Nice of you."

"Don't be such a hypocrite, Cass. You'd go out yourself if you had anyplace to go."

"No. I would not. It's his first night home, and we owe it to him to try to act pleased. One evening won't kill you."

Lotta turned her hands out. "So, I'll stay home. Only I don't know why people always figure that children owe their parents so much. I think it's the other way around. After all, I didn't ask to be born."

"Oh, Lotta. That old chestnut. Anyway, I'm not sure it's

129

true. Maybe in some other world you were banging on the door day and night, screaming, *I want to be born, let me be born!*"

"You have the queerest imagination. It sort of gives me the creeps."

Better a queer one than none at all, Cassie thought. "We'll have to set the table in the dining room, Lotta. And what are we going to have for dinner now? There are two teeny chops for you and Mother and a piece of swordfish for me, and that's all."

"There must be something in the freezer."

They went into the pantry and poked around, trying to find enough to make a meal for a man, and when Mrs. Dunne came in, she said, "That's your *father's* car out there. What in the world is he doing home? You'd think he could at least let us know. Is there enough food?"

Poor Dad, thought Cassie, making up her mind to be especially nice to him this evening.

The next day Lotta was waiting at the curb when Irene drew up in the red sports car, with the top down. Lotta stored her things in the trunk, jumped in beside Irene, and said, "Let's go."

"You running away from the law?"

"From my family. Daddy got home last night without advance notice. He wanted us all to be delighted, and it didn't work out that way."

"Oh, my," said Irene sympathetically.

"Now he's cross as a bear. Mother broke a date to go to

the movies with Mrs. Fitzsimmons last night, and then she tried to get Daddy to go with her because it ended yesterday, and he exploded. He says he has to go to the movies all the time on the road to keep from being lonely, and he'd be darned if he'd go to one when he was home, and why couldn't he just be in the *boozum* of his family for a while, and—oh, you know. He starts out being a jolly good fellow and in no time he's snarling at everybody."

Where her father was concerned, Lotta relaxed her rule about not discussing family problems. Irene often went into *much* worse detail about her father, the sort of man who had a study full of pictures of himself with something dead at his feet or hanging beside him—some animal or poor fish he'd dispatched. Cassie would loathe him.

"You're usually pretty good at pouring oil on troubled water," Irene was saying.

"With Daddy I just run out of oil. I tried. Even Cass tried—" A smile tugged at her lips.

"Something funny?"

"Oh, that Cassie. She'll be arrested someday for malicious mischief, and she still won't know why it happened or what she's done."

"Did she say one of her sayings?" Irene asked, and she too began to smile. Cassie did come out with some pretty hair-raising remarks. Her brother Vincent claimed that all Cassie lacked was social dexterity. "She's too candid for anybody's good, including her own," he had told Lotta, "but she'll learn in time." Lotta and Irene weren't at all convinced that she would. Social dexterity, diplomacy, whatever you called it,

131

was something you either did or didn't have, in their opinion. The two of them had had it since the cradle, but Cassie never seemed to get even within hailing distance.

"She said," Lotta explained wryly, "after Mother and I had got his feathers all smoothed down, 'Well, Daddy, I *must* say, everything Mother says about you is true.'"

"Oh, my word," Irene gasped. "Did she really?"

"She really did. So Daddy turns on Mother and says, 'And what is that supposed to mean? Just what do you say about me that's so true?' Mother tried to put across some business about how she said he was overworked and unappreciated. Which, as a matter of fact, she does say sometimes. But it wasn't what Cass had in mind, and Dad knew it, and Mother knew it, and nobody was fast enough to cover up properly. It was an awfully tense roomful."

"What did Cassie have in mind?" Irene asked with amusement.

"Oh . . . Mother says that life is so much more peaceful when he's on the road that she's getting so she dreads his visits. You never know what's going to offend him, that's the difficulty. I suppose it means he's sensitive and all, but if that's sensitivity, I'll take a thick skin any day. And speaking of thin skins, J. H. is mad at me again. He really was impossible yesterday over the phone."

"Well, that's what you want, isn't it? To get him to say something so bad that you can be too hurt to forgive him?"

"My, you're perceptive," Lotta said coolly.

"Comes of my association with you, no doubt."

They drove along, reveling in the attention they received

132

from passers-by on the street, in other cars. Once they stopped for a light near a telephone repair truck. A linesman leaned against the cab, folded his arms, and sighed, looking at them. "Now that," he said to a fellow worker, "*that* is what I like about the spring."

The two girls laughed and waved as they drove off. It was a beautiful spring day, very warm for April, with a wistful fragrance in the sunny air and a tentative laciness on the trees. Lotta drew a deep breath and thought how lucky she was. To be young, to be pretty, to be out of love and so ready to fall in love again, with all the exhilaration and tumult that the beginning of love implied.

"I like the *start* of things," she said, putting her arms in front of her, stretching luxuriously.

Irene didn't misunderstand. "Still hearing from Brad every day?"

"I don't mean him. I don't think I do. I just feel—free. For anything."

"I wonder if I could take over J. H.," Irene mused.

"I doubt it," Lotta said seriously. "Not for a while. Unless, of course, because of your association with me."

Irene laughed. "You know, Lotta, you are without any question the most conceited, most self-confident person I have ever known. And that includes my father, who I really did believe took the cake."

"He won't mind sharing with me," Lotta said imperturbably.

"Please don't go getting your hooks in my *father*," Irene said, only half playfully.

"Don't be crude, dear. Anyway, I like young men." One day, she said to herself, Irene's *brother* is going to look and see me, for the first time really see me. She wasn't, actually, in any hurry for that. Meanwhile—well, meanwhile she had nothing and no one in particular in mind. Brad was nice, but not thrilling and already too attentive. Lotta liked to overcome resistance. She also liked the times in between, when she sort of rested and thought things over.

When they got to the Donaldson house, a little girl opened the door to them. She wore a skirt with so many petticoats it gave the effect of a tutu, oddly inappropriate above her sturdy, little-boy legs.

"I'm Ella," she said as though admitting it.

"Well, happy birthday, Ella," Lotta said. "We're Irene and Lotta."

"I know. You're going to give me my party."

"We're going to help your mommy," Irene said, faltering before the bland, nine-year-old stare. "She's giving it. We are the assistants." This was the impression they always strove to give the children.

"My mother isn't here," Ella said.

Lotta and Irene exchanged glances. It sometimes, very rarely, happened that the mothers decamped altogether, and the girls found that sort of sad. Not for themselves. They often could handle the children better that way. But it did seem to them that a mother should accord a child's party the importance of her presence.

They followed Ella into the house, through a large foyer, into a spacious, silent living room. Herds of furniture stood about, covered with heavy block-print linen. There were great copper bowls of lemon leaves and ceramic bowls filled with early daffodils. The fireplace wall was entirely mirrored, a dark-gold crazed mirror that reflected dimly. A brass fan filled the hearth. The wall to the right was lined with French doors, all open to a flagstone terrace.

"Jazzy," said Irene.

Lotta turned toward Ella, still at the door and watching them with the air of a bored museum guide. "Did your mother leave us a note or something? Some instructions?"

Ella poked in the pocket of her skirt. "Maybe I left it in the kitchen. Do you want to come with me or stay here?"

"We'll go with you," Irene and Lotta said together.

They followed the small erect back through a swinging door at the other end of the foyer, down a hall, through a butler's pantry, into a kitchen that Lotta immediately envied for her mother. A sort of palace kitchen, with everything on a palace scale. Was it because this house was so huge and clean that it seemed emptier than any other she'd ever been in? Irene's home was big, and more simply furnished, but it didn't give the impression this one did that if you shouted an echo would shout back.

Ella was wandering around half-heartedly looking for the note.

"Did Mrs. D. tell you she wouldn't be here?" Irene whispered.

Lotta shook her head. "She said for us to get here by two, and we'd get directions then. I didn't know she meant by mail."

"Why, that poor little girl."

"Doesn't seem to bother her any."

"Maybe," said Irene.

"Here's the note," Ella said. "George and I have already set the table up on the terrace. We thought you'd like to have the ice cream and cake part out there because it's a nice day. But of course it's up to you," she said without much interest.

Well, Lotta said to herself, I was asking for challenges. Of course she had not had quite this sort in mind, but a challenge was a challenge, whoever offered it.

"Well, now," she said cheerfully. "Who's George? Your brother?"

Irene giggled. "There's always hope, isn't there?"

"George is our cleaning man," Ella said. "He went home. It's his day off, and he only came up at all because it's my birthday."

"That was very nice of him," Lotta said, ignoring Irene. She opened the note.

"What does it say?" Irene demanded as Ella drifted away again.

"Let's see . . . 'Dear girls.' Forgotten our names probably. 'Sorry to be away for the festivities, but it simply could not be helped. Ella will tell you where everything is. Be sure it's all over by five o'clock. A clown cum truck is due at four. Thought you'd welcome a break. Have a happy. Money *enclosed*. Ten for you, ten for clown.' What does *cum* mean?"

"It's Latin. Means 'with.' "

"She's overpaid us. We're only supposed to get five between us. Clowns come high, I must say."

136

"Maybe she's overpaying him, too. Maybe it's conscience money. I think we're going to earn it."

Lotta got out her notebook. "'Eighteen children, assorted,' I have here. I hope there aren't any gate crashers. Ella," she called across the room, "would you like to blow up balloons while Irene and I set up the auction table?"

"All right." Ella wandered back to them. "What's an auction table?"

"Oh, it's *fun*. We have all these mysterious packages—see, right in this bag—all different shapes and sizes, and we give you each some poker chips, and then we conduct an auction. You can bid for the package that looks tastiest to you."

"Tastiest? Is it something to eat? Because we won't need it. Mother bought an awful lot of food."

"That was just a manner of speaking," Lotta explained, and Irene suppressed a sigh. "Here's a little doohickey that blows up balloons. You put the—"

"I know how it works," Ella said. "You give me the balloons, and I'll take care of them while you do the other things. You'll find most of the stuff in the butler's pantry. I think you'd better get at it, don't you? The children will be coming at two-thirty."

"Holy mackerel," said Irene as she followed Lotta to the kitchen. "She's the head mistress of a girls' school under some sort of spell, that's what she is."

"This is her *ninth* birthday? Let's make a note not to take her on next year. She'll have us sitting in a corner going without ice cream."

"I'm sort of sorry for her."

137

"She apparently doesn't have the sort of childhood babies cry for. But maybe she doesn't want it."

They abandoned the problem of Ella's attitudes as being beyond them and concentrated on her party. After much experimentation they had evolved a system. Loud, physical, tiring activities first. Then, when the children were—hopefully—tired, the flute and piano (if the house had a piano) to provide a background for singing. After the refreshments came games involving paper and pencil. Refreshments and the quieter games could be stretched out until the parents began arriving to bear their young ones away.

Today they decided to conduct the entire affair out-of-doors, gambling that the unusual warmth would last. With the long living-room windows open, Irene could sit at the piano in there and be heard easily on the terrace. They set up the games on the lawn, a broad level of green that only after a couple of hundred feet began to slope downward toward a swimming pool—fenced in and empty. They strung crepe-paper streamers and beribboned balloons from tree to tree and along the terrace wall, piled brightly wrapped favors on a small table, which they set out on the grass, and then on the terrace set the long trestle table with a bright paper cloth and napkins and thick glossy paper plates and cups left by Ella's mother.

Birds sang in lilac and forsythia bushes, and the steady soft spring breeze lifted and fluttered balloons and streamers. The girls were done in good time and stood back to survey their work with satisfaction.

"Very nice," said Ella. "You girls do a good job."

Lotta and Irene looked at each other, looked away to keep from giggling, and thanked their young charge. Irene's right, Lotta thought. Only a head mistress could get that particular inflection—the sort that makes even a compliment sound like something you haven't quite earned.

The children came.

First two, then one, then all, it seemed, together in a rush. They'd come in their party clothes, their offerings under their arms, using their high, expectant, party voices. Nine-year-old children were not hard to please, and it certainly didn't bother them that there were no mothers present. Usually at least one mother hung around the party to be sure her child behaved or was happy or came to no physical harm, or whatever it was that this sort of mother hung around for. But today not a one.

"You know," Lotta said, watching the children tumble and collapse and struggle up laughing in the lobster race, "maybe we exaggerate. About Ella's loneliness, I mean. Maybe, underneath, all children would be just as happy if their parents weren't around."

"Ever?"

Lotta wouldn't commit herself. "Did you notice that not a single mother stayed to oversee today?"

"This is the Yacht Club set. I recognize several offspring. The parent blooms are at the club."

"Yachting?"

"Among other things. I don't know about my own, but I can certainly do without other people's parents. Especially at a birthday party. I think this is just dandy." She rang a little silver bell (she and Lotta had decided that whistles would not strike the right note at the sort of party they intended to be known for) and said, "Fine, now. Peter appears to be the winner. Let's all clap hard for Peter, the lucky lobster. . . ."

After the lobster race came blindman's buff, pin-the-tail-on-the-donkey, and a boisterous, ranging hide-and-seek, during which they had a terrifying few minutes of thinking they had mislaid Ella. Lotta finally ran her down in her room, where she'd elected to "hide" on her bed with a book.

"Don't you like the party?" Lotta cried out, unaware of how despairing she sounded. Ella looked at her kindly, slid off the bed, and put a hand in hers.

"I like it fine. Just fine. I wanted to read for a bit, that's all. But I won't leave again."

Only slightly reassured, Lotta got on with the auction. She was the caller and had always felt she made a pretty good one.

"*Now* . . . what'm I bid, what'm I bid, *lay*-dees and gennel-*mun* . . . make me an offer." She called in a singsong voice, holding aloft a red bundle. "Look . . . look . . . *look*it! This most mysterious, most fanatical, rampant, packagey-looking red-wrapped THING! What'm I *bid* for this enigma? Gimme, gimme, *gimme* . . . A BID!"

The children roared, pushed one another, held up their poker chips, and shouted their bids. Irene used auction time to bring out piles of dainty sandwiches, a many-colored mold of fruited jello, pitchers of lemonade and ginger-ale punch. She left the cake (store-bought and wildly elaborate, with a paper circus surmounting it) in the kitchen. When she'd finished, she joined Lotta, who was now supervising a peanut race with a satisfied smirk.

"What gives?" said Irene, following Lotta's gaze.

Ella's stern little face had at last relaxed and she'd flung herself into the party with the ease of a habitué. Lotta and Irene had no way of knowing whether or not she was. They had not had her as a guest at any of their other parties, as they had had some of the children here today, but that didn't mean she never went to any. On the other hand if she assumed this prim, superior air very often, it didn't seem likely she'd receive many invitations. She reminded Lotta of Cassie, whose social life was less than sparkling. The other children were party experts. They knew the games, one another, the atmosphere, the rules. They were rowdy within reason and quite sure they were having a good time.

"She's *playing*," Lotta said. "Look at her push that peanut with her nose."

"Just like a child," Irene agreed.

After the peanut race, to quiet the noisy, excited children, Irene played the piano softly while Lotta went down a row of upturned faces, wiping each with a damp cloth. Then she took her flute and joined Irene to lead the children in singing. Easy, gentle songs, and piping little voices . . . it was Lotta's favorite time of a birthday party.

During the refreshment hour, when Lotta was briefly in the kitchen preparing to get the ice cream from the freezer and serve it before she lit the candles on the cake, loud prancing music suddenly approached the house.

She ran to the window to see a carousel climbing the long driveway—a little, garishly decorated affair, mounted on a truck, that wound slowly and stridently, its music box skirling. It came to a halt in a wide paved area between the garage and

141

the house. A clown sprang from the driver's seat. He wore a red-and-yellow domino, a frill at his neck, a pom-pommed hat. Dangling from his hand was a hoop stretched across with red tissue paper. His face under its half-mask was inscrutable beneath lavish make-up. He stood facing the house but making no move toward it.

Suddenly the music stopped, leaving a disproportionate silence in which the stirring of high branches and the quick movements of birds became noticeable. The clown snapped to attention, leaned into the cab of the truck, and once again "The Entrance of the Gladiators" assailed the afternoon.

Irene came rushing in. "What on earth *is* that?" she asked Lotta, who pointed out the window. "The clown? Oh, lordy, I'd forgotten all about him. We'd better put the ice cream back in the freezer. And we'd better get him to tone that down. He'll have the police after us."

"Do you think that would give our parties cachet?"

"I think it would give them what-for. Let's go out and stop him."

"Ah-ha!" cried the clown when he saw them coming. "Huming beans. I was beginning to think I was the last survivor." He shouted over the music and began to caper as the children appeared, running full tilt from around the house. "And still they come!" he bellowed, slapping his thigh, reaching over to open the door of the truck.

"Monsieur! Vos amis sont ici. Attendez!"

A small brown poodle with a frill just like the clown's around his neck sailed through the hoop, shredding red tissue to tatters. He then rose to his hind feet and turned

142

carefully, waving his paws for balance, in three full circuits. The children shrieked and ran around as if possessed, clambering, at the clown's invitation, onto the truck's little merry-go-round with its six dashing small horses.

"Gently! *Gently*," the clown admonished. "Plenty of opportunity for all. Girls first, girls first, young gentlemen . . . lots of time. Who, may I inquire, is the birthday person?"

"Oh, me, *me!*" said Ella, her little sharp-featured face radiant. "It's me!"

"Ah . . . well, a happy sixtieth birthday to you."

"I'm not *sixty*," she protested, laughing.

"That wish is for later on. Right now—" He leaned over and scooped her up in his arms, set her, wildly wriggling, on a sky-blue horse. "There. You are now riding the lead horse. Make him know you're the boss and you'll find he goes under you beautifully."

"How do you know he's the lead horse?" grumbled a boy, doubtless vexed at the necessity for manners. "They're all in a circle."

"I got it from Monsieur here," said the clown in a hollow whisper. He gestured at the little dog. "He's in the confidence of all wooden horses. They tell him things they'd never dream of telling you and me."

The boy grinned and leaned over to pat Monsieur while five more girls sat exultantly on the other five horses. The clown slammed shut the wire gate to the carousel and began to spin the cage, slowly at first, then faster and faster, while the children shouted encouragement and the little dog ran about barking and the music blared on and on.

"Golly, he does it by *hand,*" Irene said. "He must be awfully strong."

Lotta didn't answer. She stared at the clown. Tall, graceful, powerful, and, under all that make-up, quite unreadable. Who was he? One second she'd think she must know him, the next she knew he was a stranger. It was mysterious and thrilling, like a Mardi Gras encounter.

"Do you know him?" she asked Irene after a while.

"How would I know if I knew him? He could be my brother or a man from Mars. Do you suppose we can get him to take that stuff off?"

"I sort of doubt it."

The boys had their turn on the carousel, and then some boys and girls together, and after a full half-hour the clown, noticeably panting now, put his white-gloved hands up before him and called, "Enough! No more. These steeds are tuckered out. They must head for the stable and their warm oats."

"Ah, they're wooden," said the same carping boy.

"And what do you know of the languor and hunger that go at a wooden heart?" said the clown, stooping down to thrust his vermilion nose into his heckler's face. "Learn to see beyond your proboscis, boy. That's my advice to you." He turned to Lotta and Irene. "On further thought, if *you'd* like a ride, I'm sure these chargers could be prevailed upon once more."

"Oh, no, thank you," Irene said. "I'm afraid of horses."

"And I never ride alone," Lotta said. "But thanks." She tried to read the face beneath the clown's paint. Steady blue eyes looked out of the mask and seemed to be smiling at her frustration. "Will you have cake and ice cream with us?" she invited.

The clown hesitated.

"Oh, please, please, please," Ella begged, tugging at a white glove. "Please do stay with us."

"*Voulez-vous quelque chose, Monsieur?*" said the clown to the poodle. "*Une petite glace, peut-être?*" The dog sat up and barked. "Ah well, in that case—" He turned back to Ella. "My associate here says we will be delighted to join you."

"Why do you always talk French to your dog?" asked the carping boy.

"I'm astonished that you ask that," said the clown. "Because he's a French poodle, *n'est-ce pas?*"

This kept the children laughing all the way to the table, where the clown sat, the poodle at his feet, and regaled the company with Monsieur's history while Lotta and Irene went for the ice cream and cake.

"It seems," he began, "that as the merest pup, Monsieur here—known in those days as Petit Monsieur—made up his mind to become a circus *artiste*—"

The birthday cake was bright with cardboard equestriennes and tumblers and flags. With her clown and her cake, thought Lotta, Mrs. Donaldson knows how to carry through a motif. She lit the candles and carried the cake carefully to the terrace, where the children deserted the clown momentarily to accord Lotta and her burden that wonder they give to birthday cakes and Christmas trees, no matter how expected.

"Happy birthday to you, happy birthday to you," sang Lotta and Irene, who followed with ice cream. Clown and children joined in, while Ella, looking nine and not a day older, flushed and smiled and giggled. Monsieur sat up to whine musically, which sent the children into further gales of laughter.

"He sure is the hit of the party," Irene whispered, eying the clown. "Maybe we could join forces, the three of us."

"He charges ten dollars. We'd never get any business at that price."

"Well, we could ask him. Maybe she's overpaying him too."

"You ask," Lotta said.

"For goodness' sake, what's the matter? Don't you like him?"

"How can you tell if you like somebody who isn't there? He isn't himself, he's The Clown."

"He's an awfully good one," Irene insisted.

"Yes."

Irene gave up. She'd never seen Lotta so speechless before, so subdued in the presence of a young male. She looked closely at the clown. Tall. He moved well. He had a nice voice and a sort of dashing way about him. None of it seemed sufficient to have stunned Lotta into silence.

But even after the clown had taken his blaring departure and the parents had come to collect their children, Lotta remained unnaturally quiet. Ella's mother still had not returned, so Lotta and Irene did the dishes while they waited.

"You can go," Ella told them reluctantly. "I'm used to staying alone. It'll be all right."

146

But they couldn't leave a little girl in that great empty house on her birthday, so they waited for Mrs. Donaldson's arrival, and left only in time for Irene to drive while it was still daylight.

Mr. Dunne was in the living room reading a magazine when Lotta came in. He tossed it aside and called out, "Well, how's the career girl?"

"Fine, Daddy."

She wanted to go up to her room and think but walked instead to the side of her father's chair. She seemed to be the only person in the family who could put him in a good mood. If he stayed long, even she couldn't bring it off. But this was only a surprise weekend visit, and it was worth a little effort to keep him contented.

If, of course, Lotta said to herself, sitting down on an ottoman and beginning a description of the party, if after all I do to get things calm and pleasant, Cassie doesn't come in and raise a storm again. It seemed to Lotta that she was constantly trying to smooth things over, like tracks in sand, after Cassie, who didn't even have the grace to recognize it. She thinks *I'm* selfish, Lotta said to herself. Does she ever consider that all that unasked-for honesty is selfish in its way too? That dumb remark last night got everyone in the house upset. Wasn't that selfish?

She gave her father a detailed description of the afternoon, including the carousel, but spoke of the clown only briefly. Mr. Dunne listened with happy inattentiveness. Generally he used the time when other people were talking to plan what he'd say when he interrupted, but he let Lotta talk on, not because he was much interested in what she was saying, but just

147

to have her with him and seeming pleased to be.

Very often as he drove the hundreds of miles his territory covered, or spent lonely evenings in hotel rooms far from home, Mr. Dunne was overwhelmed with a feeling of separateness. Lying on a bed somewhere, too dully tired even to turn on television, he'd stare at the ceiling and think, What am I doing here? What's the *point?* He had no actual friends— just fellow salesmen he met on the road, maybe had a drink with, and then forgot as they forgot him. He had a family, but he sometimes felt it was that very fact that made him feel so cut off, so alone. Vincent was a stranger to him, Cassie hardly less so. His wife tried too hard to pretend that his home-comings were delightful, his leave-takings a sorrow. Mr. Dunne, not looking a fact head-on, but from the corners of his eyes, suspected that possibly the reverse was true. In all this there was only Lotta. Lotta loved him and was glad to have him home. Anyone could see that. Like—take right now. She'd worked hard today and could've just waved and gone up to her room. But no, she'd come right in here and sat down with him and was talking comfortably, without that look of being anxious to get away that Cassie always had.

"Lotta," he said, not noticing that he interrupted, "Lotta, you make up to me for everything."

Lotta, lost in a private reverie even as she talked, realized that he'd said something, took a chance that a smile would be sufficient answer. It seemed to be. She went on talking to her father and thinking about herself. They spent a very happy hour together.

148

Chapter Seven

David looked up from a letter he was reading. "This cousin of mine in Mississippi," he said to Vincent. "He tried last week to go to a white movie house. All by himself."

Vincent whistled. "He's got nerve."

"He sure has, the fool."

"What happened to him?"

"He's in jail, man. What do you think, they made him mayor?"

"What'll happen to him now?"

David lifted his shoulders. "Nothing, I guess. According to my aunt's letter they told him he'd just lost his head for a while, and he's going to be a good boy from now on. He agreed, so they're going to let him out. Maybe he's out now."

149

He crumped the letter, tossed it in a wastebasket, leaned his head back wearily.

"Well, what could you expect him to do, Dave? Does every Negro in the country have to be a martyr?"

"You're asking me? *I'm* not going to college in Mississippi, am I?" David said bitterly. "I'm not trying to study in a rain of brick and spit and curses, with Federal men and the National Guard helping me to be a symbol. I don't want to be a symbol, see? Or a credit to my race. I want to be me, Dave Gates, and if I fail something it was because I didn't study hard enough or the work was too tough for me, and if I make Phi Beta Kappa it was because this fellow Gates was smart and worked very hard, and color had nothing to do with it either way, see?"

"Sure, I see."

"Oh, sure. I know you do, Vince. You do, lots of people, white and black do, and I'm not going to be sucked into hating any race. I see what it's done to white people and they aren't going to make me like them—excusing your presence, old man. But just now and then . . . I get fed up with this credit to my people business. I get it from my parents all the time. I must work harder than anybody else, and walk straighter and act nobler and never forget I stand for my people. I just stand for myself, that's all."

"Nobody just stands for himself."

"Myself, a human being. I'll take my share of being responsible for that, and believe me, that's no small responsibility, seeing how the human race conducts itself. I'll take my share of being a tasteless, thoughtless, excitable moron

150

who has occasional moments of wisdom and beauty. Come to that, I'll take my share of being responsible for the end of the world when we blow it up. But that'll be because I was a man, not a colored man."

Vincent nodded. They both believed that only one end lay ahead for the world, believed it so completely that they rarely talked or even thought about it. Enoch argued with them. He placed his reliance on the balance of fear, on massive deterrents, on his own strong sense of indestructibility.

"I guess," Vincent said, "that you and I just don't feel the way Enoch does, that something as important as ourselves and our plans can't be subject to nuclear disruption."

David laughed. "He astounds me. He pulverizes me. He's as bright as the next guy, brighter than some, and he still thinks there's some way for us to store up all these missiles and megatons, with country after country getting its own little old nuclear reactor, and still come out of it as if we'd just been adding to the preserve shelf in the basement."

"Even the preserves blow up, in time," said Vincent. "Anyway, ours did at home."

"So will ours, cousin, all over. It'll be the biggest pickle-bust in history."

"And the last."

"Definitely the last."

Inexplicably this sort of talk reassured them. It was, Vincent thought, a sort of foxing of the gods—the Olympians had always been notably foxable. If they thought all these poor mortals were prepared to accept their doom, the contrary, irrational immortals might very well stay it.

151

Enoch, coming in just as the conversation began to languish, sparked it again by suggesting that if they felt that way they ought to get out and do something about it.

"Like what?" said Vincent. "Assassinate Mao Tse-tung? Deactivate a Polaris submarine? Do what?"

"Well, picket something," Enoch said vaguely. "Join a protest group. Write letters to Edward Teller telling him what you think of him. You can't just sit here in this room explaining to each other how you're against the bomb. You go out and walk in a picket line and make yourself heard."

"On the contrary," said David. "We don't have to join anything to be against the bomb, and joining something isn't going to head it off either. You could walk till your feet were just under your ears, but the fact remains—the hand that rocks the nuclear reactor rules the world, and there's a new hand every day rocking the hell out of it. You and I don't have *anything* to say."

"Well, I don't agree," Enoch said. "I mean, I agree we don't have anything to say about it, but I don't agree that *it* is going to happen. I mean, look at it sensibly, both of you. You sit there saying so casually that the planet is going to be blown up, but do you know *what* you're saying? Do you realize that means the end of—of Greek architecture and Beethoven symphonies and skiing and dog shows and round-the-world cruises and electric swizzle sticks and—"

"Hold!" said Vincent, lifting his hands. "We get the point. We're with you, maybe ahead of you. The difference is, Enoch, that we think Greek architecture and Latin diplomas and even labor-saving methods of bending the elbow aren't going to count for much when one of these countries, ours or Russia or China or someplace we never even heard of, gets pushed that fraction of an inch too far."

"Besides," said David, "do you really think that the human being is so constructed that he'll be able to keep his finger off that button forever? One day he'll just have to push it, to see if it really works, and then—*pow*. The moving finger detonates and then moves on and there won't *be* any piety or wit to call it back, and there go your round-the-world cruises."

"Out of all the guys in this house," said Enoch, "why I had to pick you two to room with. . . . I come in here after a hard daily struggle, looking for peace and companionship and maybe somebody to have a beer with, and what do I get?"

David stood. "The beer I'll go for."

"Companionship," said Vincent, leaping up. "That's the ticket."

"Well," Enoch said lightly, "beer and companionship give life tone, even if we can't have peace. Let's go, men."

They walked across the campus through a misty spring twilight. Here and there, in the old Georgian houses and the new Gropius-type buildings, lights sprang up at windows. They could see into various rooms where people were studying, talking, moving about. White people, Vincent thought. And the strollers or determined walkers, the cyclists and motorists they passed, they were white, too. It seemed to him astonishing and shameful that he had not, until just now, realized that David was one of such an infinitesimal number of Negroes in this college. And then he thought that perhaps it was good he hadn't noticed. David wasn't much given to talk about his color or the problems that color faced him with at all times. Tonight had been an exception because of his daredevil brave cousin.

But the problems must always be there, even if you did go to a Northern college where they kept them tamped down or pretended they didn't exist. One of Vincent's friends, a Jew, had told him that while on the surface there might seem to be next to no difficulty being Jewish in a predominantly Christian school, the problems were there, like rocks just beneath the surface of a smooth-appearing body of water. Places you wouldn't go to, clubs you couldn't join. Even the fraternities that were supposed to be absolutely simon-pure unrestricted had tacit quotas. "How would you like to be part of a quota?" this friend had asked Vincent, who hadn't replied. What reply was there? And yet that fellow, being Jewish, still could walk through a crowd unnoticed. Being different wasn't with him every second of the day, inescapably imprinted on his skin, as it was with David.

What was wonderful about David, about the American Negroes generally, Vincent thought, was the poise and dignity with which they endured being made to feel at all times different from, less than, other Americans—while, of course, paying their taxes and if necessary losing their lives in battle on a strict basis of equality. It wasn't a wonder that some of them snapped. The wonder was that all of them weren't berserk. When that pit of hell opened in Oxford, Mississippi, why hadn't every Negro in the country, confronted with this violent and ugly rejection not only of a man's skin but of everything America was founded for, said that it stood for,

154

why, faced with it, hadn't the Negro Americans turned on every white man with equal viciousness and hatred? Why hadn't David, in an access of frustration and loathing, moved out on him and Enoch, or vilified them, or killed them? He hadn't. They'd even been able to discuss it, though Vincent and Enoch (but especially Vincent, since he was the American) were tongue-tied with shame, and David almost eerily objective.

Yet they were friends still, and would be, Vincent thought, as long as they were together and possibly after that. They'd weathered differences of opinion, of attitude, of upbringing, background, and temperament. Enoch, wealthy and spoiled; David, handsome and branded for life; Vincent—he never knew how to describe himself—well, say Vincent, good-humored and insignificant. They were friends. If you could take three people like them and bring them together so that they were understanding of one another, tolerant of faults, generously aware of good qualities, usually patient, and nearly always glad of one another's company, maybe there was hope yet that the world's diverse people—given time—could reach some decent, even happy, understanding.

Given time. Aye, there's the rub, said Vincent to himself as they turned into a tavern and sat at a scarred wooden table that bore the inextinguishable testimony of seventy years of students searching out their souls in this place. Here where they sat had sat generations of young men now grown or old or dead, in whose veins the blood had raced, in whose brains myriad concepts had been born and withered or flourished, in whom had been all the hopes and horrors, all the optimism and despair that flesh is heir to. Theirs then, ours now, thought Vincent. Whose tomorrow? Anyone's?

"Us youths," Enoch declaimed, licking a beer-froth mustache from his upper lip, "need something to pit ourselves against, something to rebel against. That's the mainspring of our wellsprings."

"Shouldn't think there was any lack of scope for rebellion in our times," said Vincent.

"What's a mainspring of a wellspring?" David inquired.

"I'm not sure," said Enoch. "But my father's full of them. All two of them. I'd sort of like to examine him for clockwork if there was some way to do it without letting him know. But the trouble is—the jist of it all in a nutshell is—I can't be a proper rebel where he's concerned, because he didn't move with his times."

"How's that?" asked Vincent, puzzled and amused.

"You see," Enoch confided, turning his beer glass to make a series of circles on the wooden table top, "you see, my father is a reactionary. I'd put him slightly to the right of Louis the Fourteenth. Well, so—that's where he threw me off balance. Because according to my timetable, *he* was supposed to be the flaming liberal, and I'm supposed to react by being a reactionary. Do you get my point?"

"You mean," David said, his mouth curving in a downward smile, "you're a monarchist yourself."

"Well, not exactly," Enoch protested. "Sort of a democratic monarchist, if I may put it that way."

"You may put it any way you wish," said Vincent. "Of course, it doesn't make sense, but don't let that stop you."

"How would your father put it?" said David. "Is he a democratic monarchist, too?"

"Heck, no. He's not for monarchy at all. He doesn't have that much style. He's a bourgeois capitalist, nineteenth-century variety."

"Not forward looking, eh?" said David.

"Forward looking? My father was born with a firm fix on the past and his gaze hasn't wavered *once*. From a position of unassailable astigmatism, he wages a valorous war against progress."

"Well, then," said Vincent, "your role is obvious. Rebel against that."

"But there's no real kick in it," Enoch complained. "It's pusillanimous. In essence there really isn't enough difference between us. We're both just materialists."

"There's an admission for you," said Vincent, thinking of the many young and enthusiastic right-wing types on campus. "You know something, the way things are going, pretty soon a reactionary will be a Roosevelt Democrat."

"By *George*," Enoch said enthusiastically. "I believe you've coined an epigram, Vincent, old man. Let's have a beer on it."

The tavern was full and noisy. In a far corner a group of young men was doing part-singing. A burly fellow, one foot on a chair, strummed a guitar.

> *Oh . . . Mary, don't you weep, don't you moan*
> *Oh, Mary . . . don't you weep, don't you moan*
> *Pharaoh's army got drownded . . .*
> *Oh, Mary . . . don't you weep.*

157

They were good, and the sound of their voices, the *plink-plunk* of the guitar moved Vincent to a strange nostalgia for a storybook college life that *was* only in storybooks, for him, in any case. A sort of Scott Fitzgerald world, heightened by the sharp smell of beer, by the dim and gaudy lights, by the group of girls (coeds, they'd be called) now entering. Light-moving girls in tweed and cashmere, with shiny hair.

"I say, there's Mouse," said Enoch, half rising. "Mouse! Mouse! Come into my trap. I've lined it with eiderdown just for you."

A small girl, a very small, trim girl with tawny hair that had a white streak in it, looked across the crowded barroom, saw Enoch, sent him an oddly resigned smile, and said something to the girl with her. They came to where the three young men were getting to their feet.

"Mouse," said Enoch, "I'd like you to meet some unimportant acquaintances of mine. Nobody you need pay attention to. Just squeeze in beside me here and we'll let the rest of the world go by."

"Hi, David," said Mouse.

"Oh," said Enoch. "You know him?"

"How could I not know David?" she said with a laugh.

"Yeah, how could she not?" David demanded. "I'm distinctive, Dad. Not just a face in a crowd."

"And you're Mercutio," said Mouse, turning to Vincent. "I think you were *mar*velous. You were the most dashing Mercutio I ever have seen."

"Now, just a mo," Enoch said. "We can't have things getting out of hand. Bear in mind, please, that *I* pulled one of

158

many strings I keep handy to get him that role, and *I* this very instant past invited you two over here. Let us preserve a sense of balance—"

"This is Christobel Compton," said Mouse. "Enoch Burke-Runciman, David Gates, and—"

"My *word*," said Enoch, transferring his gaze to the tall and willowy girl beside Mouse. "Christobel Compton. Your parents certainly had their wits about them. You'll have to go on the stage, my dear, that's all there is to it. Everyone will think you made the name up, but you and I will know the truth and that will be all that matters. Here, squeeze in beside me, and we'll let the rest of the world go by."

Christobel sat with Enoch, Mouse slipped in between David and Vincent. She turned immediately to David and said, "How am I going to find out your friend's name, aside from Mercutio? Is Enoch tight?"

"Oh, no," David said. "Just high-spirited. As usual."

Mouse laughed. "What *can* it be like—never to take anything seriously?"

"It crosses my mind from time to time that it may take more out of a guy than following the normal temperature chart," said David. "And this is Vincent Dunne, Mouse. If you," he added, "have any more name than Mouse, I've never heard it."

"Oh, dear. Oh, well . . . it's Daisy Prescott."

"Why the Mouse?" said Vincent.

"One of those childhood things that cling. My father said I looked like a mouse—a field mouse, you understand, *not* a house mouse—and so it began, and so, unless I do something

159

about it, it will ever be. But can you imagine being forty and called Mouse?"

Vincent, looking into the small heart-shaped face surrounded by that tawny soft hair with the snowy streak, could see what her father had meant. She was delicate and tiny-boned, and he imagined she'd move quickly and shyly when alarmed.

A waiter approached, wiping his tray with an apron. He was a student, and like all working students, gave Vincent a pang of guilt. Telling yourself you had to work too hard keeping your grades up to handle a job in addition was sort of useless if you didn't keep your grades up. I'll have to start working year-round, he said to himself.

"What'll it be?" said the waiter, yawning.

Enoch asked for another beer, David and Vincent skipped, and the girls ordered lemon squash.

"Straight?" said the waiter.

"On the rocks," said Mouse and Christobel.

"Okay, ladies. But we'll have no disorder, please."

Mouse giggled. "It's all right. We're used to the stuff."

The part-singers were replaced by a plaintive balladeer on the juke box. The crush of students, chime of glassware, swell of voices, grew. The room became hazily, smokily blue. David spied a friend of his and left.

Looking after him, Mouse said, "He's awfully nice."

"He's more than nice," said Vincent. "Sometimes I think maybe he's actually great. In the real sense, you know."

"Do you think that because he's your friend or because you are otherwise biased?"

"Oh, you mean, he's colored, so I give him more than the benefit of a doubt?"

"Something like that."

"I don't think so. I think, as things stand, we do have to give a Negro something more than strict justice. We have so much injustice to make up for that maybe some overcompensation is called for. But Dave . . . no, we take him straight, for himself. He wouldn't have it any other way, and I have too much respect for him not to respect his wishes, if I make myself clear."

"Oh, you do." She sipped her drink. After a while she said, "I've never seen you act, except that one time. How is that?"

"Because that one time constituted my stage career."

"Really? You were awfully good. Didn't it get into your blood?"

"Nope. I'm a major disappointment to Dave and Enoch. They're natural Thespians, maddened by the glamor of the stage. It didn't quite get to me. I enjoyed it, understand. But the fact is, I felt sort of silly."

"Amazing. No one ever could have guessed. That Queen Mab speech . . . you were marvelous."

"It's a great speech."

"How did you happen to do it at all, go on the stage?"

Vincent grinned. "You make it sound pretty imposing. I did it on a dare. Those two challenged me to try out for some role or other, and I've always liked Mercutio . . . so, I tried out. I got right up there on the stage and read some, and they took me. I haven't quite recovered yet. I mean, I thought maybe I'd get a walk-on part because of knowing two such wheels in the drama department. But *Mercutio* . . . well, it was great fun," he said reminiscently. "Great."

"David was a perfect Romeo."

"That was the best part of all, really. Not the best *part*, that is, because I never really can take to Romeo—"

"I know what you mean. Juliet would have had her hands full if they'd got out of that tomb alive."

"Sure she would have. But that Dave *got* the part, that was perfect. And he was perfect. He was practically resigned to being Othello again, or Oberon, if he could talk them into it. But I said if I'd take his dare, he had to take mine, so I thrust him into Romeo's doublet, and man, did he fit."

"He's so handsome, of course. And a good actor. Lisa Favor, the girl who played Juliet, is wild about him."

"Or thinks she is."

"What is that supposed to mean?"

Vincent shrugged. "Dave says she—and another girl who pursues him and everybody knows it—just sort of have an idea in their heads. I mean, he says it isn't him, Dave Gates, they're in love with. It's his symbolic self. He represents their freedom to love as they please and do as they please. He's their emancipation."

"Maybe he's wrong. Did you ever think of that? Maybe Lisa really does love him. It'd be kind of hard on her if he was so determined to be a symbol that he forgot he was a man."

Vincent smiled at this version of David. "Well, there's one other thing. He isn't in love with her. He says she's fun to be with, and he either goes out with white girls up here or no girls at all, because that's all there is. But he brought the girl he's in love with up to our Fall Weekend. She is quite a girl."

"A Negro?"

"Yup."

"I wonder if he disapproves of mixed marriages," Daisy said reflectively.

"Disapproves? Oh, no. Not theoretically, that is. He approves of them the way I do. If you look at it sensibly, the only way we're going to straighten this mess out is to get it so mixed up that nobody'll know *who's* marrying his sister. That's just common sense. But personally and individually—"

"Yes?" Daisy said coolly. "Personally and individually, what do you feel?"

Unperturbed by her tone, Vincent frowned over his answer. "Well," he said at length, "I wouldn't have the stamina to face the pain, or the peril, of such a marriage. Not for myself, not for the woman, not for my children."

"But then what's the answer?"

Vincent shrugged. "You can't seriously be asking me that, can you?"

"No. I guess not. How did David's girl like it up here? Did everyone accept her all right?"

"You might say we overaccepted her. We practically broke our fool necks being casually hospitable. They took it fine. Dave and his girl, Marie. They're used to nervous white people."

"You're nice, too," said Mouse.

Vincent blinked and looked away briefly. A feeling of warmth, gentle and radiant, ran through his veins, a sense of

163

wonder and surprise. *"On guard!"* said a voice in his mind, but he knew it was already too late for warnings.

"No, but you have to understand," he heard Enoch saying; "my father is a man of exceedingly high ideals. Now *if* you have a lot of high ideals that you find it inconvenient to live up to, then who has to live up to them? Why, your son of course. Your first-born son. It's called primogeniture," he said owlishly.

"I don't think so," said Christobel. "The law of primogeniture, while it does relate to the eldest son, is—"

"Let's go," Mouse whispered to Vincent. "I really don't think I can bear to hear about Enoch's da any more this evening."

Vincent settled his part of the bill and he and Mouse, with a wave for David but none for Enoch, who'd forgotten them, went out into the misty night.

"Whew," said Mouse, taking a deep breath. "An hour in there and you practically forget what air is."

A small wind ruffled her hair and Vincent, watching the tendrils stirring, realized that he had to look down at her. Such a little, lovely girl.

"I think I'll call you Daisy," he said, and caught his breath a little. He had so easily assumed he'd be seeing her to call her anything at all. And yet, he was sure. He was going to see Mouse again and call her Daisy.

What a marvelous, glorious, splendid thing life was. He filled his lungs with the soft night air and felt the rampant running of his blood, like sap in a spring tree. I, Vincent Dunne, he said to himself. *I, Vincent.* Only last fall he had been . . . what? A member of the audience, indistinguishable, lost, nobody. And then in a flash he had bypassed the walk-on condition, had leaped to the stage, a full-fledged and dashing Mercutio. He had caught the eye of a mouse. I, Mercutio Vincent Dunne.

For the first time in his life he seriously wondered what it would be like to be the hero of the play.

Chapter Eight

In the afternoon, when school let out, the girls walked or took buses. The boys tried to hitchhike, all but flinging themselves into the flow of traffic in their determination not to walk.

"You'd think," Cassie said to Fritzy, "they were lost in the polar regions. You'd think their only hope of survival lay in an automobile ride back to civilization."

"They're pretty lazy," Fritzy agreed. "You'd think characters who could run around a track for hours, or up and down a ball field, could manage a few blocks home, wouldn't you?"

They passed J. H., wildly signaling. His house wasn't more than half a mile away.

"What's the trouble, J. H.?" Cassie called. "You been un-horsed?"

He turned his troubled face toward her, and away, as if the sight caused him pain. A car drew up; J. H. leaped in and was off.

"Poor thing," said Fritzy. "I guess you remind him of all he's loved and lost."

"Any boy who goes out with Lotta should know what's ahead. In a town this size how could he avoid knowing? She's run through just about every presentable male in the high school. Her standard of presentable, that is to say."

"Where does she do her hunting these days?"

"She has some boy in a prep school at the moment."

"Must be fun," Fritzy said.

Cassie had no opinions on that. "Why do you suppose J. H. is carless?" she said. "He looks like half of a centaur without that automobile under him."

"He got two speeding tickets, so they took away his license for a while. Anyway, that's how I heard it."

"Speeding? J. H.? How unlike him. I suppose Lotta's driven him to recklessness and low companions."

"That should please her."

"Oh, I don't know," Cassie said contrarily. "She's not a femme fatale. Just a fickle girl. Anyway, why shouldn't she be fickle? She's at the age for it."

"Heavens, I couldn't care less," said Fritzy. "Want to go down to the Candy Stick for a coke?"

Cassie hesitated. It was a warm day, and a coke would be pleasant. But the Candy Stick, forgathering place of high-school students, made her conscious of something she generally forgot or was indifferent to. Boys never flirted with her. No young male ever glanced her way and suddenly focused, as they did with Lotta, or Irene, or even Fritzy. Their eyes slid past her without a trace of hesitation. It was easy not to mind this when you were not reminded of it. Only a masochist would put herself in a position to be publicly weighed and found wanting in this fearfully important ritual of high-school sex responses.

"Thanks, no," she said. "I have to work."

Fritzy twisted a silky curl at her cheek. "Work. Really, Cass. You should do something to get yourself left back. You're going to go to college emotionally immature."

"No. I'm already emotionally mature."

"Oh, Cassie," Fritzy said with affection. "You're a baby. A bright baby, of course. But I think you should seriously consider failing a subject so you won't get out of school at such a lollipop age."

Cassie smiled a little. "You can't fail subjects deliberately. At least, I couldn't. Anyway, I want to get out and away—"

"Away from what?"

Cassie wouldn't commit herself on that. Could you say that you wanted to find a world where people only listened to beautiful music, only read the finest books, only held the most elevated and impersonal conversation, preferably in several alternating languages? Could you say that you wanted to live where going to art galleries was as much a part of life as looking at television was in Forest Acres? Well, you could, but didn't have to.

168

"I want to be able to pick my own clothes," she said, glancing down at Lotta's baby-blue spring suit that she'd already gotten paint on.

"Lotta graduates this spring," Fritzy said. "Is she going to college?"

"She didn't get accepted anywhere."

"Oh, my. What a shame they don't give scholarships for charm and beauty."

"Quit picking on my sister, will you?"

"Picking on her? I said she was charming and beautiful."

It wasn't what you meant, Cassie thought. You meant she's flirtatious and vain. Which she is. Only that isn't all there is to Lotta. But it's funny, Cassie went on to herself, walking away from Fritzy without remembering to say good-bye, it's funny how families will do this sticking up for each other. No one would call us Dunnes a close family, and we nag and fret one another to shreds, yet I don't like it when Fritzy says something about Lotta that I say all the time.

I wish, she thought fiercely, that people would be rational and predictable. I wish everybody would make sense all the time. As this was extreme, even for Cassie's earnest point of view, she left off thinking about it, quickening her steps toward the house.

It was empty. Her mother was at some church function, and no doubt Lotta was out with her prep-school beau, Brad Whatsiz, who was home again for some reason. Prep-school boys seemed to be home more than they were away, and Cassie wondered if this wouldn't be sort of exasperating to their parents, who paid such terrible amounts of money to

169

get their sons prepared. Brad, like all of Lotta's men, seemed to Cassie to be just this side of having no personality at all, but at the moment Lotta appeared to be in love. He certainly was. He wrote to her every single day. When Cassie had realized this, she'd asked Lotta how she could tolerate such excessive attention.

"It's proof of his love," Lotta had said. "Not that you'd know anything about it."

"That's not love, it's persecution," Cassie said firmly. "Do you answer him every day?"

"I rather feel that whether I answer him once a week or four times a day, it's none of your business, Cass."

"Right you are. I just couldn't help wondering."

"Please make an effort. A determined one."

"All righty."

As it was not an absorbing subject, Cassie did forget about it. She had to think about J. H., because of seeing him from time to time. He seemed to be, and probably was, in anguish. "Lotta certainly is the 'Belle Dame Sans Merci' of Heywood High," Fritzy had said one day, and at Cassie's cold stare had added, giggling, "You know, the beautiful girl who won't say thank you." Cassie didn't think J. H.'s torment a laughing matter, and yet part of Heywood High, any high, was this sort of pain, was it not? Part of growing up? Maybe the fact that she was missing it altogether herself was one of the reasons she seemed immature to Fritzy, who had already spent sleepless, aging nights over at least two boys.

At home she debated doing her kitchen chores or school work, either or both of which she ought to do. Then she went

170

upstairs and stood, hands on hips, looking down at the turtle in his confining casserole.

"It's a grand spring day out," she informed him. "The very day for you to strike out on your own."

He stirred a little, lifted his tiny head, then sank into immobility again. The painted heart on his shell, more meaningless now than ever, seemed to Cassie's discerning eye to be wearing away a little. Give him the pond in the nature preserve and running water, and no doubt in a few weeks it would be gone altogether and he free to grow up unblemished.

"Come along," she said, and lifted him out. He wriggled his tiny feet wildly before withdrawing them and his head as if in total hopelessness. Cassie took a book, went down to the kitchen, where she put the turtle in a pliofilm bag with some water, took two apples and some stale bread, and walked to the park.

Today, for the first time in months, it was crowded. Toddlers toddled beside their mothers, children ran about shouting. Here and there people lay on the grass, offering themselves to the warm spring sun. A few old men and women sat dreamily on benches, watching perhaps their own thoughts, perhaps the activity around them. The brash drake was almost embarrassed with opportunities for successful cadging. He waddled desperately from one outstretched hand to another, trying to take advantage of all.

Cassie walked around the pond a way. She had hoped to perform a little ritual in releasing the turtle, to signify that this parting was not unimportant. After all, he, nameless and

171

defaced, was still the only pet she'd ever had. For a long time Cassie had held this against her parents bitterly. They never had allowed their children to have pets. She didn't mind much anymore, but it might have made a difference in her life once, to have had the sort of uncritical love that a dog or a cat could give.

Too late now. She didn't even call the turtle hers. (Lotta occasionally said, "How is my turtle faring?" but she was addicted to possessive personal pronouns. She even called the cleaning woman who came to their house every two weeks, and scarcely spoke except about detergents, "our Helen.") Well, the turtle, Lotta's turtle, whatever turtle. Cassie opened the bag and let him slip into the pond with only a whispered, "Toodle-oo. Grow up now." He hovered just under the surface of the water for a moment, then with a flick of the four tiny feet, a downthrusting of the loop-shaped head, shot toward the depths.

Cassie stood up, sighed a little, scattered her crumbs for less aggressive birds than the drake, and walked slowly to the deer enclosure, where the young buck gracefully accepted an apple and a few caresses through the fence.

"You aren't really hungry at all," Cassie said to him, gazing into the smoky purple eyes. "You're just being polite, aren't you?"

He arched his neck, took a few steps away on his slender legs, turned as if to be sure she wouldn't mind, and then bounded up the hillside, the white flag of his tail flashing. Perfect manners, Cassie said to herself, and began to eat the second apple as she walked along a path leading into the woods.

Sunlight struck through the trees, the young delicate leaves creating a dappled, restless pattern in the air, on the ground. The little brook chirruped between its banks, and Cassie crossed and recrossed it, hopping from stone to stone in the filtered light, filling her lungs with the warm and musky odors of earth and pine and water. Some bell-like bird call rang through the woods, and the wistful mourning dove asked over and over her unanswerable question. At length Cassie settled on an area of spongy moss and opened her book, the first and still the greatest of the governess stories. Knowing it almost by heart, she could open at any page and go on from there. . . .

"I hastened to Mrs. Fairfax's room; there was a fire there, too, but no candle, and no Mrs. Fairfax. Instead, all alone, sitting upright on the rug, and gazing with gravity at the blaze, I beheld a great black-and-white long-haired dog, just like the Gytrash of the lane. It was so like it that I—"

She slipped into the rook-haunted, storm-menaced manorhouse of Thornfield, into Jane's first days there. Sometimes Cassie felt she knew Jane Eyre as well as she knew herself and could not distinguish which of them was so regretful to be "so little, so pale, so plain-featured."

Yet, insensibly, her attention strayed from the pages. She found herself watching a dragonfly frisking above a silky sweep of water, his body like a little spear, four thin wings, pale as air, whirring at his sides. He hovered, darted, disappeared, and she read again, farther on in the book. For a little while, to make herself cold and uneasy—knowing that just the turning of a few pages could dispel the gloom—she mused over that terrifying man of God, the polished, calm, and icy St. John Rivers, whose fanatic vision, bent on Jane, demanded that she "rush down the torrent of his will into the gulf of his existence." And so, of course, lose her own. Then, for sheer delight, she read that most delicate, charming, lighthearted of love scenes, that between Jane and her blind Vulcan, Rochester, in the sunny meadow at Ferndean.

"Well," said a voice from across the brook. "I wondered if we'd meet again."

Cassie looked up with a smile. She too had wondered, since their encounter in early spring, whether this boy and she would have another. She had done a portrait of him shortly after that meeting. Using a muted puce-colored paper, she painted an emblazoned, dazzling peacock borne on the bent backs of two human beings, representing his parents, toward a castle in the air, pasted in the upper left-hand corner. The peacock was scattering school books behind him, and in a plump balloon over his head were the words, "I will not do anything productive." A little shriveled balloon above the parents' heads carried the legend, "You'll do something productive or we'll know the reason why."

Looking at him, Cassie smiled again. He didn't seem peacocky in the least, and she thought, as she had thought before, that her portraits were really caricatures, one-sided representations, quite possibly unkind.

The boy hopped across the brook, settled on the moss beside her, and several minutes passed in agreeable silence. Presently he picked up a stick and carefully laid back the fronds of a fern, revealing a shining black salamander, stippled with white. It crouched, little legs and wide webbed

174

feet splayed out, staring up from under heavy gray lids. The loose skin at its sides sucked rapidly in and out. Another moment, and it slid from sight.

"I love this time of year," Cassie said. "A nice fresh start for the world."

He nodded, saying nothing.

"Are you still sponging off your parents?" she asked, and stopped as if she'd bitten her tongue. "Excuse me, I shouldn't have said that. I'm afraid I'm very blunt."

"You can say anything you want. And I am. Sponging off them."

"Have you been thinking all this time?"

"Every waking minute. I don't have too many of those because I sleep so much. Anyway, thinking doesn't seem to get me anywhere."

"Well, but what do you do?"

"Does everybody have to do something?"

"That's how it seems to me. I could be wrong, of course," she added, not for a moment thinking she was.

"I do something," he said reflectively. "I sleep a lot, as I mentioned just now. That's very time-consuming if you go at it with sincerity. Once in a while I get a little job, and quit. And of course there's all this thinking to take care of."

"What's the thinking about?"

"What a crazy world it is. About how all the problems are so tremendous that there's no point trying to solve any of them. Not *my* problems, you understand. The world's." He picked up *Jane Eyre*, put it down again.

"Have you read it?" she asked. She always wanted to know

175

what people read. It helped to give them substance for her, to make them less strange.

"Nope. I saw the movie on television one night. You're sneering, in case you don't know it."

"Jane Eyre," Cassie said, "was a spirited, tough person. She had wit and principles and a good springy backbone. They turned her into a . . . a whiney doll with the values of a prig."

"That sounds very defensive. Almost self-defensive, one might say."

Cassie shied from his perception. "What sort of things do you read?" she asked, picking up the stick he'd dropped and turning back the ferns in hopes of uncovering another salamander.

"I don't read at all. It would get in the way of my thinking. I want it all to be firsthand."

Cassie burst out laughing. There was peacock in him after all. All his thinking to be firsthand, indeed. "Do you really believe it's possible to think without reference to what anyone else has thought?"

"I can try."

"Maybe that's why you aren't getting anywhere."

"Blunt is a word for you, isn't it?"

"I'm sorry. I don't mean to offend you. Or anybody. I usually do, of course."

"Not me, you don't. I never get my feelings hurt. That's part of my code."

"What's the rest of it?"

"That's what I'm trying to find out."

"You're trying to find yourself," Cassie said soberly.

176

"You seem to think that's funny, but essentially—yes, I'd say that was it."

"People our age are always trying to find themselves. It's gotten to be like homework. Only sometimes I think—"

"Go on," he said when she paused. "I told you I don't bruise easily."

"I was going to say it sounds very mystical and fervid, all these young people searching out the real thems. Theys? But, maybe there's a simpler answer. Maybe we—" she said, not meaning *we* but *you*, "are just plain lazy."

"I take it you aren't trying to find yourself?"

Cassie hesitated. "No. Not really."

"Why not?"

"Maybe I don't like the idea of what I'd find," she said lightly. When he just shook his head, she added, "All right. I don't like the idea of that much public and private homage to my personality. It's embarrassing. The school I go to is full of people trying to find themselves and generally it seems to mean ignoring other people's selves and talking a terrible lot about your own."

"What about 'Know Thyself'? Don't you believe in that?"

"I just think you can know yourself without forgetting everybody else. And without making yourself the central point of all the conversation."

"You sound like my grandfather."

"Oh?" She didn't know how to take that. "Does he live with you?"

"I live with him."

"I thought you lived with your parents."

177

"No. I live *on* them, *with* my grandfather. As a matter of fact I can't live with my parents. I drive them crazy."

"Why?"

"I guess because of the way I feel about things. Like leaving college after two weeks."

"That was because you couldn't stand the college kids," she reminded him.

"Not just that. It's a waste of time and money for me to go to an institution of learning. Classes bore me. Since practically nobody knows anything or believes in anything, how can they teach anything? I'll teach myself perhaps. If I find anything I want to learn. And in the meantime I like to sleep late. When you're asleep you don't have to decide about anything. If I'd stayed at home, my father would want me to rise at dawn and overcome an obstacle every morning."

"Well, you have to start overcoming some sometime. What are you going to be, if you ever grow up? What sort of work appeals to you?"

"No sort of work appeals to me. I hate it all."

Cassie looked at him in exasperation. "You seem so—so pleased with yourself. Don't you have any conscience?"

"My grandfather says I have. He says it's more my accomplice than my guide, but I have one."

Cassie laughed. "I'd like to meet your grandfather some time."

"How about now?"

"No, thanks." She got up, dusted off her skirt, tucked *Jane Eyre* under her arm. "I have to go now."

"Look, if I told you my name, and you told me yours,

we'd be introduced, wouldn't we? We've known each other long enough for that, haven't we?"

"Cassandra Dunne."

"Aaron Holmes. And now that that's over with, may I drive you home?"

"All right. I could walk, but—well, thank you. That would be nice."

They walked to the parking lot, to an old, abused-looking station wagon that belonged, Aaron explained, to his grandfather, who used it in his work but when he had time off allowed Aaron to take it now and then.

"What does your grandfather do?"

"He's a gardener. Not a steady one anymore. He's pretty old."

But he works, Cassie thought. And no doubt gets up early.

"I know just what you're thinking," the boy said, coaxing the old car along.

"I wouldn't be surprised," Cassie said drily. "It's the inescapable reaction after what you've told me about yourself. How do you feel when you roll out of bed and face an old man who's been up and maybe working for hours?"

"Well," he said reflectively, "at first I used to feel terrible. I was eaten up with remorse, if you'll believe me—"

"Oh, I do," she said, "I really do." She knew that feeling herself. Each time she hurt her father by not being able to welcome his appearance, hurt her mother by being contemptuous of the things her mother valued, she suffered that kind of remorse. It did not prevent her from hurting them again.

"But, you see, you'd have to understand my grandfather,"

Aaron continued. "He's not like other people. He never seems reproachful or angry, the way my father does. And he doesn't get that wounded-doe look my mother has—" The car stalled and he broke off to give it his attention.

Listening to the engine cough and protest, Cassie thought, as she had before, that having children must surely be the rashest, maddest, most certainly disappointing venture of life. You must always expect that your children are going to be a comfort and a joy. No matter that just looking around should convince you the opposite was going to be true, *yours* would be different. And then you wound up with a son like this, a daughter like herself. You had Vincent, who almost goaded you into pain and rage, or Lotta, who smiled and purred and wouldn't care if you dropped in a hole and disappeared. Well, all that wasn't entirely true, but true enough to be able to say even if you did not entirely believe it.

The car bucked forward, seemed to resign itself to running, and Aaron resumed his defense. "But Granddad, you see, doesn't react that way. No matter what time I come down, he just says good morning and hands me some orange juice. I mean, it's just not an atmosphere that promotes guilt feelings."

"Maybe your grandfather doesn't care about what happens to you as much as your parents do. Have you considered it that way?"

"Well, but he does. In his way. He's really concerned about me, and about the whole world, but I think he's given up."

"That doesn't worry you?"

"Naturally. But the fact remains that it's pleasanter to

live with someone who loves you but has abandoned your character than with someone who's always trying to make something of it."

You're really sort of a horrifying person, Cassie said silently, then wondered if possibly he was not so much horrifying as even more truthful than she was herself. Except that in someone else it *was* horrifying.

"Maybe," she said, "it comes down to your being honest about yourself, while I'm honest about other people, so that you sound worse but actually have more character than I have."

He didn't pretend to misunderstand. "The way I figure it, Cassandra, is people wear these—disguises—all the time, hollering, *This is me; this is how I am; take me at face value.* I made up my mind I just wouldn't do it. Of course it's made me a social outcast, but I don't care. At least right now I don't care."

"What about when you do start caring? Suppose it's too late to change?"

"That'll be just too bad. I'll tell you something, Cassandra. I think we live in such a phony, hoked-up world that probably I won't ever care if society likes me. I guess I'll care if some people do. Like Granddad. Like you, I shouldn't be surprised. But generally speaking I don't have any use for people."

"Is that really true? You aren't just saying it to be shocking?"

"Nope. I mean it. And the longer I live, the more I mean it. I think we're living in a great big crazy world where everybody wants to own the latest model of something whether it's good or bad or beautiful or ugly or even whether it works. I'll tell you something else. . . . I think everybody's even lazier than I am. Take the average business clod on his way up the ladder—working his thick head off, but do you think he's stopped for one second to figure out what he's working *for?* Like heck he has. He's too brainwashed for that kind of thinking. He hears the latest slogan that tells him what he wants and believes it must be true. That's laziness, in my book. Laziness to the point of being half dead his whole life, even if he does bring home papers every night in a dispatch case and play golf all weekend and build bookshelves in his spare time. Where do I turn?"

"Huh? Oh, the next block. We live halfway down."

They drew up before her house, and he turned and looked at her steadily in a way she already felt familiar with. Then he smiled. "I'm glad we ran into each other, Cassandra. Could we have a date or something?"

Before she was able to formulate a reply—being with him was rather like running into something and having the breath knocked out of you—Lotta and Irene pulled up behind them in the red sports car.

Lotta jumped out, gave the old station wagon a brief glance, waved to Irene as she drove off, and started for the house. Then she turned slightly, saw Aaron at the wheel, and hesitated, her mouth opening prettily, like a photographer's model saying *cheese.* Slowly she walked toward them, her blue eyes fixed on Aaron's face.

"You *are,*" she breathed softly, as she approached. "You

certainly are. And I've thought about you so much." Unguarded and guileless, she laid bare her heart. "You are my *clown!*" She leaned down and brought her wondering, lovely face close to his. "My clown," she repeated.

Cassie clutched *Jane Eyre* and grappled with a pain the nature of which she could not comprehend.

Chapter Nine

"This is nice," Rebecca Dunne said, looking around the Palm Court and back to her sister. "Just lovely. You were a darling to ask me."

"I'd ask you oftener, only you so rarely seem to be able to get away from—whatever it is you can't get away from. Although with Roger gone practically all the time, and the children all but gone too—"

"What does that mean?" Rebecca interrupted sharply.

"Nothing, yet. Except that Lotta and Cassie are fully grown and able to look out for themselves. You should be thinking of yourself now. You ought to be planning."

"Planning what?"

"What to do with yourself when they're really gone. Look at it sensibly, dear. Vincent is as good as a man, and men do

184

not hang around the old homestead, especially men who don't get along with their fathers—"

"Are there any boys"— Rebecca Dunne would not call her son Vincent a man at this stage in his life; he wasn't even twenty yet—"any boys who *do* get along with their fathers? Everywhere I go, everyone I talk to—just about the only thing I hear anymore is how boys don't like their fathers. I mean, don't get along with them. It's like a disease."

"I imagine it's no different than it's always been. Look at *Sons and Lovers* or *The Way of All Flesh*. Or *Oedipus Rex*, for that matter."

"Oh, for heaven's sake, Muriel. You sound just like Cassie. I don't get my experience and my references out of books. I get them from life."

"Well," Muriel said mildly, "the people who write the books get them from life too. What will you have? Fruit salad? Their Chef's Salad is divine."

They ordered Chef's Salads and black coffee. Mrs. Dunne sighed with pleasure at the waiter's attentions, at the richness of the linen and plate, the sparkle of glassware, the brightness of women's hats. She didn't like salad but felt chic ordering it. She intended to wave aside the pastry tray she saw passing a few tables away. The women there had all smiled and flicked it from them with slender fingers, ordering more black coffee. Of course, Becky thought ruefully, she would have felt happier if she'd weighed fifteen pounds less and had worn a hat like Muriel's. She put a nervous hand to her carefully waved head.

"Where's the orchestra?" she asked.

185

"Orchestra?" Muriel echoed.

"You told me once they had a nice little orchestra here, a string orchestra," Rebecca persisted, almost as if she'd been in some way deceived.

"Oh, that. Yes, they do, but I'm sorry, Becky, not today. They have it every day but Monday."

"Oh." Rebecca Dunne sighed. It would have been pleasant, sort of like the things you saw in movies, to have a string orchestra as a background to all these hats and conversation. "Oh, well, who wants music on Monday?"

Muriel pleased and surprised her sister by laughing. "That's marvelous, Becky. And *quite* sensible. If we all had one day that we expected nothing of—no music, no cheer, no checks in the mail, *nothing*—why then we'd be justified in expecting more of the other days, wouldn't you say?

"Ah, here's lunch." Giving up any attempt at the impersonal, Muriel asked, "Is Lotta feeling blue about not going to college?"

"I don't know. She's always so sweet-tempered that it's hard to know, if she doesn't *tell* you. And lately she's gotten sort of quiet. She's going to that school prom, you know, with Bradley R. J. Kingston. We got her a dress that we had *no* right to buy, it cost a fortune; but goodness, I said to her, you're only young once and you aren't going to go up there with those debs and whatnot and feel ashamed the way—" Rebecca broke off unconsciously, looked around the Palm Court and back to her Chef's Salad. "I wasn't going to have her feeling inferior."

"It's unlikely that she would."

"Well, just the same . . . I should think colleges would take something into account besides people's marks, wouldn't you? Cassie, of course, will probably get a scholarship to any school she wants to go to. I can't remember when she'd gotten anything but A's in anything. It's funny, Muriel," Mrs. Dunne said, putting her fork down and fixing her sister with bewildered eyes. "It's so strange, about children. Here is Cass, so awfully bright, and Vincent is too—even if he won't work hard so he never gets the sort of grades Cassie does, but he could—and Lotta so beautiful— And I can't seem to think that Roger and I had anything to do with it. I mean, they are our children, but I feel so apart from them since they've gotten older. It's so *funny*," she repeated sadly. "I keep remembering what it was like when they were little and needed us, and it doesn't seem so awfully long ago, and at the same time it seems like another life. I get so lonely for them." Tears swam in her eyes. Ashamed and self-conscious, she burrowed in her bag for a handkerchief. "Sorry, Muriel. It's . . . it's just that I never get a chance to talk to anybody."

Muriel looked at her fondly, helplessly. What help was there for women like Becky, who tried to build their lives on something as fleeting as the childhood of another human being? It was as if they could not see what was so plain to be seen, that children are children for the barest breath, that their childhood and their need for you—this clinging, dependent parent—is not only finished with before you are ready (probably you could never be ready) but even, in these times, before they are.

"Sometimes," Becky was going on, "sometimes I'm not

even sure they *like* us." She got the words out reluctantly and looked to Muriel for help.

"Now you don't mean that," Muriel said robustly, and then wondered if honesty wouldn't be kinder. That sort of rallying reassurance rallied only for the time one heard it. Plain talk might at least have the staying power of a truth faced head-on. "Well, what if they don't like you, now and then, once in a while? No, now listen, Becky. . . . Did you—honestly, now —did you always, at all times, love and like our parents?"

"Of course I did. Why, when I remember how close we all were, how we went to Mother and Daddy with our problems and joys, how you and I never had words—"

"Sometimes I wonder if you and I actually did share the same childhood," Muriel said, shaking her head.

"Muriel, it's almost as if you took pleasure in—in—" Mrs. Dunne took a deep breath, picked up her fork, and said coldly, "This is an excellent salad. Thank you for recommending it."

"Becky, I am very sorry," Muriel said remorsefully. "I don't mean to hurt you."

"No. Nobody means to hurt anybody, I guess. Still, it happens all the time, doesn't it?"

"I'm afraid so. It's just that I do feel—I'm convinced— that if you'd accept the fact that people, especially people in the same family, can't always feel one unvarying emotion about other people—" She stopped, a bit put out at the use of all those *peoples*. "A human being isn't carved out of a solid block of one material, Becky. He's changeable, he contradicts himself. His needs change, and he changes, and none of it means that he doesn't love—oh, his mother, his sister.

188

But it does seem to me that most of us are so busy trying to satisfy our own hungers it's no wonder we sometimes forget that others are hungry too."

Mothers don't forget, Mrs. Dunne said to herself. But it was not a thing she'd say to Muriel, who had no maternal instinct at all and would probably give that airy, irritating laugh and say something perfectly awful. Oh, there's no one, she thought bleakly. No one to talk to, no one to understand. I shouldn't do this. What am I *doing* here, being lectured by Muriel in her feathered cloche and her size twelve suit?

"I had a birthday card from Vincent," Muriel said. "I thought it was charming of him to remember." She suspected that Becky had reminded him to remember, and would be glad to hear he had. "How is he? Is he doing well at school?"

"Roger says he's going to have to do better. Roger says that either he gets his grades up in the fall term or he's on his own, sink or swim."

"The trouble with that is that when parents tell their children to sink or swim, they always expect them to swim. What if he starts sinking, what will Roger do then?"

"Oh, Muriel, I don't know. I don't want to think about it." She was getting tired of her Chef's Salad. Luncheon with Muriel always seemed such a gay idea and always turned out like this. "Did you know Vincent has a Negro roommate?" she said suddenly.

"No, I didn't. That's splendid. Or is it? Do they get along?"

"Apparently. He's one of these newfangled Negroes, I guess."

189

"New fang— Rebecca, what on earth does that mean?"

"Well, you know—always wanting his rights and all. You understand that I'm not saying he shouldn't have them. Whatever Roger thinks, I feel that Negroes—everybody— should have their rights. It's just that—oh, there's so much *talk* about it lately. So much ugliness. Was everything easier, nicer, when we were children, or do I only remember it that way?"

Muriel lit a cigarette, blew out the match and stared at it, finally said, "Things were more suppressed, I guess. Easier to ignore. I imagine they weren't nicer." What was sad was that Rebecca meant no unkindness, intended no injustice. She was merely doing what she could to remain blind to all but her immediate problems.

"I believe I'll have one of those nice little pastries," Rebecca said defiantly.

"Darling, of course." Muriel signaled the waiter.

"I suppose you aren't going to," Becky said grimly, eying the tray. It was hard to choose, everything looked so good. Perhaps the strawberry tart, or that apricoty-looking thing—

Muriel hesitated, then said, "Of course I'll have one. The strawberry tart, please," she said to the waiter.

Rebecca felt almost tearful. It really was as if Muriel went out of her way to upset people, to make them feel *wronged*. "I'll have that," she said dully, pointing at the apricot concoction. "Please," she added. The strawberry tart looked much better, but what difference did it make?

"What would Lotta like for a graduation present?" Muriel asked. "I want to get her something really lovely and unnecessary."

"That would be nice. A little luxury of some kind would cheer her up."

"Cheer her up? Lotta?"

"Oh, dear—I hadn't meant to say anything. Well, maybe you'd be the best person to understand. You were as popular in your day as Lotta is now, so probably you had the same problems."

In my day? Muriel thought uncomfortably, but Becky picked that up immediately. "Of course, I don't mean you aren't very well liked now too, dear," she said, happy at this chance to condescend. "But young girls are different. Everything is more important to them, they take things harder—"

Muriel looked speechlessly at her sister, who obviously meant every word. "What is Lotta's problem?" she managed at last.

"It's going to sound peculiar," Becky said with a laugh, "but the problem is too many young men. I mean, she felt terrible about having to break up with J. H., but he'd gotten to be almost a nuisance, jealous and demanding and behaving practically like a husband. A girl like Lotta can't be expected to put up with that. And then Bradley R. J. Kingston all but *swooped* on her. He is utterly mad about her, writes every single day and—"

"Every day?" Muriel interrupted. "Are you sure he isn't pathological?"

Rebecca almost smirked. "Quite sure, dear. And then, you see, Cassie brought Aaron to the house—"

"Aaron? That's a new name."

"I'm trying to tell you. Aaron Holmes. Cassie met him in that nature preserve she goes to, the park. Cassie *is* the sort of girl who goes into trees to read. So, anyway, she met Aaron, such an attractive, strange young man. Actually, he comes of a very good family, but he lives with this old grandfather, who's a gardener in a windmill—"

"How can he be a gardener in a windmill?"

"Muriel, if you would just listen. He lives in a windmill with his grandfather, who's a gardener, but he wouldn't have to be a gardener, he's just independent apparently, because his son—Aaron's father—is a successful business executive and could easily take care of his father only he won't. The grandfather won't, I mean. Get taken care of. He bought this old windmill near the Connecticut River. It doesn't run anymore. The mill, I mean, though at one time it did. So old Mr. Holmes just lives in it, and Aaron lives with him, doing absolutely nothing as far as I can make out. He *is* an odd boy. Disapproves of everything. Rather like Vincent, in a way . . . laughing at everybody's values and scorning business and money. At least Vincent does go to school and will be able to get a job one day. I can't think what Aaron is going to do if he doesn't snap out of it. He seems so aimless and lonely. I'm sort of sorry for him, except that he really seems sort of happy at the same time, you know? He certainly is not the sort of boy you'd expect Lotta to fall for—"

"Lotta? I thought you said Cassie brought him home?"

"She did. And that's really why Lotta is so upset. I mean, she wouldn't hurt her sister, not deliberately I'm sure, but she couldn't help falling in love with Aaron, could she? I mean, you can't reason about love—"

"She took Cassie's boy away? Why, of all the—of all the

192

unsporting things to do," Muriel said sharply. "She might as well play tennis with the net down."

"Muriel, I will thank you not to talk about Lotta that way. She didn't ask for this to happen, and she's just miserable about it. And she doesn't even really want to go to Bradley's prom, only she can't very well get out of it. The poor girl is really very unhappy."

"I'm *out* of words. How is Cassie? Is she miserable?"

"How can anybody tell how Cassie is taking anything? She doesn't seem to care at all. She's friendly with Aaron. She's even friendly with old Mr. Holmes. We've had him to dinner with Aaron a few times and he's very nice. He lets Cassie keep her paints and things at the mill and she's doing flower studies. She even gave him—" She broke off nervously. "This *was* a delicious lunch, Muriel, and I can't thank you en—"

"I take it Cassie gave him one of those portraits?" Muriel said. She was hurt, and determined to be amused. It was beyond her why she wanted one of the things anyway. They showed an odd and vivid talent but were not works of art. Probably if she did have one, she'd feel obliged to hang it and might not want to after all. Just the same—

"Children," she said to her sister, and signaled the waiter for the check. "*Children.* I want to tell you, Rebecca dear, that I admire you more than words can convey. That you keep your sanity and balance at all, trying to juggle Roger and three youngsters, trying to cope and understand and not spend *all* your time feeling hurt and betrayed . . . well, I consider you, and every other mother, just a little lower than angels."

193

"Why, Muriel," Rebecca Dunne said. "Why, I—" She didn't know what to say. "We just do what we can, that's all. We go from day to day and do what we can."

"That's what I mean."

They went through revolving doors into the delicious warmth of the May afternoon. Around the Pulitzer Fountain pigeons strutted in aimless, circular sentry duty, crooning plumply. People, free for lunch hour, or simply free, sat contentedly on benches, letting the fine mist from the fountain blow across them. They read or smoked, talked to one another, or just did nothing, just were there. A couple climbed into one of the horse-drawn carriages and the rig clopped off, driver straight and satisfied, passengers pleased and self-conscious, horse light-footed, even a little proud-looking.

"What a *day*," Muriel said, taking a deep breath of that air like no other—the breath of city spring, leafy, tarry, mild, and acrid at once, heady as a cocktail. "Beautiful."

"Yes," Mrs. Dunne said absently. "Yes, it's lovely. Well, Muriel—"

They smiled at each other fondly and parted with relief.

Muriel Ferris walked east, going home, not hurrying. She had taken the afternoon off, hoping Rebecca would want to stroll or shop or come back with her for tea and a little quiet talk. Silly of her. Rebecca would never stay late in town. The wonder was that she made it in at all. Muriel insisted, of course. She'd telephone, off and on, until Becky had to agree. "Becky, you cannot stay there in your—" she wanted to say rut but knew better, "—in your cocoon. You need to see something of life besides children and a deck of cards. Come

194

in," she'd say, turning to wheedling. "It's going to be a lovely day tomorrow, and I am in the mood for lunch at the Palm Court." Rebecca would say that Muriel certainly didn't need her company for lunch or anything else, but would relent when Muriel said, on the contrary the company of her sister was just what she needed.

I do need it, Muriel said to herself now. Becky is the only person, really, that I have to talk with. Except that we never do talk to each other. Not about each other. Our talk is always of the children, of whom I am fond, of whom I am very tired. Becky never, it appeared, got tired of being a mother. One would think a few hours off, a little time spent thinking of something else, looking at something else, would send her back refreshed. Muriel supposed that what Rebecca said of her was true. She had no maternal instincts. Observing women who did, and who had the children upon whom to expend these instincts, Muriel could only feel delivered. They seemed so drained and apprehensive, mothers. Especially those with children in their teens. They looked clawed and courageous and uncertain, like lion tamers who've lost the spirit for the job. It seemed children, like lions, grew treacherous as they aged.

She stopped at an open-air market and bought some short-stemmed roses with petals smooth as French kid. They wouldn't last long, but the odor was heavenly. Sniffing, she walked up Third Avenue. Crowded, noisy, nervous, it was a street she loved. She loved Manhattan, with its way of being a thousand different places at once, loved its upthrusting buildings, its glass and steel and stone skeleton, its blaring, supercharged restlessness and drive. A vulnerable city, for all its strength. Dependent on trains and trucks and boats to keep it fed, warmed, clothed. Helpless to do a thing for itself. Like a scientific or artistic genius, who can grapple with soaring questions of the mind but can't find his rubbers or work a can opener. Vulnerable, too, in another way. A target, *the* target, if the unthinkable should occur.

Sometimes she tried to picture this island of stone and steel, of chromium and glass, with its millions of inhabitants and commuters, its asphalt arteries, its slender trees, its hidden nervous system through whose ganglia flowed power to keep alive the lamps, the furnaces, the shops, the slums, the machines—she tried to picture all this laid waste beneath a cracked and glaring sky, level beyond rebuilding, smoking, dead, destroyed. It could happen. You had only to think for a moment to know that it could happen, and yet everything within her and the people she knew and the strangers she passed must assemble to resist such an admission.

These days there were always thoughts of war and death. You pushed them from you, worked hard, went out a lot, said (truthfully) that you didn't read newspapers anymore because why always be reminded of horrors. But you didn't need to read to be reminded, and she imagined the most determined hedonist, the stubbornest escapist, the completest ignoramus, didn't go through a day—or anyway, a night—without realizing that it is not only late, it may already be too late. Without knowing it, the world might last month, last year, this morning, have entered irrevocably upon the final path.

I have less to lose than most people, Muriel thought, going into her empty apartment, finding it not depressing, merely empty. And I have much to lose. No wonder Becky is nearly out of her mind. No wonder the children are testy and restless and pleasure-mad and resentful. At bottom we're all scared to death, and it doesn't bring out the best and the bravest in people, to be scared.

Rebecca caught a downtown bus. She was already enduring the first pangs of what Vincent had told her psychologists called *angst du gare*. "Meaning," he'd explained, "that the minute you get to the railroad station you start worrying about what's happening at home."

They have a name for everything these days, she thought, on her way to the railroad station and anxious about home. It seemed to her she was never really free of apprehension. Psychologists were mostly men, and didn't care what something was just so they could label it. She wondered how many of them felt, as she did, as countless mothers must always feel, this unremitting sense of peril. Not for themselves. She didn't really think she worried for herself. Sometimes, in the darkest and most private part of her being, she admitted that in many ways she would just as soon the whole thing were finished, for her. "The whole thing?" they might ask. "What whole thing?" She was too skittish and shy to say, "Life . . . I wish somehow my life were over, and then I wouldn't have to worry anymore." Because they—Who were they? Well, never mind who they were, they were there—they would think something completely wrong, such as—they'd think she meant suicide, and that was ridiculous. She just, at times, was tired. She only wanted some rest from this ceaseless fear that something, somehow, would happen to her children. "Well, they've been perfectly fine so far," they would say to her. "Why worry until something does happen?" But that was how they thought, and that was why they could never understand. That nothing had happened so far was no guarantee that something—*terrible*—wouldn't, wasn't happening right now as she ran into the station, ran across the crowded, massed, *impeding*—

"*Please!*" she said desperately to a man who seemed determined to block her path. "Please get out of my way! I'll miss my train!" And she thrust past him, thrust him almost bodily aside, and made—just made—the gate before it closed.

In the grimy car that was not a smoker but smelled of dead smoke and dust, she settled in a seat, her heart pounding, hands shaking a little. That salad hadn't agreed with her. Or seeing Muriel hadn't. Something hadn't. She had a headache and a faintly sick stomach and a feeling that she had lost something, left something somewhere, overlooked something important. How could they say that just because nothing had happened yet, nothing would? Fools, all of them. They knew nothing. Cassie and Vincent—how could anyone know what a mother would feel about them? Dear to her so that it was like anguish looking at the plain, clever faces, wishing she could have given them beauty. Vincent had a lot of friends, but girls hurt him, and would hurt him more. Women would hurt him, and there was nothing, nothing she could do to protect him. Cassie had almost no friends at all and said she didn't care. Didn't she care? How could she not care? How much had this business of Aaron—oh, how I wish we'd never laid eyes on *him*— How much pain, how much sense of failure was Cassie covering up?

And Lotta—could anyone ride so high, so carefree, and not come tumbling down and be destroyed?

They think—and she knew who these "they" were, these three children of hers—they think I don't know anything, can't understand them, have never felt what they feel. They shut me away. I'm not part of their lives. A housekeeper, a snoop, a necessary evil. They're nice to me, and shut me out, and think I don't know. And Muriel is wrong. We *were* close to our mother; we shared with her, made her part of things. Marriage or no marriage, Muriel is an old maid. Not just a single woman. A single woman can be warm and loving, can suffer for others. Muriel's an old maid all surrounded by herself and comfortable as people can be who have only themselves to think of, worry about, only one death to be afraid of.

I'm afraid for my children all the time, she thought. They're at the mercy of automobiles, of perverts, of all these crazy men with their bombs. And nothing can rescue them. Or, anyway, I cannot. Luck could save them. But could even a parent hope that her children would be lucky all their lives? The best you could do was wish it. And nobody reaches my age, she thought wearily, still believing in wishes.

The train gathered speed as it rushed out of the city toward the suburbs. Staring through a grimy window, Rebecca Dunne, after a while, smiled faintly. In spite of the troubles that beset her, she could not help being pleased at having amused Muriel. Who wants music on Monday? Thinking it over, it was sort of funny at that.

199

Chapter Ten

"Guess what?" said Irene as she and Lotta drove away from the school parking yard.

"You've been accepted at Harvard."

"No. At least, that junior college I told you about accepted me, but that's not what I mean. Guess again."

"You've had a proposal."

"Gee, I hadn't thought of that. No. Try again."

"Oh, Rene. I don't want to."

"My, you're touchy these days."

"So?"

Irene tapped the horn lightly, waved to J. H., going in the opposite direction. "He seems to be perking up, wouldn't you say?"

200

"How would I know?" Lotta asked sharply. "I don't see him, except around school, where he won't look at me." She studied Irene's profile, started to ask a question, changed her mind.

"Aren't you going to guess?" Irene persisted. "It's something nice."

"Who for? You or me?"

"Both of us. Oh, well, you're turning it into such a production, you'll be thinking it's something important, when actually it's only fun. We're going to have a party! There."

"That's fun?" Lotta said in a pained tone. "We have two booked now, and telephone calls still coming. There must be more kids born in the summer or something. And I'm beginning to think there isn't a mother in this county who's willing to throw the affair herself, for her own child. When I have children, I intend to give them their parties *myself*."

"I wasn't talking about that sort of party. Though, come to think of it, Lotta dear, we're going to have to discuss that."

"Discuss it? How?"

"Later. Listen, what I'm trying to tell you is, *I'm* giving a party. For graduation. And this time we're going to be catered to. Mother's throwing the whole bash, and all we have to do is look pretty. Sounds good?"

"Oh, sure. Sounds great."

"Well, I must say . . . you don't. Sound great."

"Sorry."

"Lotta, what's the matter with you? We're going to *graduate*. Life is finally opening before us, and you're mooning around as if they'd just run off the last reel."

Lotta swallowed painfully before forcing herself to smile at Irene, forcing a note of gaiety into her voice. "I guess I just can't take things as casually as you do, Rene. After all, a whole part of our lives is ending, and some people can't just say 'Okay, next slide' and move on without *any* reaction. However, I'll try not to show it since it bothers you."

Resenting the implication that Lotta had sensibilities she lacked, Irene was without a ready retort. She had no sentimental feelings about closing this particular chapter in her life. The end of high school seemed to her to call for nothing but jubilation, and she strongly suspected that Lotta felt the same. That sweetly mournful manner was a red herring. Only what was she trying to hide? If I were a good friend, Irene thought, a really good friend and not just half of a relationship that Lotta and I have found convenient, fun, and mutually beneficial, I would try to find out what is troubling her. I would offer my hand, my help.

But she realized, analyzing herself in a detached, uncritical fashion, that she didn't want to get involved in somebody else's woes. She wanted to be cheery, to look forward to all the wonderful things that lay ahead. Why should Lotta have woes, anyway? she wondered, and then recalled that apparently the poor dear was never going to have the fun of college. Still, Irene found herself irritated that her lighthearted, impulsive, gaily egotistical friend should, practically overnight, have taken to sighing and looking wistful. It wasn't fair. It just about required that a friend either turn sad and sulky too, or be really concerned. Irene would not do either. She hadn't the time, or the will, to bear or share burdens. Espe-

202

cially not now, and it was maddening of Lotta to do this when they could have been cutting such a swath together. Irene was happy to share pleasure and diversion with Lotta. She'd share her car, her clothes, her confidential opinions on love, life, men. . . .

Apparently, all of a sudden, that wasn't enough. Could Lotta, by any chance, be regretting the loss of J. H.? But she had Bradley R. J. Kingston, and that divine-looking, peculiar Aaron Holmes. Or did she have them? Irene refused to admit a flicker of satisfaction as she eyed her friend's expressionless face.

"You never said what sort of time you had with Brad that weekend. Was it a ball?"

"What? Sorry, Rene. . . . I was thinking."

"Skip it."

They drove on, presenting a felicitous picture, the yellow-haired girl and the brown, their young faces smooth and pretty, the little sports car gleaming. Irene had a fine, flirtatious ride of it. She told herself she was sorry about Lotta. They'd had a lot of fun together. Certainly, Irene thought, I've learned plenty from her. She felt generous, admitting that. Who but Lotta had taught her the value of the first-class returns on a sweet disposition, an uncomplaining nature? Before knowing Lotta she'd had a terrible temper and a tendency to get her little feelings hurt. Now she was almost indistinguishable from Lotta herself, so honey-tempered was she, so affable and darling. Come to that, at this point you could say she'd surpassed the teacher. This thought flowed through her like good wine. She thought she was sorry to see

Lotta brought low, but in truth it was one of the sweetest moments of her young life.

She wanted, Lotta realized, to know if I had a ball that weekend. That should be easy to answer. She had not. She'd had an awful time. But tell Irene? Not to be thought of. Rene wasn't a person you shared doubts and confusion with. She wasn't someone you went to and said, "I'm so unhappy . . . help me."

Bradley R. J. Kingston was being prepared at a pretty posh school, and the weekend should, in sober fact, have been a ball. There'd been herds of boys, all striking a nice clean note of breeding and self-confidence. Somehow they'd even all looked handsome, though obviously an entire senior class could not be. But for that nectar-gathering honeybee, Lotta, what should have been a field of flowers had been a desert.

Any place, now, that did not contain Aaron Holmes was barren in Lotta's vision. Since the day he'd driven Cassie home in that disreputable station wagon, she'd wandered about perplexed and distracted in a dream of Aaron. She thought about him all the time, she didn't understand him, she adored him.

He'd come in with them that first evening—only a few weeks ago?—and had been, with no difficulty at all, persuaded to stay for dinner.

"Shouldn't you let your grandfather know?" Cassie had asked, but Aaron had explained that there was no telephone in the mill, and that in any case his grandfather only looked for him when he saw him.

Mrs. Dunne came home a little late, pleased at having won

the table prize that afternoon. "A grand slam, doubled *and* vulnerable, and if I do say so, brilliantly played," she announced from the hall, and then, coming into the living room, smiled at Aaron warmly. "Why, Lotta dear," she said. "Who's this?"

Aaron came to his feet as Cassie said, "He's a friend of mine. I found him in the woods," and Lotta said, "This is Aaron Holmes, Mother. He's my clown. Remember I told you about the clown at the Donaldson party?"

Lotta had not, in fact, mentioned the clown except in passing, but she could rely on her mother to back her up when she made statements like this. Mrs. Dunne never looked even momentarily at a loss.

"Of course," she said now. "Lotta's talked of you so much. And now here you are. Isn't that lovely."

"I've asked Aaron to stay for dinner," Lotta went on possessively. "I got steaks out of the freezer, and if you, Momma darling, hurry, you'll have time to make one of your marvelous lemon pies."

"Fine, fine," said Mrs. Dunne, happy to be imposed upon. "Cassie, dear, come along. I'll need a little help."

Cassie, looking momentarily rebellious, had stared fiercely at Lotta, then inquiringly at Aaron. Then, as no one spoke, she'd followed her mother to the kitchen, and Lotta had settled on the sofa, legs curled up, chin on palm, to question this charming creature that Cassie had so fortunately found for her once again.

"Isn't it simply marvelous," she said disarmingly, "that Cass and you met. I mean, if you hadn't, you and I wouldn't

205

have again. Or maybe we would have. Where have you been clowning lately? I've looked for you at birthday parties since, but you never, never come."

"Oh, that was a one-day stand," Aaron said. "I did it for fun. And the ten bucks."

"And the little dog?"

"He belongs to the fellow who owns the carousel. Monsieur, I have to admit, works harder than I do. Come to that, just about anybody does."

Lotta found his attitude entrancing. "You mean, you just don't do *any*thing? Don't you go to school?"

"I tried for a couple of weeks, and quit. Couldn't stand the college kids."

Lotta laughed with pleasure. "And do you really live in that windmill?"

"You've seen it?"

"Everyone in town has seen it, I imagine. Sometimes I've wondered what use it was being put to now." She let her eyes tell him what excellent use it was, in her opinion, being put to. "I'd love to see it sometime."

"Any time. I asked your sister to go by there with me this afternoon, but she insisted she had to get home."

"Cassie would. She's a martinet about duty and all that. Just the opposite of me. I'm afraid I'm . . . sort of lazy too."

"I take that with a grain of salt, after seeing you handle those kids that afternoon. I think it's extraordinarily energetic of you."

Lotta pouted slightly, let the pout become a smile. "I need the money, you see. Or I did. I was hoping to use it to pay

206

part of my college expenses. Only now it appears I'm not going."

"Why not?"

She leaned forward a little, tipping her blond head so that she looked at him with an oblique and fetching glance—a practiced glance, one that had not yet failed her—and said, "Because I didn't get accepted anywhere. So there." She sat back and laughed lightly. "And now I don't care, though I thought at first my heart would break. Maybe I wouldn't have liked the college kids either. And I'm not a student. I've always preferred people to books."

"I sort of feel that way myself."

"Yes, I rather thought you did. When can I see your windmill, Aaron? I'm consumed with curiosity."

"Tomorrow afternoon?" he suggested. "We can ask Cassandra if—"

"No, no," said Lotta, shaking her head. "*Don't* do that, Aaron. She'll only have to figure out a way of refusing again. Cass is awfully shy, and she hates visiting people, really hates it. I'm simply stunned that she even agreed to let you drive her home, because Cassie is *no* girl for accepting strangers. Goodness knows, she hardly even accepts *us*."

"We got along quite well," he said, frowning slightly. "She's a very interesting girl."

"*Isn't* she, though? Really so bright and studious. She quite puts me to shame. But don't torment her by insisting that she visit you. I know her so much better than you do, really," Lotta said, feeling not the smallest stir of disloyalty or dishonesty. What she said was true. Cassie did not take to strangers, and if she wanted to visit people, why didn't she ever visit? Except for Fritzy, Cassie practically didn't even have any friends, and if a person didn't have friends, it was because the person didn't want them. Nothing could be clearer or truer or, at the moment, more reassuring.

Because Lotta wanted Aaron for herself. She supposed, in some detached portion of her mind, that if Cassie had been the kind of girl who liked boys, who wanted them to like her, some sort of sportsmanship would have been called for in this situation. I mean, Lotta said to herself with simple vanity, how could Cassie hold a boy after he'd met me? I should have to do something drastic, like being rude to him or trying to appear homely. This was one time to be glad Cassie didn't have the sense to know a find when she'd found it.

She clasped her slim ankles and looked at Aaron and sighed happily because no sacrifice was called for. Cassie had been —an instrument, that was it. She had met Aaron and inevitably brought him home. (She had never, to Lotta's knowledge, let anyone else drive her home. J. H. said once that he'd offered her a ride in an absolutely bucketing downpour, and Cassie had just laughed and said she liked walking in the rain. "She wasn't walking, she was treading water," J. H. had said. *Poor* J. H., Lotta thought. I hope he isn't suffering too much.) So, granted all these perfectly factual facts, it became exquisitely clear that Cass had met Aaron only so that Lotta could find her clown again.

"Do you believe in predestination?" she asked Aaron now.

"You mean the theory that everything in our lives has been decided ahead of time, that we can't do a thing but follow a course already laid out for us?"

208

"Well, I didn't mean it quite so—so strictly," Lotta said, but of course could not say what she did mean. It would be too un—immodest, and Lotta always knew where to draw the line between bewitching candor and immodesty.

"I don't believe in it at all," Aaron was saying. "I believe in free will. I believe that a man is not only capable of making choices, but is responsible for the choices he makes."

Lotta moved a little restlessly. Yes, this would be the sort of person Cassie would allow to drive her home. Serious. Well, serious or not, he was the most desirable young man that Lotta had laid eyes on in—in at least a week, she said to herself with a silent laugh.

But as the evening, and then the days that followed, came and went, she was less and less inclined to be amused by her feeling for Aaron, and at the end of a week she had a feeling that perhaps she'd never laugh again. She was in love, absolutely, consumingly, for the first time in her life. What she had felt for Ray, for J. H., for Brad, for a couple of others —all that was nothing, was a faded facsimile of an emotion. Aaron was her love, her god, her everything, and she could hardly care (and certainly couldn't understand) why love, when it came to her at last, seemed to take all the lightness and laughter out of life. Only when she was with him did she feel alive at all. The times between stretched like endless empty highways. And yet, when they were together, when he came by casually, unannounced (he never made a date, never said ahead of time when or if he'd be back), she had to be content with the fact of his presence. She had to try to understand, finally, that Aaron did not—yet—feel for her anything of what she felt for him. J. H., she thought, would give years of his life to keep me anxious and moody and tormented with longing this way. She even had a time of tenderly brooding over J. H. If in losing her he suffered the way she did now at Aaron's indifferent friendship, then she could not help but brood over him, worry about him. Poor, darling J. H., she said to him in her mind. I'm so sorry, so truly sorry.

Poised on the edge of expectancy, she contrived, when not with Aaron, dreams of fulfillment, in which his eyes lost that curiously distant expression and fixed upon hers, seeing her at last. Oh, one day his gaze bent upon her face would recognize the warmth, the depth, the constancy of her love, and he would take her in his arms and hold her and kiss her—that kiss she was in anguish to have—and he would say, finally and at long, long last, the words she would surely die for lack of. How many boys had said them to her, how often, and how meaningless they and their words were now.

Meanwhile, letters from Bradley R. J. Kingston arrived daily, and Lotta, not knowing what else to do, stopped replying, which should have but did not stop him from writing. The week before Senior Prom he telephoned.

Cassie had answered and called upstairs, "Lotta, for you. Brad."

"Tell him I'm out, won't you *please*, Cass?"

Cassie had turned to the phone again. "She'll be right here, Brad." She put the receiver on the table and walked away. Lotta, coming downstairs slowly, thought how much had changed in a short time. She and Cassie had quarreled in the past, and they'd never been close sisters. But now it was as if Cassie had erased Lotta right out of her life. She scarcely spoke a word to her that was not required. She never teased or corrected her, never laughed with her. We live like strangers accidently berthed together, Lotta thought. Strangers who have not taken to each other and do not mean to improve upon the acquaintance. She was so certain that this should not have bothered her—when had Cassie's opinion, good or bad, mattered?—that it was almost unbearable to find how much it did matter.

I don't seem to know anymore what I'm doing about anyone or anything, Lotta thought, picking up the phone. I only know that I'm in love with Aaron, and he's taking too long, too long to fall in love with me, and it hurts.

"Hello, Brad," she said wanly. "How are you?"

"How am I isn't the point," he said anxiously. "I'm getting hives waiting to hear from you, Lotta. What's wrong?"

"I—nothing. That is, I've had a cold."

"In your hand?"

"What?"

"Does a cold prevent you from writing to a guy?"

"Oh. Well, I'm sorry, Brad. I just haven't been feeling marvelous."

"You're going to be all right for the prom, aren't you?" he said in alarm. "Look, Lotta . . . you can't back out on me now. I mean, I've been looking forward to this for months, and I've told everybody, and what'll I look like— Lotta, you *are* going to be here next weekend, aren't you?" He was beginning to sound shrill, and Cassie, who'd come back in the hallway (deliberately? Lotta couldn't tell) heard every word.

"Well, that's the thing," Lotta began slowly, wondering

211

how to put this so that Brad wouldn't be hurt, realizing there was no way. He'd have to be hurt, because she couldn't possibly go up for that prom weekend. Who was Brad, anyway? She could scarcely recall his face. She owed him nothing, and he wouldn't be the first boy who'd been stood up or hurt. Who was Bradley R. J. Kingston that he should be spared all hurt? "I don't think—"

Cassie leaned forward, cupping her hand over the mouthpiece of the telephone.

"You," she whispered, "are the most selfish, egotistical, self-involved human being I have ever met, and if you disappoint that boy at this late date, then I'm going to tell Aaron exactly what you're made of, see? And he'll believe me, don't think he won't, even if he isn't bright enough to figure you out himself. You may be crazy about him, Lotta, but you don't know a single thing about him except that he's hard to get. But *I* know him, and I'll know what to tell him and how to tell him, and he does *not* take to people who hurt other people. So now inform Brad very nicely that you've just made a spectacular recovery and will be there in your gorgeous dress and your very best spirits when he expects you. *Have* I made myself clear?" she asked, removing her hand.

Lotta, for the moment more stunned than angry, said, "You're absolutely raving mad. And you wouldn't dare."

"Don't rely on that," Cassie said in a cold tone, and walked away.

"Lotta, Lotta! What's wrong?" Brad was yelling at her desperately. "I'm paying for this call, you know."

Lotta delayed another instant, and then said, "Yes, yes . . . I'm here, Brad. Sorry—something interrupted."

212

"Well for the luvva mud, you could at least give me your attention when I'm paying for it."

"Yes, of course."

"Lotta, are you coming or aren't you? What's wrong? What—"

"Brad, of course I'll be there. You don't think I'd disappoint you at this late date, do you?"

Brad, too relieved to hear she wasn't breaking the date to quibble with her manner, said, "Okay, that's great. Did you get the timetable I sent you? Well, take the train I marked, and I'll meet you at the station. And look your prettiest, girl, because you're going to be the prettiest girl here, and I'm all set to crow."

So duly on the train he had selected, dressed to look her prettiest, carrying in a pale blue suitcase borrowed from Irene the dress they hadn't been able to afford but had bought anyway, Lotta went to Bradley's Senior Prom.

She told herself she carried it off well, because most of her responses in a situation like this were automatic. She laughed and widened her eyes and lowered them. She expressed wonder and enthusiasm as he guided her over playing fields and campus, into laboratories and gymnasiums, into the dormitory where she and the other invited girls would spend the night, or as much of it as would be left after the dance. She looked divine in the expensive dress, she danced untiringly. She had always loved to dance. Aaron claimed not to care for it, and that seemed to her a mark of superiority, but still she loved it. Brad was as good as J. H. She flirted circumspectly, enough to massage Brad's ego and not enough to wound it.

It all meant nothing. It was an endless period of hollow

213

time somehow to be gotten through, and while she went through the lines and gestures that were second nature to her, Lotta longed till she ached for Aaron, wondering where he was now, who was with him, what he was saying or thinking, what was in his thoughts—or who was. When she thought of Cassie, she trembled with fury, and once Brad caught her at it.

They were on the terrace, between dances. Lotta, weary from hours of painstaking gaiety, watched the couples walking around the campus grounds, having punch and cookies in the room behind them. She wondered how many of these girls this weekend were with boys they loved, really wanted to be with. Quite a few, probably. Girls their age usually were in love, or thought they were. They knew nothing of Aaron, of how Aaron could make a girl feel, of how he could undermine her self-confidence, wreck her joy, leave her sleepless, hungry for words or kisses that never came. They knew nothing of how a person like Aaron could, without meaning to at all or even knowing he'd done it, come between two sisters, turning one of them viperish and wicked—

Brad's arm went around her. "You're shivering, Lotta."

"No. Not really."

"I guess you did have a cold, at that," he said, sounding faintly pleased. "I mean, crimers, Lotta, I thought maybe you'd changed your mind about me."

"Changed my mind?"

"That you didn't, you know, *care* anymore. But, heck, if it was just a bad cold . . . Say, I'm awfully sorry. Maybe we better go inside again. In a sec, that is." He attempted,

214

clumsily, to draw her against him, to pull her face around to a kissing position. Lotta stiffened and then thought, Oh, what the heck. He deserves a kiss for the weekend, for being so devoted, for—just for wanting so badly to kiss me.

But she could not, after all, have been very convincing, because when the weekend was over, she never heard from Bradley R. J. Kingston again.

Now, riding beside Irene in the gleaming sports car, Lotta thought with bewilderment how everything had turned about since Aaron's arrival. Even before Cassie had found him in the wood, he had changed Lotta in some way, she now realized. The clown had won her first with his lazy, lithe strength, his unreadable, tantalizing face. She'd thought of him often after Ella Donaldson's birthday party. And wasn't it then, around then, that she'd begun to perceive the flaws, the crudities in J. H.? Perhaps a little earlier. Still, you could almost believe that she had been shedding J. H. in a preparatory sense—getting ready for the coming of Aaron, as if she'd known he had to arrive one day, and soon, and that when he did she would have no room in her life for anyone else.

Only why was it taking him so long to love her?

"Rene," she said suddenly, "let's drive by the mill. All right?"

Irene slid a sidewise glance at her passenger, pursed her lips knowingly, and signaled a right turn to the traffic behind her. "Sort of kid stuff, isn't it, my pet? Cruising past the one and only house in a gale of giggles?"

Why in the world did I used to like her so much? Lotta wondered. Yet this was Irene, her dear and good friend, who

215

had often been caustic in the past. It had seemed amusing. Then, of course, the barbed tongue had flicked in other directions, toward other targets, and that made all the difference.

"Suppose we just don't giggle," she said, trying for a light tone. "And I won't then remind you of the times we've circled Tony Winter's house like a couple of satellites looking for an orbit."

Irene clucked. "Dear me. How well we know each other, Lotta."

Know each other? Lotta thought. Do we know each other at all? It was simple to guess why Irene was slipping out of the attendant-lady role she'd carried off so well in high school. She didn't need it anymore. She didn't, in a word, need Lotta. She was moving on to another court, where Lotta wouldn't be queen, where Lotta wouldn't even be a memory. That's fair enough, isn't it? Lotta asked herself. I'd forget Irene quickly enough. I *will* forget her when she leaves for her junior college. Maybe we'll meet from time to time and talk of the olden times, but Irene and I do not have between us whatever it takes to make people friends in spite of space and time, even quarrels and wounded feelings.

Knowing all this, why did the change in Irene come as such a painful surprise? Why, when she loved only Aaron, did the suspicion that perhaps Irene and J. H. now found each other compatible and Lotta just a part of the past, offend her this way? Not so very long ago if she'd thought Irene was seeing J. H. she would have asked right out if it were true. Knowing herself, she suspected she'd have seen to it that J. H. turned his eyes back in the direction toward which he'd

216

trained them for so long. She wouldn't relinquish any heart, even one she did not want anymore, that easily, and to Irene. And now? Now—perhaps she was afraid to ask. Not sure if she could do a thing about it if Irene said, "Yes, J. H. and I are madly in love, and you see, Lotta, pet, it was inevitable, because he and I have similar interests, similar aims, and you aren't part of what we're going on to. So sorry, sweetie."

What do I do now? Lotta wondered. When Irene goes in the fall, and J. H. is gone, and Ray, who doesn't speak to me anymore anyway, and Brad, who doesn't write—when all, all are gone, then what becomes of me? If Aaron doesn't love me, what then? If he does? Aaron, she had learned, was not a person to rely on. She doubted if even love would make him reliable. It might make him less so. Trying for the first time to see into, to sense the reactions of, another human being, Lotta had been successful in comprehending that Aaron would not accept responsibility. The rest of him eluded her. That sunny, seeming openness had fooled her. But Aaron, for all he talked, in the end was as secretive as Cassie. He turned out not to be talking about you or himself at all. What he was talking about she could never quite tell.

At that moment the mill came in sight, its long-unused arms starting up against a blue, cloudless sky. Old Mr. Holmes kept it shining and tidy, surrounded by flowers.

"Oh, but it's adorable," Lotta had cried out on her first visit.

Mr. Holmes had looked gratified, but what he said was, "It's a toy, a conceit. That doesn't affect my pleasure in it, but I cannot take it seriously."

217

"Rather the way he feels about me," Aaron had said, and Mr. Holmes had not contradicted him.

Today as they approached the sideroad leading to the mill Lotta abruptly held up her hand. "Stop, please," she said. "Before they see us."

Irene pulled up, turned off the engine, and they stared across a stretch of meadow, watching Cassie and Mr. Holmes as they strolled about the small garden, talking companionably. Mr. Holmes, in an old cardigan, a beret sitting raffishly on one side of his head, gesticulated with the pipe that he was never without. Cassie strolled beside him, nodding at intervals, then shaking her head. She wore faded shorts, a shapeless blouse, and her hair from this distance looked like a clump of mustard weed. The old man and the girl looked peaceful and animated at once, like friends of long standing having a brisk argument.

"Well," said Irene, fluffing her hair. "Shall we advance?"

"Cass and Mr. Holmes are friends," Lotta explained. Irene made no reply. "They play Scrabble together, and Cass has given up portraits in favor of flowers. She comes over here a lot, and even keeps her oil paints and things in the mill."

Irene yawned. "I didn't think she and Aaron were dating, if that's what you're taking pains to tell me. Do you want to drive over or not, Lotta? I have things to do later on. Oh, look. There comes the other member of the seed-eating crew." Irene found Cassie's vegetarian inclinations terribly funny, and she pretended to think that all Cassie's acquaintances shared the persuasion.

"Aaron is not a seed eater. I mean, a vegetarian," Lotta

said tartly. "And besides, I fail to see what's so funny about people who are." She spoke as if her attention were on the subject and not on Aaron, who had joined the two in the garden. "Let's go back, Rene."

"But the light of your life is over there. I could drop you. He'd jump at the chance to drive you back." No matter that Irene herself was very nearly free of the spell of Lotta, she still had to assume that any young man Lotta desired was as good as wrapped up and delivered. This was the way it had always been, and Irene tended to judge by the past rather than through fresh observations.

"Cassie is there," Lotta said. "I am simply not up to an afternoon of Cass." She knew a twinge of guilt and anger, saying this. The words were true. They had nearly always been true, and were more so now. But only now, only recently, would she have said them. It was not part of her nature and not part of the picture she had of herself to speak slurringly of her family.

Oh . . . everything has *changed* so much, she cried silently, desperately. When had her life become so somber and uncertain? Had loving Aaron lost her that old self, that confident, cocksure self? She wasn't even sure that she was beautiful anymore. J. H. seemed to be able to glance at her and look away as if he hadn't seen. J. H., who for months hadn't been able to wrench his gaze from her face. Brad had given up with little sign of struggle. Irene was looking prettier all the time, and Lotta had a superstitious impulse to wonder whether her friend, her so-called friend, wasn't some sort of vampire, drawing the color and loveliness from Lotta into herself. She shuddered and said, "Would you mind driving me home, Rene? I have sort of a headache."

Irene backed up smoothly and started back the way they'd come. "Maybe you should see a doctor. There always seems to be something the matter with you lately."

Lotta, looking for concern or affection in the remark, fancied she heard only impatience. She made no reply and did not speak at all until she was on the sidewalk in front of her house.

Irene said, "I'll come by in the morning, and we'll make plans about the party, all right?"

Lotta nodded. She felt choked, as if speaking at all would be a risk. She managed to say, "Super," and turned, forcing herself to walk slowly toward the house when what she wanted to do was run and be through the door and up in her room before the tears came.

Mrs. Dunne was in the hallway, vacuuming, when Lotta burst into the house. "Why, darling," she said. "Darling, what's the matter?"

For the first time since she'd been a little girl, Lotta flung herself weeping into her mother's arms.

Cassie had seen the little sports car parked on the road at the other side of the meadow. She hoped Aaron hadn't. Not that he'd gloat or feel triumphant. Quite the contrary. He'd be uneasy, perhaps annoyed, probably sorry. Lotta's terrific, single-minded, obvious feeling for him (Cassie called it a crush but conceded that to Lotta it probably hurt like love) was completely unwelcome to Aaron (which anyone but Lotta would be able to see), and he didn't know what to do about it.

Mr. Holmes caught Cassie's eye, and she realized that he, anyway, had seen the car. They exchanged a helpless glance and went on talking about flowers, strolling happily, followed by Mr. Holmes's silver tabby cat. They admired the tulips, claret-colored, saffron, peppermint striped, and the beds of golden jonquils.

"When you leave," said Mr. Holmes, "I'll give you some for your mother. Have you chicken wire at home?"

"Chicken wire?"

"To hold the flowers up."

"We use those spiked things. The flowers stand up straighter."

Mr. Holmes shook his head vigorously. "No, no, Cassie. You mustn't do that. Do you think anything can give the best of itself when it's stuck on a pin? Let them sway a little and get out of order. Don't impale flowers."

Cassie felt chagrined that she had never thought of this. He was right, of course. He seemed always to be right, and Cassie found this not vexing or irritating but simply beautiful.

Aaron had gone to the far end of the garden, where he now prepared to sunbathe. Stripped to trunks, he lay down on an old blanket, an ancient straw hat over his eyes. His breath came and went evenly, peacefully.

"He seems to be asleep the second he touches the ground," Cassie said. "He's like a cat."

Mr. Holmes looked down at the silver tom, absently pawing a leaf. "In many ways," he said, sighing. "Self-contained, self-serving, unreachable except through self-interest, and completely enchanting, with that way of making the least gesture of affection or attention seem an accolade. Of course, like the cat, people either love him or can't tolerate him. No in between."

It seemed to Cassie that Mr. Holmes was in between. He seemed both to love and be unable to tolerate Aaron. She said as much, but Mr. Holmes answered that he could always tolerate his grandson. "And always love him too. Which does not make me myopic. I see Aaron's faults quite clearly, as his parents do. I don't try to correct them. As they do."

"It seems to me," Cassie said, "that that's a fault in you. If you love somebody, don't you try to help him, to give him the benefit of your experience?"

"Oh, come now, Cassandra," said the old man, shaking his head. "Use that wise brain. Do you believe that anyone ever learned from another's experience? You can learn facts. Arithmetic. Why it's a good idea to look both ways before crossing the street. That sort of thing. But the person you are, and what's good or bad for that person—unhappily each human being has to learn all those things for himself. If my experience or my advice could help Aaron, I would offer them at any price, even the price of his affection. But since they can't help him, I retain his affection and am required to watch helplessly while he—"

"While he what?" Cassie prodded.

"Finds his way."

"He can't find it flat on his back."

"That may be deceptive too. I'm inclined to feel he's thinking much of the time, gathering his strength and his wits for the battle ahead."

Cassie still thought he was just asleep. But as she loved

222

Mr. Holmes, she made an effort not to blurt out thoughts like that. Tact, which had once seemed to her simple dishonesty, now appeared to have other facets. It could be consideration, could be kindness. It could, indeed, be grace. She decided Vincent would probably be pleased to find she'd learned this, and on the heels of that thought realized that it had been some time since she'd turned to Vincent in her mind for approbation or criticism. In the past weeks it had been Aaron and his grandfather from whom she'd desired response. She didn't approve of Aaron but wanted approval from him quite as much as she wanted it from Mr. Holmes, whom she considered the perfect human being.

By now she'd forgotten a period of exhilaration and pain she had known because of Aaron, a time like a foretoken, so swift and brief that it scarcely disarranged the surface of her life. He was terribly important in her life, and she decided that she loved him like a sister. She always had been a loving sister.

"But what's going to happen to him?" she said now to Mr. Holmes. "He's bright. He has a *lovely* mind. Is he really going to use it doing little clown jobs, or supermarket jobs that he quits or gets fired from in a week? Is that how he's going to live?"

"I don't know what he's going to do. I'm like you, Cassandra—I want to see people use their gifts and wits, get pleasure from them. But you can't force a boy to—to do anything. The draft board can force him, and I suspect it'll be putting the arm on Aaron pretty soon if he doesn't go back to school. But his friends and relations can't force him to do a

223

thing. Aaron is lonely and frightened, like most of us in our time. He's also bored—like too many of us. And that's a great pity. There hasn't been enough challenge in his life."

"He isn't going to find it here, is he?"

"He won't be here forever." Mr. Holmes settled in his deck chair, took up his book (George Bernard Shaw), and, smiling at Cassie, dismissed her.

She wandered a while, came to a halt at last beside Aaron's recumbent form. He was lying on his back, the straw hat tipped over his face, and was not, after all, asleep.

"Sit down," he invited, not removing the hat.

Cassie settled on the grass beside him.

"You turn a lovely rose-brown color in the sun," he said. "It's most becoming."

"Thank you," she said, pleased.

"Not at all. You know, Granddad's right. He says you have natural elegance, very composed and grand. We like it."

She didn't reply to that. There was a long pause, and then Cassie, emboldened by the gentleness of his voice and the fact that she couldn't see his eyes, said, "You know, Aaron, you have hurt my sister. Badly."

His chest lifted and fell with a sigh. "Not really. Or if I have, maybe it's good for her."

"Your grandfather says the only thing that's unforgivable is cruelty. Would he call that cruelty, I wonder?"

"You confuse cruelty with the human condition," Aaron said, and sat up, pushing the hat back on his head. "You have to be evil to be cruel. I'm not evil. I don't know anybody who is. Hitler was. I guess all dictators are, because they really don't think people matter. But the rest of us know they

224

matter, and what happens to us—well, lots of it is painful or distressing or sad or maybe even unbearable, but not as a result of somebody's malice. It's just part of being alive, to suffer and be hurt. And to cause it. Everybody thinking 'me first' isn't cruelty. It's human nature, and that's a long way from being beautiful."

"I know," she said in a low voice. "Only—only you *did* seem to be so—so taken with Lotta. So fond of her. At first. And you changed your mind so quickly. She isn't used to having things like that happen to her, and I don't like to see her so unhappy."

"Neither do I. I think it would be just dandy if everyone could be happy all the time." He lay down again. "I tell you, Cassandra, no good can come of a day that starts with getting up."

"You shouldn't have started out liking her if you weren't going to keep it up. You shouldn't have taken her out at all."

"Baloney."

"Well, why *did* you?"

"Take her out? Because she's so awfully pretty. She's just about the prettiest girl I've ever seen. It was irresistible."

"For a while."

"That's right. For a while."

"But how could you find somebody—resistible, practically overnight?"

"Cassandra, you are a very pushy girl. But since you push, you shall have an answer. Because that extremely pretty girl is uninteresting. You asked for this," he said, sitting up again. "Lotta is a dull person. Maybe one day she'll get over it, but right now she is literally not interested in anything but little conversations about love and Lotta. I tested her. I'd start talking about a subject as far removed from the subject of Lotta as I could possible manage, and in two sentences flat, sometimes one, she'd have it back to herself. I'd say I understood that Chief Luthuli *could* have remained in Sweden when he went to accept the Nobel Peace Prize but that he chose to go back home. And she'd say, 'Who's Chief Luthuli?' and I'd say, 'He's a South African leader who's been under house arrest, except for the trip to Sweden, for five years,' and she'd say that since she can't go to college she feels under house arrest herself. This was repeated in no end of ways, and I got tired of it. Have I made myself clear?" He turned to Cassie. "Oh, hey, Cass, I'm sorry. I've been brutal, haven't I?"

Cassie, tears falling down her face, shook her head silently. He hadn't been brutal, except as the truth was. And she had pushed him into speaking. Only, it seemed so sad, so pitiful— Lotta using all her cute little wiles on someone who found them a bore.

"And it isn't just Lotta," she sniffled. "It's *life*. It's *too* sad."

"I know. Where are you going?"

"To get my paints," she gulped.

"Cassandra, I'm so sorry. For making you cry, and about Lotta, too. You believe that, don't you?"

"I should think you incapable of deception," she said loftily.

Aaron gave her a wry smile. "Want me to get your easel for you?"

"No, thank you. I can handle it."

"And everything else?"

"I didn't say that."

226

"No. But you have that determined air. A Cass who walks by herself. What do you think about when you're painting?"

"Nothing. Maybe that's why I like to paint."

"Is that a fact?"

"I think so. I mean, I think I don't think. It's more like feeling, responding, than—" She frowned, considering her words. "When I'm painting I don't get snarled up in knots trying to make sense out of a world that won't make sense."

"I wish I had something like that."

"You do," Cassie said, glad of a chance to get back at him a little. "You have your twenty daily hours of unconsciousness."

"Whew. Downright is scarcely the word for you, Cassandra. Why do you object so to my escape hatch, when you admit you have your own?"

"Because yours is wasteful, I guess. It's a way of life for a sloth, but a sloth isn't overfurnished in the head. For a grown-up, intelligent person to wrap his tail around a branch and then just *hang* there—it's debasing."

He pushed the hat forward again, over his eyes. "I believe I'll just lie down here and turn your words over in my mind. Who knows, I may decide to rise with the roosters as a result. If Granddad will get me a rooster."

In spite of herself Cassie laughed, and as she went for her paints it crossed her mind that this indolent, lonely, bored young man stimulated her more than anyone else she'd ever met, no matter what their enthusiasms or rising hours. Not in a way Lotta would understand, not in a romantic way. By understanding her, knowing her mind, seeing what it was she hoped to be and to have.

227

Aaron knew what brilliant world she wanted to live in. He could paint it in colors as dazzling as her own, and he said she'd find it one day.

"It'll be like opening a door, Cassandra. One day you'll see that door and throw it open, and there your world will be."

"Like Alice's garden?"

"Oh, your world will be real enough, and I don't think you'll have to contort yourself to get in it."

"What about your world, Aaron?" she'd ask.

But Aaron would never discuss his world or his future, except to laugh about them.

"Maybe I'll be a clown forever," he'd told her once. "I like it in back of that mask."

For a couple of hours now, Cassie worked on her painting. A section of the windmill, a splash of garden, and the silver tabby. The cat was a lovely model, paying delicate, intermittent attention to his grooming and then lazily lying down at the foot of Mr. Holmes's chair. Cassie painted in a mindless state of joy quite unlike the intense concentration she had brought to her portrait collages. She didn't do those anymore. It was as if they'd served their purpose and now had none. Mr. Holmes had asked for one when he saw them, and Cassie had let him take what he wanted. Next time Aunt Muriel came to the house Cassie intended to offer her as many as she wished to have. Knowing the way people reacted, she was willing to bet that now Aunt Muriel would no longer want any.

Chapter Eleven

"I have ten hearts, a thousand arms! I feel too strong to war with mortals—BRING ME GIANTS!"

"What say, Vince boy?" David asked over his shoulder. He was trying to squeeze a jacket into a suitcase too full for an additional handkerchief. "Certainly never thought the day would come when I had too many clothes."

"Has it?"

"Either that or I ought to invest in a second suitcase. Why should we bring you giants?"

"I feel as Cyrano would have felt if he'd acted like a man of sense."

"If Cyrano had acted like a man of sense, there wouldn't have been any play. Which, of course, is true of practically all plays. If some of those cats like Oedipus or Othello had asked a few simple questions in the first act, *pfft*—no drama."

"Leading to the conclusion that only the foolish and the misdirected are worthy of the dramatist's pen."

"You have a point. Until you stop to remember that all men are either foolish or misdirected. Which is why we have the Human Comedy. Can you fit this jacket of mine in your suitcase and keep it for me over the summer?"

"Why not pack it in your trunk with the blankets and stuff?"

"Because I lack foresight. Because that trunk is full. Because when I get what's left around here in it tomorrow, it's going to break down. So now can you find room for this garment which I am going to need badly come fall?"

A few weeks earlier Vincent would have said, "Assuming the fall does come, I'll try." Now he merely said, "Hand it over," and, making an attempt at neatness, crushed David's jacket into his suitcase.

Love had made Vincent invulnerable. It had given him a sense of permanence, both personal and worldly, that he had not known since childhood. As he had then, when his parents' loving presence had made existence secure, he felt now that nothing could threaten a world that contained Daisy. To think of her made annihilation, even the concept of annihilation, incredible, absurd, unworthy of discussion.

David, having several times run in headlong astonishment into this new conviction of Vincent's, had given up all attempt to discuss the world's perilous condition. He felt no less threatened himself, and that menace included, of course, Vincent and his Daisy. But there was something wonderfully

230

joyous and even powerful in Vincent's new belief that God was in His heaven, all was right with the world. David observed his friend's metamorphosis with pleasure, with the same happiness he would feel reading a splendid play or poem. It occurred to him to wonder why he, who certainly felt for Marie all and anything Vincent felt for Daisy, could not find that sort of weatherproof, bombproof unassailability in love.

The answer was not far to find. No man of color could feel impregnable in this world, and love, far from strengthening his defenses, toppled them. James Baldwin had said, "How many lives are being wrecked, and wrecked silently, while we sit here talking?" All the lives in Harlem did not seem too wild a guess. No American man of color could be unaware of the inexorable penalty he would pay for that color all his life. He could not find refuge in loving a girl equally threatened, with the prospect of bearing children and rearing them under the same promise of punishment—evil, pointless, unending. He and Marie, indeed, had sworn to each other never to have children, but David put no stock in that. When people loved, the need to create something out of their love was stronger than promises, stronger than fear. For a moment now, in this room with his white friend, looking across the summery campus where he had, for a while, found a refuge that could not last, David apologized to his children for wanting them so terribly that he could not spare them existence.

"Hey, Dave, what's the matter?" Vincent said anxiously. "Don't you feel well?"

David turned from the window. "Nothing's the matter," he said evenly. "Not a thing. Everything's copacetic."

He looked at Vincent and thought that it really was the

most remarkable example of the pure power of love he had ever seen. Vince even looked taller. Maybe he was, maybe he wasn't. Maybe it was just the way he carried himself that gave him greater stature. His skin seemed to be all cleared up and the eyes behind the glasses had lost that cold, forlorn look David had often spied there when Vincent's guard was down.

Enoch and I have witnessed a miracle, David thought. We've seen the sort of thing that happens to a crumpled old caterpillar when the sun and the proper season touch him with splendor and send him winging into life. Enoch—no surprise—hadn't noticed particularly. He knew Vincent was dating Daisy, and after an initial period of mild rancor—it seemed that he himself had dated Daisy and had not been the one to call a halt—he found consolation with Christobel Compton and thereafter was affable about Vincent's arrangements. More than that he seemed not to see.

"I guess that's it," said Vincent, looking around the room. Their trunks were in the hall, where on the following morning they could stow away the bedclothes necessary for this one last night. "Dave, does it seem right that another year has gone? Didn't it go too fast? I feel as if we'd just *un*-packed, and here's everything ready to be shipped out again."

"You remember how slowly time went when we were kids? How long it was between holidays, or birthdays? And now—"

They fell silent, a little frightened at the acceleration of life, at this feeling that there wasn't going to be enough time for all they wanted to do.

"Excuse me, could you tell me where Enoch Burke-Runciman's room is?"

232

The question was accompanied by a gentle knock on the open door, and the two young men turned to find a gangling tweedy figure in the doorway.

"This is it, sir," said Vincent.

The man's mild blue eyes kept straying to David, but he addressed Vincent. "I'm his father. He's, ah, expecting me, isn't he?"

Enoch had said nothing to that effect, but Vincent didn't see why Mr. Burke-Runciman had to know that. "Oh, sure he is. He's around someplace."

"I told him I'd be here, to drive him home, you know. He didn't answer my letter, of course. I never do hear from Enoch unless he's wrecked something, failed something, or wants money." Mr. Burke-Runciman stared again, openly, at David, and a frown furrowed his already deeply creased brow.

"Oh, excuse me," Vincent said edgily. "We should introduce ourselves. We're Enoch's roommates. This is David Gates, and I'm Vincent Dunne."

"My *word*," said the man. His jaw dropped open slightly and the blue eyes were all at once shallow as he continued his study of David. "My word."

"Gentlemen, if you'll excuse me," David said suddenly, "I just remembered three hundred and forty-six things I have to do, none of them in the immediate vicinity." He strode toward the door, where Mr. Burke-Runciman practically hopped to get out of his way.

"Enoch never said," the man told Vincent querulously.

"Never said *what?*" It was too late, as it often was, to spare David's feelings. One could only hope he was used enough to

233

this sort of thing to despise it. That he was above it did not guarantee his thickness of skin. "A thick skin and a tender conscience, that's what makes a good man," he and Dave had long ago agreed. True enough, but a tough combination to find and probably impossible to develop. As it was too late now to spare David, the next best thing was to try to abash this man. "Never said what?"

Mr. Burke-Runciman was not abashable. "Why . . . Well, that David—that his roommate Gates, was—that is to say, is an African."

A short laugh from the hall told Vincent that David had been too curious to get out of hearing. "Hold it, Gates!" Vincent yelled. "I'll bear you company."

"Oh, but see here," said Mr. Burke-Runciman, lifting a hand to arrest Vincent's flight. "What about Enoch?"

"He'll be along," Vincent said, brushing past.

He caught up with David just outside the house. "So that's old Senior, father of old Junior, eh?" he said in a jolly tone.

"So it would seem," David replied, not breaking his stride. "African, he says. That's me—the playboy of the non-Western world. I should be so lucky. Maybe I ought to have told Mr. Fisheyes that I'm a black *American*, and as Mr. Baldwin so neatly puts it, all of Africa's going to be free before I can get a lousy cup of coffee."

"Not here at school, Dave. It's not like that here," Vincent said, and felt the words were weasly.

"I graduate next year, old buddy, remember?"

"Yeah. I remember."

Suddenly David laughed. "After a year and a half of hearing

about the paterfamilias of the Burke-Runciman clan, nothing he said should have taken me by surprise. But he did, you know. He looks so—genial. Doesn't he? At first, that is."

"Nice and gentle. Like a watchdog taking the afternoon off. Come on over to Daisy's with me."

"Why?"

"She's got a picnic for us. Bread and cheese, apples and wine. We're going up in the meadow and think long thoughts about the death of youth."

"I'm not going to horn in on your last afternoon. Nice of you, and all—"

"Dave, will you quit digging your toe in the dust and come on? Daisy and I have our last evening—if that's how you want to put it, though it's my feeling that Daisy and I aren't ever going to have our last time together, not for years, not this side of the tomb— Anyway, we'll see each other tonight. So come on. Let's hie us up the meadow, reciting dithyrambs."

"Okay," David said, laughing. "Have you proposed to Daisy? Is that what you're saying?" He sounded pleased.

"I haven't said, Will you marry me? But I guess she knows."

"Girls like to hear it. I proposed to Marie on our second date."

"You did? Why aren't you married? I'm beginning to feel like an old bachelor on this campus, going into my junior year without my lines."

"Marie thinks we should wait till I'm out of college. I think she's wrong, but what Marie says goes."

"Maybe she's right. I don't know, Dave. One minute I think we'd better grab everything we can while the grabbing's good, and the next I hate the whole sort of *gulping* attitude. I want to live as if there were time to do it decently, not like a hog who knows the ax is coming. Even if I don't believe there's time, I'd like to live as if there were. And then, of course, there's economics. Daisy doesn't have any money, I don't have any money. We'd have to try to sponge off our parents, *if* they'd agree, which I strongly doubt."

"That's what Marie says. I may marry her anyway this summer. And go to work."

"Leave college? You'd be a fool. You're too close to graduation, Dave. To quit now—"

"I don't mean quit. I could get a job. Marie isn't going to college, and she could work. I'd have to leave here, of course, and live in the city where I could find work. I'd go to school at night."

"Are you serious?"

"I think so."

They stopped for Daisy, and the three of them walked over the campus, up a hillside to a plateau of meadow grass, where they could look across the campus buildings to the river moving languidly in the valley. Two boats were out, crewmen readying for the regatta at Derby. Even from this distance one could hear staccato directions from the coxswains, the slap of wooden seats thrusting forward, then back. The boats skimmed the glittering water with smooth precision, long oars flashing in unison, all the powerful young bodies moving as one man.

"That's a beautiful sport," David said lazily, munching on a piece of crusty bread torn from the loaf.

236

Vincent, lying back with his hands under his head, enjoying the rough touch of grass against his skin, said, as if there'd been no interruption, "If you do leave, Dave . . . we'll miss you. We'll miss you badly."

"Leave?" said Daisy. "What are you talking about, you two?"

"Dave's going to drag Marie protesting to a preacher and settle down in the city to the life of a married drudge." The words weren't out before he regretted them. Sitting up, he said, "That was crass, even for me. I guess I just don't like the idea of your leaving, Dave. I often come all over gauche when I'm confounded."

Daisy nibbled an apple. "It's a proven fact," she said, "that people who get married in college immediately become better students and—oh, more sensible. The rah-rah and the college kid stuff disappear."

"I guess so," Vincent said, "but something else goes, too. A sort of—time of discovery. What's that line? 'I went from homework to housework.' Something like that. A cartoon I saw. Well, that's what happens. There ought to be a time in everyone's life when he just strikes out, on his own, by himself, and *finds out.*"

"Finds out what?" said David.

"Anything, anything, Dave. Don't you see? You've got that one time, when college is over and you're on your own, risking only your own pride and income. If you've got a wife, and children maybe, you can't rush around the world taking chances for them, can you? But you can take them for yourself."

"Anyone would think," Daisy said reflectively, "that you disapproved of marriage, Vincent."

He looked at her in astonishment, his natural modesty conflicting with a suspicion that Daisy's remark had been most personally pointed at their own relationship. Even as his heart lifted with a sudden, illuminating joy, he realized that he meant what he'd been saying. He wanted a time of his own before he married. He wanted to take some risks, poke around the world for a while, find out, if he could, what sort of world it was before he settled for a part of it. What a contrary creature a man is, he thought ruefully. A few months ago to have a girl like Daisy all but direct him to propose to her would have translated him to a heaven where freedom and risks and something of his own were assets too negligible to contemplate.

And now? Now he loved Daisy with all his heart and hoped one day she'd marry him. But not yet, not for a while.

He met Daisy's eyes. She smiled, tossed him an apple, and told him she understood without speaking a word. Vincent felt his eyes sting, his knees against the grass tremble a little. His whole being seemed to melt with tenderness, with an almost painful joy. But I never knew, he thought, until this very second, what happiness is. Happiness—pure, perfect, not to be mistaken for anything else. And now I know.

Heat shimmered in the air, grasshoppers shot out of the dry grass like tiny rockets, and somewhere in a distant tree a bird sang a reedy repetitious song of summer.

David, looking across the valley, smiled to himself, and in a great youthful upsurge of feeling recanted the bitterness, the

238

pessimism, of a little while ago. Our day is coming, he said to himself, and could not care just now whether Daisy or Vincent or any white person shared it. *Our* day. Not blood, bigotry, or brutality was going to stop a dawn already breaking. Many a dawn had come up in thunder and violence. But after that came the morning, and the long day. Now he could only remember, like an objective observer, that he had a short time ago apologized to the children he would one day have for giving them, unasked, the gift of life. Oh, but life, for all its pain and sorrow, was the greatest thing to give, a splendid thing to try, and his children had a right to it. His children, and Marie's, born to a new day.

"I propose a toast," he said, pouring the warm red wine into paper cups and handing them around.

"To what?" said Daisy.

"To," said David, "whatever each of us is thinking."

Daisy looked at Vincent and wondered how she ever could have found that dear and beautiful face homely. I think I'll drink to vision, she said to herself, lifting her cup.

Vincent simply drank to Daisy, and David drank to Life.

"*Dum vivimus, vivamus,*" he shouted, and tossed down the wine.

"Translation, please," said Vincent.

"While we live, let us *live!*"

"Oh, I'll drink to that," said Vincent, and thought, We will always be friends. I suppose that's what life is, what gives it meaning, the friendship, the love, that you get and you give.

The moment seemed to hover, as though arrested in flight,

but presently they were eating again, laughing, and the intense awareness of one another, the heightened sensitivity that had brought them close to the essence of themselves, of what they were and what they needed, ebbed, as it had to. You couldn't go on feeling that way, Vincent thought. It would be excruciating, an insupportable measure for so frail a vessel as a human being. He wondered rather jealously if there were beings, somewhere in space or in time, who could exist on a level like that.

"Do you suppose there is life on other worlds, out in all those galaxies?" he asked.

"In my opinion," said David, "it's far more likely that there would be than that there wouldn't. I can't make myself believe, even as I sit with two of my favorite earthlings, that it's all empty except for us. It seems to me that only the most astounding ego could believe us the sole inhabitants of all time and space." They thought awhile, and David added, "Besides, I guess I want to believe in a race of beings more intelligent and merciful than we are."

"Why do we always assume they'd be more so?" Daisy asked.

"Probably because they couldn't be less so and have survived at all," Vincent said. He didn't see how anyone, even optimistic Daisy, could disagree with that. All you had to do was look around you. Consider David, he thought, and what is done to him and for what reason. You might as well condemn a man for the color of his hair. That would be as rational, as insane. Yet it was done. Look anywhere around you—at the filth of the streets and the streams, the spoliation

240

of fields and forests. Everything plundered, stripped, made useless or dangerous. Read the newspapers, listen to conversations in the street. Watch the way parents behave toward their children and young people toward everyone older. Consider man's inhumanity to man, his brutality to the beasts, his malevolent disregard of the earth's needs, or his own. To say nothing of simple courtesy.

"We're making a greater effort to preserve the whooping crane than we are to guard the few courtesies we have remaining," he told them. "And I am not being irrelevant."

"I had a cat once," Daisy said. "She hated the rain. If we opened the back door for her to go out, and she found it was raining, she'd hunch back on herself like a caterpillar going into reverse. And then she'd turn and run to the front door, assuming the sun would be there. I remind myself of her: I'm always sure that the sun is shining somewhere if I can find the right door."

David and Vincent laughed, finding her not persuasive but charming. For a while they were silent, knowing the afternoon was going, but reluctant to leave. The two boats came back around the river bend, streaking for the boathouse, as smooth and swift and flashing as they'd been going out. The grasshoppers grew bold, landing on the picnickers, then launching into space again, long legs trailing.

"You know my cousin in Mississippi?" David said at length. "He's in jail again."

"What for this time?" Vincent asked.

"They called it 'disturbing the peace.' He's been out getting the Negroes in his county to register for the vote. The trouble with my cousin is, he never waits for backing, for a group from CORE, or like that, to show up and be with him. He's a loner."

"He's a lion. How many people do we know could be that brave?"

"I'm not sure I could," David said. "But I'm going down there this summer and find out."

"You are? Suppose you get put in jail too?"

David laughed. "Cousin, it's getting so a colored man has no cachet if he hasn't spent at least one night in the slammer. My parents are down there now—not in jail. At least, I don't think they are. They're lending moral support to my aunt and uncle, who sure need it."

"Are you going straight to Miss?" Vincent asked.

"No. Have to stop off home for a few days, see about this job I've been promised."

"I mean to say, if your parents aren't there, you'd have to cook for yourself, or something impossible like that. Why don't you come home with me for a few days?"

David hesitated, and Vincent almost added, Don't worry about my father, he won't be there. He said nothing. Such reassurance would be an insult to David, to Vincent, even—possibly—to Mr. Dunne, who might be an almost mechanical bigot in his speech, even in his feelings, since he'd been brought up that way and was not in the habit of questioning himself. But he wouldn't insult a guest in his house. *Would* he? What a stupid world, Vincent thought angrily, when you can't make the simplest gesture without wondering at once if it wouldn't have been better to do nothing, to keep quiet.

242

Well, he'd asked David, he wanted him, and he wasn't going to back out now. Waiting for his friend's answer, Vincent was deeply, shamefully conscious that what he hoped for was a refusal. Because, leaving his father out of it, how would the rest of them behave? He thought he should have known, but he didn't. Since he had left for college he had almost entirely lost communication with his family, despite frequent letters from them which he read but rarely answered. His mother wrote three and four times a week, gossipy letters that sometimes interested and often bored him. His father from time to time typed long single-spaced letters of admonition and advice. Vincent read them triple-spaced and threw them away. Cassie's letters were charming, touching. Full of little drawings and determinedly bright observations. Once, only once, she had written him an anguished appeal, pleading to know why life was so confusing, so bitter, so sour-sweet, asking for answers to everything. Vincent hadn't known how to cope with that and had thrown the letter out. Since when he'd wished uncomfortably that he had, at least, acknowledged it, had confessed that he had no answers but had heard her, had cared. Too late now. He told himself that people didn't really expect answers to such letters, that by the time they reached their destination, the sender was in a different, altered frame of mind and wouldn't recognize a response if he got one. Lotta never wrote to him at all.

Aside from this mail, and an occasional phone call which he made (collect, and only because his mother became upset at not hearing from him), Vincent could go for weeks without thinking of his family. If he did, it was as a group of almost

243

statuelike figures who would, in his absence, have done nothing they hadn't always done. They would in no way have changed or suffered or grown. His father would always be that shadowy man on the road, faintly ominous, faintly sad, not really welcome at home. His sisters would be school kids, with school-kid emotions and problems. His mother would be his mother, anxious, overprotective, living at secondhand through her children and therefore exasperating them even though they loved her. And we do love her, Vincent thought—giving them some attention now that he was about to go home again. We all, I am sure, love one another, because we're a normal everyday family, and normal, everyday families love the members therein.

Don't they? Do they?

Did love countenance total forgetfulness of people? Daisy was never out of his mind for a moment, not really, not even when he thought he was thinking about the zoology final or the bomb or what use he wanted to make of his future, aside from establishing Daisy in it—and there he was, back to her again. The love of a man for a woman was different from a person's love for his relatives, but did any love allow you both to forget and then, when you remembered, to realize that you didn't at all know what these people were like that you'd grown up with?

How would they greet David? Putting his father aside, and hoping he'd stay there, how would the rest of them be? His mother was a kindly woman, but unreflective. She lived a tight little existence made up of children, bridge, and preconceptions. She never questioned her values or her judgments, grew peevish if anyone else did, and had absolutely no vision of or interest in the problems, the people, the probable destination of the world that lay outside her small radius. It simply wouldn't occur to her to invite someone of another race into her home. She almost didn't know anyone outside of her own church. "I'm sure," she would say, clearly feeling not smug but broad-minded and sensible, "that they don't want to mingle with me anymore than I do with them. I mean, Vincent, the Jews have their own clubs that *I* couldn't get into. Not that I'd want to. And I'm sure they feel the same about me." This sort of talk, though he'd heard it for years and might have gotten used to it, still depressed Vincent almost to the point of illness. And it would be completely and absolutely impossible to make her see why.

So, how would she respond to David as a house guest?

Lotta would probably object on the basis of what people would think. She cared to a pitiful extent what people thought and was pretty sure they thought just as she did, which was next to not at all. She doesn't so much think as react, Vincent said to himself, and then wondered how he could be so sure. He didn't, in truth, know a thing about Lotta except that she'd made him and Cassie jealous and angry as children.

And Cassie? Well, though he'd neglected and overlooked her, he thought that Cassie, at least, he could be sure of. She would take David, or anyone, as a person. Cassie was impatient of all kinds of people and seemed at times to wish to do without them, if that had been possible. She wanted to do her odd, secretive portraits and find life between the covers of

245

a book. But faced with a real live person of any shape or hue, Cass would see a person, not a representative of a race. Anyway, he thought she would.

What a sad, strange thing it is, he said to himself, walking down the meadow with Daisy and David. Here I've known Dave a couple of years, Daisy a couple of months, and I know them as well as I do myself—which isn't very well, I'll admit, but at least I can trust them and myself to have and abide by certain values.

But the people whose blood is my blood, whose heritage is my heritage, I just don't know at all.

Oh, Daisy, Daisy, he said to himself, suppose I had never met you. Suppose you hadn't loved me—

Why Daisy loved him was the beautiful, unanswerable miracle of his life. Why not one of all the other fellows she'd met and gone out with, any one of whom would have loved her? Why not Enoch, with his good looks, good spirits, his marvelous British voice? He'd asked her once how she'd happened to stop seeing Enoch and she'd given a characteristic little shrug she had for things she considered beside the point.

"But he's such a charming guy," Vincent had persisted, annoyed with himself but unable not to prod, to try to extract a reply.

"Vincent, darling . . . charm. Well, charm that is unaccompanied by any thought of other people, any consideration, gets to be uncharming. It becomes repellent after a while."

"Don't underestimate Enoch," he'd said, this time in earnest. "He may not be the most perceptive citizen in the world, but he's a good sound person."

246

"I guess he must be, or you and David wouldn't be so fond of him. But—for a girl, anyway—he's not dependable, you know? I don't mean stuffy dependable. I mean that I never had the feeling I could trust his responses. He's slippery. Besides, he whines."

Vincent didn't agree with her, but thought he'd protested enough. More would be folly, since he couldn't see yet how given a choice between himself and Enoch any girl would choose as Daisy had.

"He never seems real to me," Daisy had said with an air of finality. "And you do, Vincent. You are very, very real."

Daisy, Daisy—

"Give me your answer, do," he said aloud, and the other two looked at him, as if wondering who should reply. Vince flushed a little, then laughed. He felt marvelous, springy, full of confidence. He wasn't proposing to Daisy, not yet, though it must have sounded so. One day he would. "I meant," he said to David, "are you coming home with me?"

"I'd like to."

Vincent realized that was what he'd wanted to hear. He must have been crazy, posing all those objections to himself. His parents and his sisters had their faults, as who did not. But they were decent, good people and given something to rise to—like the challenge of their first Negro guest—they would rise. He didn't know them very well, but well enough, he judged, for that.

Lotta was sitting on the floor on her side of the room. She'd started to give herself a manicure, but some time ago had

247

replaced the little brush in its bottle, screwed the cap tightly and leaned back against her bed to think. Given the severe economy of the Dunnes, she could not do what she wanted to do, and that was run, escape, go somewhere new and fresh where no one knew her and she knew no one. Would anyone have believed, a few months ago, that she, Lotta Dunne, could be worked into a loveless, nervous, insecure position where flight seemed the only answer? Probably not. Yet here she was, and in a way it seemed unbelievable that she had ever been a girl who rode like a feather over the slumps and depressions that other people fell into.

She couldn't even fix on anyone to be mad at. Except herself, and that was asking much of a girl who had always found her own behavior enchanting. What *could* she have done wrong? What had happened? Why had sweet and gentle Lotta, courageously indifferent to material lacks, adorable to parents and friends, gay and pretty—*all* of that—suddenly become a person Irene Stevens was *kind* to?

"Do dance with Lotta," she'd heard Irene say to her brother at the graduation party. "She's having rather a thin time of it."

"Okay," he'd said. "Sure thing." And before Lotta could find Aaron and ask him to take her home, there had been the college brother, of whom Lotta had often dreamed, standing before her, asking for the pleasure of—

She'd wanted to shriek at him, to say something haughty, cutting. She'd wanted to say, "Thank you, but I'm not having crumbs this season." The habit of graciousness and the knowledge that she would simply turn Irene's *kindness* to condescension prevented her. She smiled and stepped into his arms, hoping that once in them, once dancing, the old ways would reassert themselves.

"How simply marvy to have you here," she heard herself saying, and her voice in her own ears sounded just as it always had. A little forward, a bit breathless. They'd always leaned toward her, to hear, or just to be closer to her fragrant hair, her soft cheek. He didn't answer immediately, so she added (*did* she sound faintly shrill now?) "To what do we owe the honor?"

"Rene shanghaied me. I had no choice."

You aren't very nice, she said to his broad muscular chest. You are not a nice person at all, and I wish—

"Excuse me," she'd said suddenly. "I have the funniest feeling . . . a little faint, or something. Perhaps I should go out in the garden."

"Yeah. Sure. Want me to go with you? Will you be all right alone?"

Shocked at his manner, she turned without a word and ran through the doors to the terrace, to the garden, to a chair by the swimming pool. It was a party that was going to last the night. Heavily chaperoned, all these young graduates were going to spend the entire night dancing and playing games and swimming in the moonlight, and a long, long time from now, having breakfast by this pool. The tables were set up already at the other side.

I'll never make it to then, Lotta had thought, her arms clasped tightly across her breasts. Submerged lights in the pool made the quiet water blue and mysterious, and though

249

it was a balmy, mothy night, full of the sound of crickets, sweet with the breath of early roses, Lotta felt chilled. A rising panic fluttered in her veins. What did she have, if what she'd had was gone? If the witchery and the charm she'd relied on so unthinkingly were lost to her—and why, why, why? —what did she have to take their place?

J. H. was back there in that room from which the sounds of music and carefree voices and laughter came to her only slightly softened by distance. He was there, paying loud and obvious court to Irene. He had danced with Lotta once (had Irene arranged that dance, too?) and had seemed not even to hear her whispered protest that it was the strangest thing she'd ever known, to have him being someone else's date. . . . "I mean, J. H.," she'd said softly, darting him that oblique glance he'd loved so well, "doesn't it seem peculiar to you?" She'd faltered when she found him looking over her shoulder —for Irene, for someone.

"Huh?" J. H. had said. "Say, who's that cat with Rene?"

Lotta had looked, as bidden, and answered dully, "Aaron Holmes. He's my date."

Aaron looked handsome, desirable. He was here with her because he was kind, because she had all but begged him to take her, because she had *not been asked by anyone else.* Aaron didn't like parties. He said a party was a roomful of people wriggling and making remarks. Cassie had laughed when he said that, and after a bewildered hesitation, seeing nothing funny at all, Lotta had laughed too. When Aaron and Cassie were together they made her feel lonely, out of touch. They said such odd and stupid things but clearly

250

thought that other people would be stupid to disagree.

"Nice people," Aaron would say, "do not eat T.V. dinners."

"Or send studio cards," Cassie would add.

"Or call famous people by their given names."

"Or belong to country clubs."

They could amuse themselves in this manner for ages, and Lotta found it all very unfunny. But, for tonight, having consented to take her to this party, Aaron was acting beautifully. He didn't dance well but was being wonderfully attentive. Anyone but me would be fooled, Lotta thought bitterly, and said to J. H., with what she hoped was a significant inflection, "He's my very, very date, J. H."

"He's that kook who lives in the windmill, isn't he?"

"Aaron is not a kook," Lotta said, in a rage at this unknown and hateful J. H. "How do you dare to talk to me this way? To treat me this way?"

"Why," he drawled, "I have no notion what you're squeaking about, girl. Is there some reason why I shouldn't *dare* to treat you some way? I mean, I haven't got a contract or anything with you, have I?" He looked at her deliberately, coldly, reaping vengeance for the hurt that had been done him.

"J. H.," Lotta said unhappily, "will you believe me if I tell you I'm terribly, terribly sorry that I hurt you?"

"You did not hurt me," he said loudly. Several people glanced their way. "My feelings weren't in the least hurt. They were outraged."

Lotta pulled out of his arms and went to find Aaron, who had disappeared, and it was then that Irene had directed her

251

brother to be gallant. And now—now here she was, alone at a party for the first time in her life.

I can't stay here, she thought, hearing a noisy group making for the bathhouses in gusts of laughter. Not here, and not in there. I want to go home. She turned wildly and started up, running into Aaron's arms.

"Hey, hey," he said. "What's this? I've been looking for you."

"I'll just bet you have," she said, all charm and grace of manner deserting her in this most needful time. She heard her own voice and knew that it had no softness in it. A harsh voice, full of hurt and anger. And she couldn't stop it. "Well, you needn't look anymore, because I'm going home, see? And I don't want to see you or anyone here ever again in my life. I hate hate hate all of you."

"Lotta," he said, holding her close against him. "Lotta, quiet down, be still. . . . Everything's going to be all right. There, there . . ." He patted her back as he murmured and gradually she did quiet down, and even giggle.

"You sound just like my mother," she said at last.

"Well, that's all right too," he said imperturbably. "Are you better now?"

"Some." She took a deep, jerky breath. "But I won't stay here."

"I think you should."

"Why? Because I'm wanted so much? Because I'm such a belle?"

"For your pride's sake, maybe. I think you'll be sorry if you leave. The night won't last forever, and you'll prefer to have stuck it out. Besides, I'd like to have a swim. You brought

252

your suit, didn't you? Good. Well, go get it on. Let's swim and dive and duck each other, and after that we can talk."

"About what?" she asked, relieved to be persuaded, still raw at the treatment she'd received from J. H. and Irene's brother. "What's there to talk about?"

"There's no end of things to discuss. Just lately my mind has been occupied with the subject of weeder geese. Did you ever hear of them? They're being used extensively in cotton-growing areas of this country, particularly in Texas, for the purpose of weeding the crops. They've just about replaced human labor in certain sections, and when you think about it, it is a most peculiar situation we human beings are in. We aren't being replaced only by machines. The geese are moving in. Pretty soon we won't have an undisputed area left. I'd like to go into this matter in depth. Then, when we've settled that, there is the subject of trading stamps to be taken up. Will they replace currency, and if so what—"

"I'll get my suit," Lotta said.

She'd stayed at the party. She and Aaron had been among the last to leave, and Irene was more perceptive than Lotta gave her credit for if she could guess that her onetime best friend had had anything but a ball. Aaron, on the surface, had been all anyone could ask for in the way of an enraptured escort. As the night wore on toward morning the college brother had begun to hover in Lotta's vicinity, and J. H. had seized an occasion to whisper something meaningful and reminiscent. She'd pretended not to see the college man, not to hear her erstwhile suitor, and her pride therefore was salvaged and assuaged.

If pride, she thought now, looking at her polished nails, is just something to show other people. She leaned her head back and a few hot slow tears coursed down her face. Aaron didn't love her. He didn't, she suspected, even very much like her. He always seemed so impatient when she talked, and he certainly couldn't care about looks in a girl when he found Cassie attractive. Which he appeared to. Cassie was an interesting, really very nice girl, but plain to the point of being homely, and how *could* a boy prefer her?

But it seemed he did. Maybe he didn't love her, but he would certainly rather be with her. Lotta, who could not sustain an unrequited love, and doubted if anyone outside of Cassie's books could, was no longer in love with Aaron. She had to be grateful to him for going to the party with her, for making it a success in her enemy's eyes. Irene, my enemy, she thought. How queer, how sad. She didn't like to think about Irene anymore, or J. H., or Brad. But she did not any longer love Aaron, and it would have been nice not to think about him either. Impossible, since he was around all the time.

Oh, I wish I could go away, she thought wearily, and opened her eyes to find Cassie standing over her like a policeman.

"What's the matter, Lotta?" Cassie said. "Aren't you feeling well?"

"I'm not sick, if that's what you mean. Except of everything."

Cassie at this juncture would ordinarily have turned away. She disliked emotional, personal discussions and never pretended otherwise. Today, however, she sat on the floor next to her sister and said, "What are you going to do about it?"

254

"Do? What is there to do? Shall we ask Daddy to send me on the Grand Tour of Europe? I wish I'd gotten into some college, any college."

"That would have been a waste of time."

"Thank you, dear. You're so sweet."

"Well, it would have been," Cassie insisted. "Your time and the college's. But that doesn't mean there's nothing left to do. Lotta, you seem to have lost all your spirit."

"Yes, I do, don't I?"

"Don't you care? You can't just sit on the floor and cry. You have to *do* something."

Unaccustomed to this sort of attention from Cassie, Lotta found that even bullying was welcome after such a long period (it seemed long) of feeling overlooked and forgotten. "What do you suggest?" she asked, faintly hopeful that practical Cass might actually have an answer.

"Why not business school, like Alice Adams?" Cassie said, and then thought it probably wasn't the happiest instance she could have offered. Alice, the belle who became a has-been before the age of twenty. Lotta might find the comparison odious. If, that was, she'd read the book.

It developed that Lotta had not. She knew it was a book, and even that was sufficient to annoy her. "Honestly, Cass. Don't you and Aunt Muriel ever have any ideas that some writer didn't have first? Why should I do what the people in your books do? I want to do something of my own!"

"I only suggested that because you obviously are good at organization, and you're very inventive in your way. A business school would get you started somewhere, and with your talents you could—"

Lotta put her hands to her face. "I'd forgotten. How *could* I have forgotten?"

"Forgotten what?"

"Cass . . . do you know what she's gone and done? Irene? She's refused to do any more of the parties with me. She's tired of it. And here am I, with two of them on my books, and either I have to phone the mothers and cancel or try to handle them alone, which I can*not* do, and that—that *person* has no sense of responsibility or loyalty or—" She broke off, pushing her blond hair into disorder.

"I could help you," Cassie said. Lotta stared at her. "Couldn't I? I can't play the piano, but I could do—oh, paper cutouts and collages with coffee grounds and shells, things like that. Children like that sort of thing."

Lotta looked at this stranger with her sister's face. "Would you really, Cass? It would just about save my life."

"Why would I say I'd do it," Cassie asked stolidly, "if I didn't meant it?"

As Lotta was always saying things she didn't mean, she prodded Cassie once more. "You're positive? I mean, I wouldn't want to tell the mothers okay and then—" She stopped at Cassie's expression. "All right, Cass. Thank you, and I do think it's marvelous of you."

"I should think it'd be fun," Cassie said. She got up, stepped across the string, and immediately fell silent.

Lotta finished her manicure in an elevated frame of mind. I'll do these two parties, she said to herself, and that'll be the end of that enterprise. Maybe Cassie is right, maybe a business school, a two-year course in a really nice, tony New York business school, would be the place to start. Maybe Aunt Muriel would let me live with her. That would save us money, and I like her apartment. I'm sure she would, Lotta decided (correctly, but without wondering whether Aunt Muriel would relish the arrangement). Her natural presumption was already reasserting itself. Let Irene and J. H. have the joy of each other, she thought, but as for me, I'm going my way.

She smoothed the cover on her bed, from which the toy kittens had long vanished. They had been replaced by a stuffed panda from Brad, and now it too was gone. Lotta had been waiting for something, from someone, to fill the empty spot.

"You know," she said now to Cassie, who was reading, "I believe I don't want any more stuffed animals." Cassie just refrained from saying, "That's progress." She settled for a cheery nod, and Lotta went on: "Another thing. I really think we should take the string away now too, Cass. It's sort of childish, don't you think?"

Cassie got up, sighing. "I guess it served its purpose." She meant that it was obvious Lotta no longer considered it a barrier to conversation, but again refrained from speaking her mind. "Something there is that does not love a wall, that wants it down—"

Lotta shrugged. Another quotation. Probably Cass would spend her whole life thinking what someone had written about something before she thought what she thought about it herself. Lotta smiled and began to tug at the string. She felt quite animated, like one who's been sick and finds the return of good health exciting, intoxicating. Sometimes writers did put things into words that other people only touched on in their thoughts, and if Cassie wanted a literary precedent for everything she did—that was Cassie's affair.

As for me, said Lotta to herself again, *I am going to live firsthand. I'll find another world, with new people, and I will be a new person, too.* She always had loved the beginnings of things, and this time it was all so buoyant and challenging she could scarcely wait to begin. She considered with pity the wan and witless thing she'd been during these past weeks. And all because Aaron or J. H. or some *boy* didn't seem to want her. She'd outgrown boys, that was what had been the matter. She'd outgrown them, and this town, and this house—everything here, just as she'd outgrown the string that she now wound up and tossed in the wastebasket.

"You'll have the room to yourself pretty soon, Cass. You can spread your things around and have some privacy."

"How's that?" said Cassie, stepping back to observe the undivided room.

"Why, when I leave for business school, of course. I'm going to phone Aunt Muriel tonight and see if she'll let me stay with her. Some of these schools have summer sessions, so I could start practically right away. Don't you think that white coat of mine would look marvy dyed pale yellow?"

Cassie agreed that pale yellow would be just the thing. By nature unsympathetic with moody people, she had tended to avoid Lotta recently, and it was pleasant to find her more nearly her old sunny and selfish self. Until Lotta had gone into repine, Cassie hadn't realized how agreeable that self-

258

confident good humor had been. Aaron held that everyone in the world, except possibly saints-in-waiting, was just as self-absorbed as Lotta.

"Most of us," he'd said, "aren't as innocent and forthright about showing it, which makes the difference. Of course," he'd gone on cheerfully, "girls, especially girls as pretty as Lotta, can get away with murder, where the rest of us have to use our heads. We have to use empathy and imagination when we deal with people, so in the end I'd say that we were actually ahead of the beauties, in terms of real friendship or understanding, you know."

Talk about *tact*less, Cassie had said to herself, but laughed. Aaron never offended her. She was both too fond of and too independent of him. As, in past months, she had come to be about Vincent. Time was when her brother's absence, his silence, his growing indifference to everyone he'd left behind, had hurt her painfully, like an internal wound that would not heal. Aaron had healed it by making a boy's will (a young man's will) more understandable to her. Boys, as they became men—in order, perhaps, to become men—left home. If not bodily, then in spirit.

"Why don't girls, then?" she'd argued with Aaron. "Even when girls leave bodily, when they go to college or get married or join the Peace Corps—practically no girl ever really leaves home, and I'd like to know why that is," she'd asked irritably.

"Maybe they're just unlucky. Or lucky. I'm not sure which. Maybe females are kinder than males. Or weaker. I don't know the answer, Cass."

Aaron had helped to explain her brother to her. Vincent

259

didn't write to them, forgot to telephone, seemed almost to have put them all from his life, not for lack of love—because Vincent was a loving person—but simply because this was how he had to find himself as a person of his own and not as part of a unit. I shall do the same, Cassie thought now, looking at Lotta, gaily and suddenly preparing to make her flight from the family. One day I'll go too. Even though girls don't go as far as men do, they go . . . and parents are left behind.

"You know," she said to Lotta, who was at her dressing table, studying herself from various angles (seeking her most executive expression?) "if I ever have any children, I'm going to start getting ready to lose them the day they're born."

"Cass, don't be morbid."

"I'm not being morbid. I'm facing facts. Do you think Mother's prepared for the time when we'll all be gone?"

"I never thought about it at all."

"Well, think about it now. What kind of life do you think she'll have?"

Lotta piled her hair high, and turned. "Does this look nice? Sort of mature?"

"Yes," Cassie said drily.

"I believe I'll start wearing it this way."

"Oh, do. Please do."

"You think I'm being hardhearted, don't you?"

"Aren't you?"

"No, dear, *I'm* facing facts. Mother's going to feel awful. But I don't really see what there is to do about it. Why don't parents just accept plain truths? You have your children, and they live with you for what really is just a fraction of their lives, and for that matter only a fraction of yours. Enjoy the time they're with you. Period."

"You know, Lotta, I think you must be one of the great oversimplifiers of all time. Don't you see they can't accept that?"

"Don't you see they have to?"

"I do not like to watch people suffering."

"Dearie, neither do I. Just don't look, that's my advice."

We seem, Cassie thought, to have got our positions reversed, Lotta and I. She suspected that neither of them entirely meant what she was saying. Lotta was not so impregnable, she herself not so compassionate, as their words would have them. Half-truths, thought Cassie. That's what we have to live by. For someone who had started out trying to live, and force others to live, in the naked glare of absolute truth, it seemed the saddest admission she had ever had to make. And I'll get used to it, she told herself. Maybe so used to it I'll forget I ever dreamed of absolutes.

She went to the open window and leaned out. A quickened breeze touched her face and she lifted her head, sniffing a fresh, faint moisture. Overhead the sky was still sunny, but in the east piles of Prussian-blue clouds were mounting, and two great sooty crows flapping past seemed to be squawking, "*Rain, rain . . .*"

Aaron worried her. He seemed to be more idle and indolent all the time. He seemed to care less and less that he was drifting and wasting time, wasting his life.

"What character I have left," he'd tell her, "is being eroded by easy living."

"Aaron, that's a dreadful thing to say and mean, if you mean it," she'd protest, and he would only laugh.

Mr. Holmes, she thought now, is a wonderful man, but he doesn't realize that Aaron, anyone young and bewildered as everyone young was, needed to be helped, even pushed. There has to be some sort of discipline, some order, she thought. Or it will all fly apart in our hands, in front of our eyes. Maybe for the time being that's more important than truth. Maybe if we survive, we'll all get to a place where truth is a climate we can endure, but meanwhile we'd better settle for some sort of order. And for kindness. Mr. Holmes is right about that, anyway.

"Lotta," she said, turning from the window, "let's make a pact. Let's try to be thoughtful and kind, always, all the time, no matter what happens."

Lotta looked at her in astonishment. "Are you serious?"

"Very."

"Oh, Cass. You do get carried away, don't you? All right. I promise to try. But I hope you know it isn't going to be as easy as falling off a log. Whatever that means."

"But *try*. We can try," Cassie said stubbornly.

"I said all right, Cassie. I should think Aunt Muriel would be *glad* to have someone living with her, wouldn't you? It must be awfully dull, having things your own way all the time." Lotta hummed as she sorted through her dresses, trying to decide what to take when she went. She felt marvelously happy, full of an electric confidence, in herself, in the future, in the world.

Mrs. Dunne, coming upstairs with Vincent's letter, found

Lotta singing in a welter of clothing and Cassandra stretched on her bed wearing a look of penetration and wonder that she assumed at each of life's discoveries.

They think I don't know them at all, Rebecca Dunne said to herself. But I know that look of Cassie's, that air of Lotta's, so well, so well. Today she didn't try to point this out to them. She was learning that they'd never believe her anyway. And there was Vincent's letter. . . .

"Vincent's coming home. He's bringing his roommate for a few days."

"Hey, hey," said Cassie, sitting up. "That's great."

"Which one?" said Lotta. At her mother's uncomprehending expression, she added, "Mother, there's an English roommate and a Negro roommate. Which is he bringing home?"

Cassie looked at Lotta, a frown gathering on her forehead. For someone who had just taken a vow to be thoughtful and kind—

"I don't know," Mrs. Dunne said, glancing at the letter. "David, he says. Which one is David? Does it matter?"

After a moment Lotta shrugged. "Not if Daddy doesn't come home, I guess."

But Cassie was staring at her mother with tenderness and awe. If this was what life was going to be like, if it was going to take you unawares and throw new and strange light on people and things you thought you'd exhausted every hue and angle of, then it looked like being better than books or painting, it looked like being the greatest art of all.

She threw her arms in the air and all but sang, "Oh, *isn't* life marvelous? Isn't it the most glorious thing of all? I feel like a balloon, like a wild bird, like a rocket headed everywhere!"

Lotta laughed at her sister and then laughed just for herself.

"Always going to extremes, isn't she?" she said to her mother.

"You should know an extreme when you see one, Lotta," said Mrs. Dunne, smiling at them.

She would always be afraid for her children, probably always a little afraid of them, and no doubt she and Roger would plague themselves all their days, wondering what they'd done wrong, what they might have done differently or better. But there's one thing we can say, she told herself, and that's that we brought up three people who are willing to face life head-on. I don't see how we could have done more.

ABOUT THE AUTHOR

MARY SLATTERY STOLZ WAS BORN IN BOSTON, MASSACHUSETTS, and grew up in New York City, where she attended Birch Wathen School, Columbia University, and the Katharine Gibbs School. She also studied at New College, North Carolina. Mrs. Stolz's first jobs included selling books at Macy's and working as a secretary at Columbia Teachers College.

As long as she can remember, Mary Stolz has loved to write. But it was not until 1950 that she submitted a manuscript for publication. TO TELL YOUR LOVE, a teen-age novel, was an immediate success.

Mrs. Stolz has written for people of all ages. Her published works include two novels and several short stories for adults, as well as many teen-age novels and books for younger children.

The author says about her writing: "Perhaps as compensation for the fact that I never learned to do figures, I discovered very early that words could be manipulated. You needn't simply read them, it was possible to move them about, choose among them, find combinations of your own, and all exactly as you pleased. That was a long time ago, but I still remember the sometimes almost unbearably exciting prospect offered by a sheet of blank paper and an idea. All through school I put words together indefatigably—verse, essays, stories, biography. I liked anything that could be written about and continued not to understand anything which needed to be figured."

Mrs. Stolz loves young people and loves to write for and about them. Her books are enormously popular and are currently published in twenty-eight languages. "But it is possible for me to say with perfect honesty that I love writing about and for young people for reasons other than the financial. Which is to say, I doubtless would write this way even if it did not reward me so handsomely. The young are *never* boring. Exasperating, mystifying, sometimes hurtful, but never, never tedious and so often delightful and electrifying. I have a gregarious teen-age son who has (conservatively) two thousand close friends. I regard them all with awe, with respect, with a deep sense of reward. I guess I can say that it was the company of him, of my seven nephews and one niece, and their many friends and acquaintances that started me in the field where I now seem most to sow, to till, to reap. It's a splendid harvest."

Mrs. Stolz's teen-age novels include TO TELL YOUR LOVE; THE SEA GULLS WOKE ME; IN A MIRROR; READY OR NOT; PRAY LOVE, REMEMBER; BECAUSE OF MADELINE; GOOD-BY MY SHADOW;

THE ORGANDY CUPCAKES; HOSPITAL ZONE; AND LOVE REPLIED; WAIT FOR ME, MICHAEL; and ROSEMARY.

Her books for younger children are EMMET'S PIG, An I CAN READ Book; FREDOU; THE LEFTOVER ELF; A DOG ON BARKHAM STREET; THE BULLY OF BARKHAM STREET; and PIGEON FLIGHT. She is the creator of the brave mice, Asa and Rambo, and their friendly enemy, Siri the cat (BELLING THE TIGER, THE GREAT REBELLION, and SIRI THE CONQUISTADOR).

Format by Chet Gilbert
Set in Linotype Electra
Composed, printed and bound by The Haddon Craftsmen, Inc.
HARPER & ROW, PUBLISHERS, INCORPORATED